"*River City One* deftly encapsulates the feeling of entering back into society after a deployment: the longing and guilt, the restlessness and regret. An unsentimental deconstruction of love and the memory of war, and how society's arbitrary demonstration of patriotism leaves you feeling like a ghost in a strange town. An embodiment of the veteran experience."

—Miles Lagoze,
critically acclaimed director of *Combat Obscura* and
author of *Whistles from the Graveyard*

"John Waters renders real a fictional account of what it's like to attempt to live an ordinary life after experiencing the extraordinary thumbprint of war. With rich prose and a touch of the surreal, Waters tells a story that will make you reflect on your own life, as all great stories do. *River City One* is an utterly human story that demands to be read."

—Kacy Tellessen,
Eugene Sledge Award-winning author of
Freaks of a Feather: A Marine Grunts Memoir

RIVER CITY

ONE

A Novel

John J. Waters

PERMUTED
PRESS

A KNOX PRESS BOOK
An Imprint of Permuted Press
ISBN: 978-1-63758-895-6
ISBN (eBook): 978-1-63758-896-3

River City One:
A Novel
© 2023 by John Joseph Waters
All Rights Reserved

Cover art by Cody Corcoran

Permuted Press, LLC
New York • Nashville
permutedpress.com

Published in the United States of America
1 2 3 4 5 6 7 8 9 10

For Henry

FOREWORD

Sixty years before John Waters sat down to write a novel to help make sense of his military service in Iraq and Afghanistan, historian Bruce Catton prefaced his seminal Civil War trilogy by explaining his own fascination with the soldiers who fought in "Mr. Lincoln's Army."

In his boyhood in rural Michigan just after the turn of the twentieth century, Catton had known some of these aged Union army veterans. After returning to their farms and villages in the time before the automobile, most of them never again ventured even fifty miles from their homes. And nothing that happened there fazed them or interested them very much.

All that was real had taken place when they were young, Catton wrote of the men who lived out their lives expecting to eventually be reunited with their lost comrades. This is not as morbid as it sounds to modern ears in our more secular age. The veterans of the Michigan Brigade and other storied Civil War fighting units across the North—and in the South—were sufficiently steeped in the old-time religion to believe unquestioningly that upon death, they would be rejoining old friends and resuming ways of living they had known long before.

The concept of an afterlife aside, hero worship and idealized tales about marching off to war were reinforced in annual parades and ceremonies in the reunited USA, just as they are today. Ostensibly, these rituals exist to honor those willing to die for their country and in that sense are certainly fitting. Yet, their other purpose is to induce heroic imaginings among young citizens who are the fodder for future wars. As such, they obscure a grim truth: "War, obviously, is the least romantic of all man's activities," Bruce Catton wrote, "and it contains elements which the veterans do not describe to children."

Yet, we return to it again and again and again. The unprecedented carnage of the First World War, which began when many Civil War veterans were still alive, undermined the notion that there is anything noble about deploying modern armies across from each other on killing fields. Nor did "the war to end all wars" deliver on its promise. It did, however, produce a grim new phrase: "shell shock."

By the time of the Second World War, the U.S. government recognized this condition for what it was, and in typical military fashion gave it an acronym: CSR. This stood for Combat Stress Reaction. It was universally known as "battle fatigue."

Today, we understand that post-traumatic stress disorder is not limited to veterans, although among those who have seen combat, PTSD is so prevalent as to be the norm. In other words, it's a mentally healthy reaction to war, if one doesn't mind a little irony with his Freud. Yes, it was the famed Austrian psychoanalyst who first delved into survivor's guilt—after the death of his father.

Contemporary clinicians have diagnosed it in those who've suffered trauma ranging from sexual assault and contracting AIDS to surviving the Holocaust and dodging airplane crashes or lung cancer.

A landmark 1991 study concluded that 46 percent of Vietnam War veterans suffered from some level of PTSD. One third of them had contemplated or attempted suicide. Is this because of the nature of that particular war? When PTSD received attention in the early 1980s, many people thought so. "Bad war, bad outcome, bad after-effects," military historian Thomas Childers noted succinctly.

Exploring PTSD is not really John Waters' objective in the story that follows, however. But the psychological reactions of American soldiers, sailors, and marines in Vietnam are relevant again for the simple reason that in Afghanistan (like Vietnam), the United States military did not prevail. Likewise, this book is not about any political factors that may have hindered the U.S. military effort, now or then. That said, the self-defeating feature of calling the current struggle the "War on Terror" is palpable. The very name implies that victory is elusive, the mission never-ending.

What about those who have charged into combat only to realize after the war's end that they were on the wrong side?

Standing on the cliff at Pointe du Hoc sixty years after D-Day, I encountered a German tourist at the same spot. He stepped aside in deference to me, an obvious American, and instructed his family to do the same. I had been gazing out at the Normandy coastline while envisioning the seven thousand ships in the Allied armada that had come to liberate a continent. What this man, who was not even alive when Hitler wreaked havoc on Europe, was thinking I can only imagine. The words that came to my mind were from Ulysses Grant at Appomattox. As Robert E. Lee surrendered, Grant found himself trying to reconcile his respect for the bravery of the Confederates, including Lee, with contempt for the depraved institution that had induced them to take up arms against their own nation in the first place. It was a cause, Grant wrote, that was "one of the worst for which a people ever fought, and one for which there was the least excuse."

As twenty-first century America undergoes one of its periodic reckonings on race, we are reexamining slavery's legacy. Yes, it's true that Jim Crow was a conscious attempt to maintain white supremacy in the South. But that's not all. I believe it was also driven by the same motivation that fueled the odious "Lost Cause" narrative as well as hagiographic books ranging from *Gone with the Wind* to *Lee's Lieutenants*: namely, a revisionist impulse to show all that killing and suffering hadn't been for nothing.

This is not to say that the battle-tested Union men who marched with Grant—or those in the Greatest Generation, for that matter—didn't pay any psychic price. We know better. More than fifty years after the fact, a onetime American soldier named Earl Crumby who earned a Purple Heart in the Battle of the Bulge, wept while describing for writer Tim Madigan the kind of details veterans do not describe to children.

Crumby's wife of many decades had died a few years earlier, but his tears that day weren't for her. "As dearly as I loved that woman, her death didn't affect me near as much as it does to sit down here and talk to you about seeing those young boys butchered during the war," he told Madigan. "It was nothing but arms and legs, heads and guts. You'd think you could forget something like that. But you can't."

Other writers have explored not just what combat veterans have to see, but also what they have to do. In *My Dog Skip*, Willie Morris' autobiographical coming-of-age story about growing up in Mississippi, Willie's next door neighbor Dink Jenkins comes back from the fighting in Europe a shell of his former self. Dink tells young Willie, "It ain't the dying that's scary, boy, it's the killing."

Willie's father is sympathetic. He lost a leg in the Spanish Civil War "and a piece of his heart" in the process.

What all these characters I've mentioned have in common—and what "John Walker" does in the pages that follow—is reveal that when they come home from war, they must learn to live again as a civilian.

America, the nation that perfected the idea of the "citizen-soldier," now has an all-volunteer military, which has evolved into a professional fighting force with its own subculture. And a self-perpetuating one. Historian Andrew Bacevich, a West Point man who commanded a combat platoon in Vietnam, has pointed out that the lack of a military draft has made it far too easy for politicians who never heard a shot fired in anger to send Americans into battle zones.

The makeup of today's armed forces also places an undue burden on the small minority of families willing to fight democracy's wars. Multiple deployments in Iraq and Afghanistan were a curse to many of these men. But not only a curse. For some, the "War on Terror" was more than a calling; it became a lifestyle. Then it was over.

Saving the world from evil makes most stateside jobs seem mundane by comparison. What are people supposed to do with themselves when their main purpose in life has come and gone before they've turned thirty-five?

"Find love, raise children, pursue a meaningful career" would be society's answer. The warrior's burden has never made it that simple. Two Spartans survived the famous Battle of Thermopylae: One of them, Pantites, was dispatched to warn Sparta's allies. He returned too late to fight with King Leonidas and the three hundred Spartans martyred by King Xerxes' massive Persian army after betrayal by a Greek shepherd. Out of shame, Pantites hanged himself.

The other survivor, Aristodemus, had been excused from the action because of an eye infection, but was still shunned by the Greeks for his supposed cowardice. He atoned by giving his life while fighting furiously—and recklessly—the following year against the Persians at the Battle of Plataea.

The modern world is less dramatic, if no less tragic. Legendary Navy SEAL and decorated Iraq combat veteran Chris Kyle was fatally ambushed at a Texas shooting range along with a friend named Chad Littlefield, a man with a passion for assisting veterans. As it happened, the mentally ill and drug-impaired veteran they were trying to help shot them in the back.

Almost all fighters in the field long for hearth and home. When they get there, they must figure out how to live again without the constant rush of adrenaline. If going to war makes them feel like heroes, then it stands to reason that the very act of returning to civilian life can make even a reflective person worry that they've abandoned the mission.

To stave away the demons, some of them write. And those of us who give up a good seat on an airplane, or stand and cheer for veterans and their families at the ballpark, or who tell men and women in uniform, "Thank you for your service," can do more. For starters, we can read their memoirs and their novels. And after doing so, we can look with deep skepticism on elected officials who are too eager to send young Americans off to war.

Carl M. Cannon
Arlington, Virginia
April 2023

CHAPTER ONE

The safety was flicked off, the hammer cocked. The gun was one inch above the seam of my pants pocket. A sudden move and the thing might go off. I closed both eyes and held my breath to slow everything down, breathing only to catch my breath. It was a couple of pounds, maybe three, and I felt it hanging, the weight of bullets pressed inside the hollow grip and tugging down on the waistband of my khakis.

The gun had been an accessory, a set of car keys slipped into my pocket on the way out of the house; I had taken for granted that it would follow me everywhere. Metal grooves and small notches of the grip filled with rust when shamal winds whipped sand into the air, the heavy rotations of a dust-off grinding blue skies into dust. Oiling and scrubbing. Oiling and scrubbing, cleaning each nook with a toothbrush to make sure the bolt didn't jam up with grit, just to make sure the thing fired when I needed it to.

I carried it inside dust-filled trucks rumbling over potholes and every cut and groove in the road. I carried it standing in line for a plate of hot food, holding a plastic tray in my hands, letting my elbow rest at my hip, in the small space between the hammer and sight posts. I took the gun off my hip only to clip the holster into the nylon straps of the flak jacket that covered my chest, setting it so high up I could rest my chin across the long steel grip and fall asleep.

But there was risk in taking it off, so I took the gun with me into the green plastic porta-shitters, the dense sound of metal striking the soiled plastic floor when I unfastened my belt, pants sagging to my knees. When I slept, when I ate, it stayed clipped into my pants, welded to my side through so many places I forgot it was on me until I saw somebody else's pistol lodged in a leather-strapped shoulder holster—dangling under his armpit like he was a police detective in an old movie—reminded me. The calm returned only when my palm grabbed onto a fistful of black grip stock. That was years ago.

Today it was new again.

"Wait for the natural pause in breath," a voice said.

The words sounded strange coming from the blonde with a pistol tucked into the top of her white pants, her breasts rising out of a pink halter top like two hot air balloons straining at their leash. She was hanging close enough that I could see the brown of her irises and the freckles splashed across the bridge of her nose. I pressed the soft flesh between my thumb and forefinger into the smooth notch and let my right hand fold around the outside of the three-inch handle, forefinger resting straight along the barrel, just above the trigger well. The rough surface of the gun's handle grated like sandpaper against the insides of my fingers. I drew in a long breath and held it.

One, two, three counts. My heartbeat thudded through the insides of my ears, each beat deepening the longer I held the breath.

The air exited as my right index finger touched the holster's release button. I swept the pistol forward in one smooth motion until my arm reached full extension. My left hand molded onto the opposite side of the pistol, cradling the gun in both hands, index fingers pointed to the target.

She was smiling.

"Slow and steady pressure—let the weapon surprise you," the voice said.

I pulled my fingertip back gently and waited for the sound.

Crack.

The hammer dropped into a bright spark of flame and the barrel jerked upward, my shoulders rocking me backward onto my heels. I exhaled then waited.

Crack.

Inhaled.

Crack.

The firing became automatic, shell casings leaping from the barrel and falling soundlessly to the ground. The empty magazine dropped from the handle and I took one long breath, relieved, noticing for the first time the smell of charcoal smoke and sulfur.

I set the pistol down on the metal tray and stepped back, eyes panning left and right. The room was small, only a few shooters standing within arm's reach of one another. A hand reached beside me and turned the switch, making the sheet of paper come flying toward me, stopping so close to my head I felt the brush of air on my cheeks.

The report was good. Five holes clustered like a honeycomb inside the woman's chest.

"Fuck yeah, duuude. I see you, Walker! You had that pistol rawking!"

I winced when his hand slapped against my shoulder and I peeled the plastic earmuffs off my head.

"How 'bout we take a look and inspect our performance, eh?" Dan unclipped the paper from the wire and traced a finger around the holes I made in the center of the woman's pink shirt.

"Center mass, from the looks of it. Center bosom."

If it was a joke he didn't laugh.

Dan studied the paper, pushing his orange-lensed shooting glasses to the top of his head to get a closer look. He rubbed the back of his tanned neck, sleeves rolled up to his elbows. I could make out three tattoos on the inside of his forearm, images I had not seen before. They were figures of men like chalk outlines drawn on the ground at a crime scene, the pictures filled in with bright pink and neon blue colors.

"Nice," he said, still studying the target. "Actually, dude, *very* nice. Tight grouping. Maybe a few inches lower than we were aiming, but...."

He took a black marker from a cargo pocket and drew circles around the bullet holes, tracing lines from the circles to small squares he drew near the woman's heart and forehead. He was a football coach diagramming an imagined play. "Tight grouping means your technique is still sound, bro, and that's gonna be your key to high performance."

The air felt thick. Smells of hot metal and powder mingled together, filling my nose and mouth with an iron taste like blood on my tongue. Again, he clapped me hard on the shoulder.

"The important thing is that we're havin' some fun. Couple of dudes just layin' waste to paper somewhere in middle America. That's how I see it. Gonna shoot those blues away in no time, my friend," Dan said, his head thrown back mischievously.

"That's enough," I said. "I was wearing two sets of hearing protection and it's your voice that's ringing in my ears."

He was here to check on me, and we both knew it. Dan made the weekend trip to see things for himself, to make sure I was still getting out of bed every morning, brushing my teeth, and going to work. He came to make sure I hadn't been burning days just driving around the neighborhood, thoughts drifting a decade into the past. I didn't want to talk about it.

"Why the goofy target?"

Dan pulled the shooting glasses off his head, placed them into a thick black case, and then slipped that case into a black backpack hanging off the side of his shoulder.

"Because that chick," he said, "she's out there. Look, you wanna fuck the chick, right? Like, we all want to fuck her—she's a babe, I got it. But if you can't shoot an armed woman just because you want to fuck her, then the bottom line is very simple. You need more training. You need to learn how to separate your feelings from your skill set, dude, because this isn't Afghanistan anymore. It's not always gonna be some haji dickhead with the black beard and the mascara and the dirty jammies. Guy was a shooting dummy. The threat is now nuanced. Dude, it's a very nuanced and fluid threat landscape out there and preparation is critical. So critical and so key."

Dan stretched out the two syllables of the word "nuanced" in a way that let me know how much he enjoyed speaking them.

"This is exactly how we're training at the academy. Intense. Realistic. The training is a ball-breaker but also highly realistic."

I nodded along, placing the pistol in a hand case and snapping shut the lock.

The sound of an M4-style long gun echoed across the tin walls of the indoor range. I looked over my shoulder and saw a man wearing a wool sweater and a pair of penny loafers. He had the buttstock of the rifle chicken-winged under his armpit.

"They got a bar on the other side of that wall," I said, grabbing the door.

"I was hoping you'd say that," Dan said. "This place weirds me the fuck out."

We met in training a decade ago. I was wearing dress slacks and sweating through my long-sleeved oxford under the Virginia sun, standing near the back of a long line when I spotted a man bobbing to the check-in desk, a white orchid stuck behind his ear. That was Dan, the performer, the artist of contradiction. The more things he tried, the more experiences he crammed into his life, the better his chances of inventing something he had never seen before. He'd said it started in a photography program at the art institute.

"Too many pre-tortured souls more serious about themselves than living life."

He transferred to a university and ran with the cross-country team, dabbled in construction, and managed the floor of an electronics store. At some point he landed his "dream job" with the National Park Service, working as an administrative assistant.

"Figured I'd be leading campers on backcountry hikes, spending days and nights out on the trail. They put me on the side of the road, man. Assigned me to the wilderness, an empty patch of grass off a dirt road nowhere near the big trail. I'm sitting on a campstool by myself spinning the same story three times on a good day. Army of Northern Virginia, heavy casualties, over and over. Turns out a sixty-five-year-old who'd just read a bio of Lee knew more about that battle than me."

He took his commission not out of patriotism, but because the military offered "a challenge worthy of my youth." That was how he told it to me late one summer night in the room we shared, lying half naked on top of our sheets, not knowing whether it was sweat or humidity that stuck like grease on our chests and necks.

"I'll join the pretender class once this body's been worn down," he whispered.

Now, watching him strut across the lobby with the black gun case wedged underneath his arm, I realized that fifteen years on, it still had not happened to him, the part about his body wearing down, of giving up on the dream of living life always on the edge of some new and thrilling experience.

"ATF is much less bureaucratic than FBI. Nimble is the word. A very nimble group," he said.

I pulled open the heavy door and stepped inside the bar. Walls at least twenty feet high and painted white were covered with television screens that glowed like electric wallpaper. The wooden tabletops were lacquered so thick they looked like sheets of glass. One couple sat in a red booth eating big hamburgers and watching one of the televisions, the crack of gunfire faint but still loud enough to notice.

When I was a kid, this building had been a department store, the place my mother took me every couple of years to refresh my dress pants and collared shirts, the clothes I wore to church on Sundays. What had once been the jewelry display case was now the counter, stretching from one end of the room to the other, a dozen handles sticking up straight like stalks of corn from the other side of the counter. Each beer was named after a caliber of ammunition. There was a .22 on the light end all the way to .50 Browning machine gun on the heavy end, each tap outfitted with a matching shell casing melted into the tip of the custom oakwood handle.

"Nice touch," Dan said, resting his elbows on the glass counter.

The bartender put two fingers around the long shaft of the brass cylinder and tugged down, releasing a dark ale into a pint glass.

"Owner does a lot of work with vets' groups," the bartender said. "You'll notice their symbols on your side of the bar; look below the counter."

I took a step back and saw a row of military insignias mounted on the outside of the bar, each one made from sculpted metal sharp enough to cut your legs if you sat too close. Rangers, Special Forces, Navy SEALs. There was a skull with a reticle covering the forehead. That one belonged to the bar.

"In gratitude for the owner's charity work with disabled veterans, a SEAL presented us with a box of empty shell casings, these here." The bartender flicked his finger against one of the brass casings. "Each one was used to bag an al-Qaeda member. An al-Qaeda fighter, I should say."

Dan glanced at me and rolled his eyes before turning back to the bartender. "Shit's crazy now, you know? Hell, I'm hearing about those terrorist dudes implanting, like, sleeper cells—in America. Fuckers wanna get their asses into one of our pro shops, put their hands on some American-made carbines. No shit, man. True story. We got extremists in the suburbs."

Dan wagged his tongue at me like we were the only two guys in the bar.

"Or was it a Taliban soldier. A Taliban fighter? Now that I think about it," the bartender said, losing focus into a cluster of television screens, his hand draped over a long brass casing. "Well, it don't matter anyway. They're all the bad guys, right?"

I nodded, pulling my beer off the countertop and following Dan to a booth in the back. There was a big square window off his shoulder and the ground outside was dark brown and unturned, still a month or so away from planting season.

"Put you behind that gun," Dan said, settling in against the wall. "Get outside your head for a few beats. Let that beast back out. Am I right?"

"It felt good," I said.

Shoulders slouched forward, I stared into what might become a thick field of tall, golden corn in four or five months. I watched the land change every year but never spent enough time on a farm to understand the timing of these things, when one season had finally given way to the next.

"What was the nickname they use around here?" asked Dan. "River City? Sorta like 'River City One'—remember that?"

"Sure," I replied. It was the code they used aboard ship whenever the internet and the phone line went dead, whenever the ship shut off its communications with the outside, leaving everyone onboard in quarantine from the world beyond. I remember hearing the captain's voice coming over the ship's loudspeaker, "We are now entering River City One," and wondering whether isolation was a place one could choose to enter and just as easily choose to leave.

Dan leaned forward, pulling down the zipper on his black fleece top stretched tight across his chest. "You gotta do something to keep your sanity out here, that's all."

"Finally, Dan. Glad to know why you took a break from the adventure to visit me."

"Easy, dude. Come on now!" He held his hands up in the air, innocent. "You gotta admit there is no action here. But if that's not what you're into anymore, then well—"

"What I'm sayin' here is that nobody in River City is crushing it, right? Just wondering if the stakes here are too low for someone of your caliber, dude."

"You know this is what we wanted," I said. "Grace and me."

I had once imagined my homecoming: accepting an invitation to return to the old neighborhood, to leave the military behind and happily nestle in among the people and places that raised me as one of their own. I had imagined that my neighborhood would be an anchor for the life to come, but things had been different.

"Speaking of caliber, you'll notice I opted for the .22," I joked, trying to lighten the mood. "But anyway, how's your ex?"

Dan winced. "I still have love for her, dude, and she knows that."

They got the marriage license at the courthouse a week before we deployed. She was a friend of his younger brother, a pretty girl at a college party who sent him a photograph every week for the seven months we were gone. Different clothes, different makeup, and always tasteful. He made a collage of the pictures, pinning them to the plywood wall above his cot in our living quarters on base, just above the place where we stacked our flak jackets and Kevlar helmets after patrol.

"But she's fucked-up, man. Seriously. Not good, and I don't say that lightly. She is a sad, fucked-up woman."

"Could there be a reason?" I asked.

"Absolutely not," he shot back, laying his palms open on the table. "I left her in good hands. In Denver of all places. Everybody wants to make a pilgrimage to the Mile High holy land. She's going to be fine."

He took a long drink from his glass and drew back from the table

"Besides, she didn't fight me on the divorce, just signed the papers, so who am I to judge?"

"Her ex-husband," I said, but sarcasm had a way of never sticking with Dan.

"Everything got better for me as soon as I realized she was my problem. She was always sad, never believing in me. Did you know that she never once encouraged me to just chase my dreams? Shit was never simple with her, always complicated. She was brilliant and dark, and very stylish, like the most stylish woman. I mean, my ex was a fashion maximalist. When everybody was wearing plaid and flannel, she wore sequins and shit, but what I'm sayin' is she never respected me. Never respected my inner power. I got out of the military because my wife thought it was beneath us. 'Dan, isn't it time for you to go to law school and put all this gear away and grow up?' she'd say. I was not a high-enough-status male for her."

"Your father is a lawyer," I said.

Dan laughed. "You're funny, man! I opened that door once. Twelve years old and stuck hangin' at dad's law office for the afternoon. Quiet as a library. I'm just trying to find a kitchen or a box of crackers or something, push a door open, and there they are."

He paused, his face twisting like he'd experienced a sudden onset of pain.

"Three old dudes sitting around a table built for ten. Room stinks of aftershave. Barbershop shit. The kind that sticks to your clothes the rest of the day. So, no. Could never see myself sittin' all day in an office like yours. I'd get an emergency before lunchtime on my first day, call it a 'feel-good emergency.' I'd bust outta that place so rabid I'd have to hotwire a car or climb a building, jump off a goddamn bridge just for the sake of feeling something." He waved his hand. "But anyway, "I just met this Latin chick online, dude."

Dan smiled, running both hands through his thick blond hair. Between the tanned skin and a light shadow of facial hair sketched across his lip, he had the appearance of a man nearing forty in laughably good condition.

"Speaking of marriage," he said, changing subjects. "You hear about Willis?"

I shook my head and pushed away the beer, having drunk no more than half the glass but considering my duty as a drinking partner upheld.

"Other red-haired guy from the battalion?" I asked. "Sure, and I remember his wife was a doctor. Not very common for that group."

"You hear what happened to him?

I shook my head.

"So Willis decides to move on with his life. Got a couple kids and a third one on the way. Moves the doctor wife and brood back up to Boston where he came from. Wife lands a job at the hospital and ol' Willis, well, he enrolls in grad school to seek self-improvement and better himself and so forth, following all the rules and becoming, like, a poster child for leaving the gory shit in the past." Dan held up a finger. "But that's not the end of the story, my friend, that's not it by a mile, because—"

"Because he starts beating his wife," I cracked. "Old gods of violence came back to haunt him?"

Dan shook his head. "No, but—"

"He beat up a classmate?"

Dan shook his head again.

"He was a violent guy, as I recall. Was it a teacher? Neighbor?"

"Can I please tell my story?" Dan frowned. "Thirty minutes on the firing line and all you can think about is violence, man. Nobody's beating up anybody. Willis got himself a girlfriend, a student. The two of them were in a small section together at school. They're working on projects for class together, studying in the library together, eating lunch, takin' walks on campus, spreadin' picnic blankets and everything. This chick is ten, twelve years younger, right? Everything's great, they're going steady for October and November. Not until December does this young lady get around to plugging his name into Google and isn't she surprised to find that the first result is, like, the baby registry or whatever for a 'Mr. and Mrs. Willis'?"

"Wait a second. Months?" I said. "It took her months to run his name through a search engine?"

Dan rolled his eyes. "Dunno, dude. Don't care either. You woulda run a background check, a credit check, a public records search, and hired a PI by the second week of fall classes, but hang with me here, okay?"

"I just find it a little hard to believe."

"So this girl says nothing to Willis about her discovery. Not one word. She lets the weeks float by like everything is A-okay." Dan paused, drawing air between his teeth. "Which is just diabolical, dude. Absolutely unbecoming of her and I'd like to get to know this young woman. Actually, Walker, could you pull a roster of grad students currently assigned to—"

"Can we finish the story." I tapped the face of my watch and tried hard not to laugh when Dan smiled.

"Young lady pulls his home address right off the class roster. Willis wants to live a double life but puts his home address on the class roster like he's *hoping* somebody catches him. She waits until Christmas Eve. Parks her car outside his beautiful four-bedroom colonial in Marblehead, painted white with green shutters. Sweet dreaminess of domestic life shit. Willis's family is sitting down to dinner when our girl rings the doorbell. Mrs. Willis gets up from the dinner table and opens the door. Girlfriend smiles and says, 'Mrs. Willis, I have a gift for you from your husband.' She holds out a turquoise Tiffany box. Girlfriend hands it over and goes back to her car." He raised a fist to his mouth and bit down lightly on his knuckles. "Mrs. Willis undoes the bow…" He mimicked pulling apart an imaginary ribbon. "…she pops open the lid…" He held his hands out toward me. "…she looks inside…" He paused.

I sighed.

"And there it is—pile of wet condoms." Dan broke into a smile. "Returned that mess to its proper owner," he said.

"Then what?" I said.

Dan blinked. "Huh?"

"I thought the history lesson was to give up your country before your family. So what's he doing now that he abandoned his wife and kids?"

Dan shook his head and pulled a rain jacket from his tan backpack. "She took him back. Pregnant again. Go figure."

"How?"

He shrugged, glancing at his wristwatch. He grabbed the shoulder straps of his backpack and thrust both arms through the loops. "Let's roll, brother. Can't stand being late."

❏ ❏ ❏

I pulled the station wagon into an empty space near the door to his terminal. Dan hopped out, adjusting the fit of his black baseball cap, an American flag Velcroed just above the brim. He wore tan and black slim-fitted cargo pants and hiking boots, giving him the look of a private security agent on some urban detail.

He pulled me in for a hug. "Take care of Grace and Charlie." He gripped my shoulders tightly then pushed himself back. "And don't forget to get out of that office sometimes, dude. Even you need a little water and light to grow."

I sat in my car and watched him walk through the revolving door and into the airport lobby, ignoring cars as they honked and drove around me.

Dan had tried and failed at several jobs, had ended a marriage, and yet he was the same person today as the day we came back, full of the restless enthusiasm that made him believe anything was possible. I knew why Dan had come here. However much we still had in common, there were problems I could no longer tell him.

I waited until I lost sight of his box-shaped pack floating through the small crowd at the terminal, then drove away.

CHAPTER TWO

I slammed the car door shut and grabbed the gun case from the back seat. My parents lived in the house next door.

My father was holding a set of gardening shears that looked like a small crocodile—part chainsaw, part hedge trimmer—a ring of sweat around the collar of his long-sleeved gray shirt. The sun's warmth was fading into the early evening winter chill. He was leaning forward, slightly hunched.

"She's got a five-amp motor and weighs in under five pounds. There's a sweat-resistant rubber handgrip right here, and she's battery powered." Dad popped out a thick cylinder from the back of the trimmer and held it at the tips of his thumb and index finger.

"Give her a charge for one hour and you get two full hours of play time," Dad said, patting his Timex. He took a hit of water from the blue hose of the pouch strapped to his back.

"You can use it," he said, taking the gun case from my hand and checking to make sure the lock was secure. "I mean it. I want you to use my trimmer!"

If he spent some time using tools, he spent more time organizing them, building a wooden tool rack that mounted to the garage wall, hanging up his shears and handsaws and drills in a particular arrangement, only to take them all down and put them back up in a different arrangement. It was all he could do after quitting smoking, keeping his hands busy and his mind occupied. Dad kept a barstool next to his tools where he sat to watch the television mounted on the wall above the tool rack that doubled as his gun safe.

He had been a salary man at Graybar Corporation for thirty years, using his expertise in engineering on construction projects across the Midwest. He specialized in the design of load-bearing structures, the kind of structures that supported freight transport. He knew how dynamic loads acted on a piece of timber compared to a piece of masonry or steel, and how many years it took for a moderate thermal load to warp a track of hot-rolled steel on a truss railway bridge. He knew everything about materials, about loads.

"Come over anytime and grab this thing from my workstation. But make sure you put it back in the charging station once you're done. You know the rules. Everything in its place."

I'd heard that phrase a few times since the retirement, ever since Dad started inviting the neighbors over to put their hands on his new materials. They would unlatch the metal handle on the wooden fence door and walk onto the polished gray surface of the sprawling patio where he might be building a bonfire or smoking a slab of meat.

"I'll think about it," I said unconvincingly, opening the front door. "I might wait 'til spring, though."

Charlie's voice stung my ears when I walked inside.

"I don't want to! I don't want to eat!"

He was sitting at the kitchen table, his curly blond hair painted the color of tomato sauce. His pants and socks had been kicked onto the rug beneath his bare feet.

Grace was sitting next to him, resting her chin on the palm of one hand. "If you don't eat, you'll never grow big and strong."

He was three years old and already I realized my presence would never be enough for Charlie. I had kept vigil by his crib for months—the whole first year practically— falling asleep in the wooden gliding chair under the glare of his baby monitor. I fed him, swaddled him, and still Charlie cried, his voice ringing out from deep inside his throat as I rocked him desperately in my arms. My son would always want his mother first.

"I left his diaper bag for you," she said. "It's outside the back door on the porch."

We used cloth diapers. The point was to save a little money, sending Charlie off to day care each day with four clean diapers and receiving him each evening with the same number, soiled. It fell to me to wash them, cleaning and rinsing the diapers before putting them into the washing machine. I would lay out the diapers on a patch of grass at the back corner of the yard, unroll the hose, then spray water at each soiled diaper until it was soaked.

"If you don't eat, I'm taking you to bed right now," I said sternly.

His face was red, lower lip trembling and bending down at the edges into a frown. On the verge of tears, Charlie bent his head down toward his plate and began to eat.

❏ ❏ ❏

"Pray for Mommy. For Grandma and Grandpa. For friends." Charlie liked to add new things to our list of prayers, animals or objects he had seen that day. Whatever crossed his mind became a part of our nightly ritual.

A metal crucifix was bolted to the wall at the head of Charlie's bed. The object made me uncomfortable. Thick as a handlebar and long as a bayonet, the crucifix showed up shortly after we moved into the house. It was put there by his mother to either ward off evil or bring good fortune, which one I couldn't tell, but it was there for a purpose.

When we finished, Charlie rolled over onto his side, hands still pressed together in prayer. "...and for the souls in purgatory. Amen."

He never asked me what the last part meant and I was happy for it. I didn't know the answer. This prayer was something my mother had taught me when I was a child, to always remember the "souls in purgatory." Charlie and I ended every night making a prayer that had no meaning to either one of us beyond the sounds of the words.

I tucked the yellow bedspread under Charlie's chin and behind his shoulders until all I could see of him were his eyes and nose, a few curls of hair, and the face of a stuffed teddy bear that poked out from under his arm.

"Good night," I said, watching him, how small he looked in bed.

Downstairs, I found Grace seated at the far end of the kitchen table, her back to the wall. The laptop was propped open in front of her alongside a calculator and a fresh pad of white paper. Behind her was the wallpaper she put up shortly after we moved into the house, a collage of numbers and Greek symbols, Σ and Δ and Π, dozens more. Each symbol was the size of a penny and canvased across the wall in all different colors, making a pattern that repeated over and over again across the cream-colored paper. I could never remember how she had explained it to me, those formulas and what they represented, at least not well enough to describe.

I lowered myself into a chair at the other end of the granite table.

She stared intently into the blue computer screen, her fingers clacking at the keys.

"Midterms," she muttered from over the top of her screen. She recoiled from the keyboard, drawing her hands back and placing them on either side of her head, squinting even harder into the screen. "Each step in the work is correct, but the answer is wrong. I can't figure it out…"

"Have you let Charlie take a look?" I joked, looking at the neat rows of symbols lining the wall behind Grace's head, wondering if that code was any hint of what might be happening inside her head.

Her blonde hair was messy but cut short.

"I see what's going on here," she said, her head bouncing to the rhythm of some new solution.

Grace had been on the faculty for only a couple of years. The lights in the kitchen had been shut off for the evening, and backlight from the screen washed her face in a blue glow that shone across the width of her cheekbones and the small, pointy nose that had always made her look years younger than her age.

"Don't push too hard," I said, counting symbols on the wall.

We met in college. It was the spring before I left for basic training. Every morning I rolled out of bed before 5 a.m., sliding my feet into a pair of running shoes before stumbling down steps onto the grassy field outside the dorm hall. Long-sleeved shirt, shorts—enough clothing to cover me up but not so much that I wouldn't feel my skin tighten against the cool morning air. I started to jog as soon as I stepped through the glass doors of the heated building, warming my legs and chest through force of physical movement, picking up speed when I reached the start line of the track.

I did three miles, twelve trips around, and I did it every morning as fast as I could. I ran the miles but I wasn't a natural athlete. I wanted to be faster and so I was diligent, running each day and writing down my split-times and finish-times in a spiral notebook, keeping track of every detail with notes in the margin:

March 15—felt leg cramp at the one-mile mark

March 16—fatigue halfway through; need light snack before training

One morning, I found her.

Sitting on the bleachers, I pulled a pen from the spine of my spiral notebook to log that morning's notes when a new group of runners moved soundlessly across the far side of the track. They had uniforms, pants and light jackets that matched, and each runner wore a pair of clean white running spikes that kicked and pushed across the black surface like painted white wheels spinning across a field. The sun had not come up and their faces were unrecognizable. There was no mistaking how gracefully she moved, the tallest one in the group, how easily she leaned onto her inside leg, rounding the bend in the track, upper body straight but not stiff as she accelerated through the curve and into the final one hundred meters. Her long legs seemed to never touch the ground. All the runners were powerful but only Grace was effortless. How easy it looked as she glided ahead of the pack.

The group slowed as they crossed back over the starting line, stretching their arms up and down and shaking out their legs in preparation for the work that would follow. I watched while they unzipped their jackets and rolled down their pants, tossing the extra layer of clothes carelessly onto a chain-link fence that ran along the outside of the red and black track.

Grace was different. She folded her clothes neatly. She put the jacket on top of the pants so the bundle of clothes fit into a perfect square before setting the stack down on the first metal bench at the end of the bleachers. It was always that way, day after day. The quick sprint around the track, arms waving and legs moving, and then the careful, patient folding of her tracksuit. She had a long, thin neck and wide-set eyes, a shock of light blonde hair pulled back into the nub of a ponytail. I watched her from halfway up the bleachers with my notebook in my hands, squinting through the morning light.

One morning, after Grace had finished her mile repeats and put on her tracksuit, I walked down the bleachers and held my hand above my head, waving to call her attention.

"Excuse me," I said. "Do the shoes make a difference?"

She scrunched her face.

I hadn't planned what to say once I got her attention.

"Do shoes make you run faster? I'm training for a competition and I want to lower my time because lower time means a better score."

She put her hands inside the pockets of her jacket and cocked her head. The muscles in her jaw clenched then eased while I waited for her to speak.

"Shoes don't make a difference, especially for whatever race you're running. It's all about mileage, how much you've run. How long is your race?"

"Three miles, but I wish it was longer."

"How many miles do you run per day?"

I told her four miles, even though I never ran more than three.

"If you want to get faster, double your miles and do it every day. You'll be seconds quicker in a week."

She looked me up and down, starting at my shoes then working up to my head and back down. "I'd tell you to lose a few pounds too, but you don't have any to spare, so just add miles." She turned on the ball of her white shoe and jogged across the field toward campus.

By the end of the school year, my times had improved. I waited for her at the track in May.

"Good for you," she said, smiling when I told her about my progress. "Running is ninety-nine percent grit. Talent shouldn't matter in the races you're running."

It didn't bother me that she was unimpressed by my workouts. Sensing I was onto something, I told Grace I was leaving for the summer and asked if I could write her a letter. She looked past me and out to the street, where cars slowly rolled down a two-lane campus road, then blinked.

"Okay," she said, taking my notebook in her hands and flattening the surface of a fresh white sheet with blue lines spanning the page. She wrote her name in a neat row of capital letters, then her phone number and address. She handed back the pen and notebook. "What's your name anyway?"

"John Walker," I said. "Like the whiskey."

"Never heard of him."

I wrote her twice a week, scribbling out letters under the red glow of my flashlight, telling her about my performance on the latest road march or obstacle course, events that could be measured in time and distance. We fell into a routine that summer, me putting a letter or postcard in the mailbox and receiving her handwritten pages in response. That was fifteen years ago. Before deployment and the long moodiness that followed. Before law school and career changes and the birth of our son.

"Have a good visit with Dan?" she asked.

She knew Dan well enough from North Carolina. She had also known his wife, having spent Saturdays and

Sundays with her at their house in Wilmington, knees in the dirt together. They planted enough medicinal plants during our deployment to stock a natural drug store, their own backyard apothecary. Neither had been inclined to join the officer's wives' gatherings on weekend afternoons, where other wives seated themselves around the coffee table at the commanding officer's colonial house on base, probing the lines of permissible gossip, mentioning this wife who refused to leave Wilmington and move her family into base housing, or that husband who everyone suspected would not get picked up in the next round of promotions, his career months away from ending. Each wife was careful not to say anything beyond the boundary's edge or risk making herself into the next piece of marketable gossip.

"Refreshing," I said. "It felt natural. Shooting, I mean. Like I was picking up where I left off. Like riding a bike. Memories and thoughts coming back. It was like I went back in time..."

A quick burst of keystrokes interrupted my train of thought. Grace closed the laptop and pushed it forward on the table as if to make sure that the work would stay out of reach.

"Good thoughts?" she probed.

"All old thoughts are good thoughts. I actually want to remember..." I stopped when I noticed my volume rising.

Grace nodded. "I was there, in case you've forgotten."

Grace had seen it all, including when she had not seen anything. When we came home after seven months, I spent all my time with the guys—"the dudes" was what we called each other—relying on each other instead of the families that waited behind for us. We were glad to show up to work before the sun rose, starting most days with a beach run then a swim in the ocean, workouts that would last two, three hours, as long it took for our lungs and legs to burn off whatever memories still lingered from the night before. After the exercise, I worked. Mostly desk work, scheduling appointments and checking in on the dudes. Did Jones see the eye doctor for his new prescription? Did Taylor make those child support payments? He had received a paycheck for the last seven months with no way of spending it, so he had to have the money. And what about Ives? How was the platoon's wounded warrior? Did he have another skin graft on his stump, or had the sores healed so that he could finally start building a callus where the prosthetic attached? The work would last until about three in the afternoon, never any longer, and, just as the day should have been drawing to a close, we'd file out the door of the headquarters building and make the short drive to the club at the edge of base.

The club was a small, nondescript red-brick building near my exit onto the highway, crowded on all sides by tall pine trees. I always called Grace when I pulled into the parking lot, telling her that I was "on my way home" though I knew it would be hours before I got back on the road. We liked the club because the lights were low and the bar was quiet. The music never rose above a whisper. By then it had been years since you could light a cigarette indoors, but the sour smell of smoke and ash still hung in the air, embracing you as soon as the door swung open.

We knew the bartender, we knew the group leaning on pool sticks under the Budweiser lamp that hung above the billiards table, and everybody was in uniform. We would seat ourselves around the big oak table at the center of the room, the same table every time, then bring over that first cloudy pitcher of light beer.

I never went for the drinking. I went because I wanted to hear stories, and this was how the dudes liked to tell them, around plastic cups of beer arranged on a rubber tabletop. The talking would last until at least nine, maybe ten, before anyone acknowledged there were reasons to leave, that there was some other place called "home" where people waited for us.

"Do you expect him to finish this time?" Grace asked. "That agent training?"

"Definitely. He says the training is a cakewalk compared to the first time. Second time around he's much clearer. Mentally he's more focused since breaking up, and I guess it turned out to be a really good thing for Dan, because she never believed in him or—"

Grace laughed harshly and clapped her hands together. "Blessing! Well, how about that. And did he blame her for the DUI that got him kicked out the first time?"

"Well, yeah," I said.

Grace laughed even harder. "He left the military because his evaluations were bad, John. Because they didn't want him, not because of anything his wife did. He got kicked out of training because he drank too much, drove his car, and he got a DUI, not because of anything his ex-wife did. I know you love your friend, but God he can be a fool for his own fantasy."

I wisely remained silent.

Grace leaned back in her chair and crossed both arms at her chest. "That guy knows how to keep things new alright. He keeps changing the past so that he can tolerate the present."

"He's a dreamer." I slipped the toe of my shoe under the black leash that hung down the back of the chair next to me and kicked it closer. "We've always had that much in common."

I pulled the collar around the neck of our black lab Rex, pushing his head down when he kicked his forelegs up onto my thighs. Grace was standing in the shadows, hands on her hips. She reached an arm across my chest and we hugged, two kids who met on the track all those years ago. The leash tightened around my wrist.

"I'll be up later," I said, and Grace nodded before turning toward the stairs.

The air outside was still and cool. Streetlamps cast orange light that reflected like sparks off the glass and metal of cars parked in driveways all along the sides of our wide, paved street. I looked to the end of the street then behind me but there were no people around. Everyone must be inside. I reached into the shoulder pocket of my windbreaker and grabbed the tin of Copenhagen, pinched a clump the size of a marble, and pressed it against the gumline below the bottom row of my teeth. The sight of it made Grace sick, so this had become another part of me I chose to keep hidden from view, saving my habit for late night walks alone through the neighborhood.

As Rex and I made our way down the sidewalk, my eyes floated from one set of windows into the next, across full lawns and over rows of neatly trimmed hedges. I liked looking into the windows of other people's homes, noticing the flash of color from a television set or family photos lining empty hallways. This was the neighborhood where I had grown up and so much of it had never changed.

When we got to the end of the street, Rex pulled me toward a stop sign while he sniffed around its edges, maneuvering his body back and forth as he looked for the right position to kick his hind leg into the air. My face prickled with sensation, a blowing breeze that felt neither warm nor cool, and my eyes went to the white two-story on the corner, through a bay window and into a room where a large television was broken into four small screens, each showing a pistol or rifle in the foreground pointing toward a bombed-out building. A first-person shooter in an urban combat game.

The words were slipping away. Almost as soon as the words appeared to me, I was stuck again, the same place I had been stuck for weeks, beating a hand against my head and trying not to remember. I gripped the leash with both hands and pulled until Rex dropped his head and shuffled back, coughing into the grass. His body brushed against the side of my leg and I put a hand on his face, then his neck, scratching the soft underside of his long jaw. We stood together for a moment, then continued on down the sidewalk.

CHAPTER THREE

ailor & Tines was the oldest law firm in the city, and I was its newest attorney. The only attorney assigned to park in the lot a half-mile walk from the Power and Light building. The only attorney who spent the winter months trudging through snow and slush, stomping my feet on the office doormat alongside the secretaries and runners who were my parking lot neighbors.

"When you move up, don't forget how it feels to start your day with wet socks," my secretary said as she slipped out of snow boots and put on flats.

Beads of moisture dripped down the insides of my black leather shoes. It might be years before I moved into the firm's heated parking garage, where months earlier I had watched Mick Ward take one crooked step out of his Mercedes, lose balance, and fall face first onto the firm's welcome mat. Ward hadn't needed to take one full step. He fell into work. He was dialing his secretary from the ground when I bent over and helped scoop him up, hooking my forearms underneath his armpits and noticing how light he was.

"Thanks, kid," he said, the sharp tone of his voice echoing down the concrete ramp. He dusted off his jacket and looked at me. "Haven't I seen you around? Wait a second..." He snapped his fingers. "I've seen you downstairs—I know who you are. You're in the cafeteria; you eat a salad by the window?"

That I had been at the firm for six months seemed beside the point. He'd noticed me and that was good enough.

The building was nothing special, a well-built cube, a box of brown bricks stacked ten stories high and taking up half a block of real estate in the heart of downtown. The only architectural flourish was an arcade walkway on the side of the building that faced the river. It was the feeling of being covered, but with a fresh breeze and sunlight that made the walkway something of an attraction in our small downtown. I stepped through the revolving door and walked past the elevators to climb the stairs. Most of the Power and Light building had not been renovated since the 1980s, as if the third and fourth floors had been holding onto their threadbare maroon carpets and beige walls as a badge of honor in the resistance to change. Only one of the three floors had been deemed worthy of a renovation. That was the fifth floor, our showcase, where light glowed in a cream aura and the only sound was the soft clack of leather soles across pink marble floors. You felt cleaner just walking around on the fifth floor. The walls and doors were built of frosted glass and cut so thick not even a whisper traveled from one attorney's office into the hallway or through the walls that separated offices. I had to set my feet shoulder width apart and pull with both arms just to open one of those enormous glass doors. It was heavy as a bank vault.

Tailor & Tines was a trial man's law firm and the attitude of the place reflected as much. There was no fussing over paperwork, no hunkering down for the slow crawl through probate or the eye-bleeding tedium of contract reviews.

"Nobody hirin' a Tailor man to do deals. No business deals here. No real estate deals or otherwise chickenshit deals for some coward's arbitration board."

Mick said this at my first all-associates meeting, a monthly lunchtime program designed to broadcast on a big television screen each associate's hourly output from the previous month, what had come to be a monthly exercise in public humiliation.

"Leave all that to somebody else," was Mick's advice. "Leave it to the old-timers, the featherheads and paperweights. Let the lesser men ride their painted rocking horses at full steam across some office room floor. Tailor men go to war."

Figurative war, but still the hardest kind of combat one can expect when business partners fall out or somebody's facelift leaves a visible three-inch seam running down the edge of her jawline. And we especially went to war when a top client's kid had too much to drink, got pulled over by the cops, refused the breathalyzer, and lost his license. If you had a bone to pick and enough downstroke to cover a $10,000 retainer, then Tailor was your first and last phone call.

And Michael "Mick" Ward was your first pick. He was five-feet, four inches tall and his head was bald and shaped like a peanut, a small head even for his small body, but his eyes shone a bright green from behind his Coke-bottle lenses, his ruddy face and scalp covered with light brown freckles. You could find him any day of the week seated behind his big desk and wearing a pressed white shirt, the kind with the soft collar that rolled down over a striped, prep school necktie. He pulled it all together with a double-breasted navy blazer with yellow shank buttons sporting a raised eagle on the outside, and always, always a shiny black pair of Testoni loafers.

"The shoes are for you, counselor," he'd say. "Nobody payin' to see you in a pair of lace-ups."

There were many litigators at the firm, men somewhere just past middle age. The kind who wore shabby shoes with rubber soles and black slacks, blue oxford shirts that bunched up and wrinkled around the elbows, neckties that never seemed to stay snug around the collar. These men represented the insurance companies. They liked calling their cases "files" and each other "filers." To them, there was always time on the clock to make one more offer to settle a file, to strike what they were fond of calling "a reasonable tone" with opposing counsel, to try one more time to "get everybody in a room together," maybe see "if both sides can't put their swords away, save everybody a lot of heartache." They were wonderful men to work for, patient and rule obedient, but none of those filers had ever wanted that big, brass office in the corner of the fifth floor. None had ever picked up his sword and started swinging just for the hell of it.

"Get me to the jury. Everybody knows Micky's a goer."

Mick said it to mediators and opposing counsel. He said it to every judge from Chicago to Denver; even a cold caller on the other end of a phone line was going to hear about how much Mick loved a jury before the line went dead. He said it to anyone who would listen, and he meant it every time.

The firm's fortunes rose with Mick. They had never been higher since last summer when he won the $50 million verdict, the big one.

"The work these people do for us, in our own back-yards," he told the jury in closing argument. "Working in poor footwear, mind you, and look at us. Take a hard look at yourselves. Look at how we bury them: at the bottom of a pile of concrete."

It was a wrongful death case, a family of immigrants living in an empty building alongside the river just a short walk from the fancy restaurants and curio shops of the Market District. The building was one of a series of one-story brick buildings used a century ago to store textiles and dry goods before the railroads hauled them west. The city had condemned the buildings where the family was living, but officials never bothered to post notices on the doors before they started the demolition. They were building a "white box" on the site, and the data storage and telecom companies behind the project were driving the city hard. Four kids and their mother were buried under rock and rebar, and it wasn't until somebody noticed a sandal sticking out of the rubble that they cleared the debris and gave the family a Christian burial.

"That one," Micky told us in the conference room the day he got his verdict, holding a Heineken, "had what I call the 'wow' factor. Tell 'em every time. 'Micky's taking your case only if it meets the 'big three'—clear liability, astronomical damages—I mean the damages got to be outta this world—and that last one, the 'wow' factor. When I saw this case, it had sparkle. I was so far ahead of defense counsel they couldn't hit me with a three wood!"

His longtime secretary, a white-haired woman called Viv, said she couldn't believe what moxie he'd brought to that case. "Such a scrapper," she told me, in awe of how much Mick risked to take on the corporation, the city, how he fought with closed fists against the big guy, not unlike that South Boston welterweight with whom he shared a nickname. "Micky Ward, the people's champ!"

So long as the people had the 'wow' factor and enough tragedy in their story, Mick would play the heartstrings. As much as I couldn't stand his bravado, the man had vision.

He intuited the arguments as much as he plotted them out. Other partners, especially the filers, labored over every draft of their briefs, poring over the placement of each period and comma, cutting sentences so short their arguments read like a children's book. These filers hammered language so flat each sentence touched down with a dull thud. "Make it sound like you're talking to your neighbor, see?" one of the filers told me. "Like it's just you and your neighbor, except your neighbor is the judge, and the two of you, well, you're just having a nice old conversation, like Otis and Andy."

I did my best, but everything I wrote sounded more like the slow grind of machinery than anything heard in Mayberry.

Mick was different.

"Make it sing, counselor. I'll do the rest." He filed his briefs on the first draft. Well, he had Viv file his briefs on the first draft, just like he had Viv answer his emails, send out his invoices, and occasionally dispatch a runner or a mail clerk to collect Mick's overdue dry cleaning. She even typed all his voicemails into text messages so he could read them while sitting in a deposition.

> *10:10—Mick, it's me Tim, your friend. It's been a while. You dodging me, Mick? You said you'd handle my mom's will six months ago. She died last week, Mick. Call me.*

> *10:30—Hey Mick Ward, it's Sam. Don't know if you heard, but I'm launching a bid to be your next mayor. Can we talk sometime, Mick? I could use a fighter like you in my corner.*

Who knows if he ever read those messages or how many he received in an average day, sitting up in that beautiful corner office with a commanding view of the district courthouse and city skyline. The office was the kind of reward 1 percent of hard-driving people achieve in their working lives, but Mick was rarely there to enjoy it, what with the schedule of meetings and consultations he kept all about downtown, walking from coffeehouse to coffeehouse each morning, holding a Starbucks grande in his left hand to keep his right hand free to greet clients, area businessmen, and local politicians.

"Bring it in, bro," he'd say, wrapping an arm around you like a long-lost friend. After he finished the coffeehouse circuit, it was on to the corporate headquarters of the regional bank or the insurance company, or all the way up to the fiftieth floor of the Paul Graybar headquarters to commiserate with Mr. Graybar himself, leaning back in his chair with fingers clasped behind his head, expounding on the wrongful discharge suit of a former senior vice president.

"Man's got no claim here. 'Cause a shooter don't pull the trigger with his eyes closed, know what I'm saying?"

People rarely did, but area business types loved the decisiveness. A firm answer today, right or wrong, was always better than the smoke-and-mirrors routine they'd come to expect from other big-shot lawyers. Mick always left the C-suite having relieved a little bit of the pressure, letting the president or the directors rest a little easier knowing Micky Ward was making their arguments.

By late afternoon it was time for "office hours." The associates were already queued outside the thick glass door, somebody waving a motion or a brief in the air, trying to choke down the panic rising up from his stomach. "Mick, can you read this? Please, it's due to the court in ten minutes!" The questions just kind of rolled from there.

"Hey Mick, how do we get around this hearsay objection?"

"Do you like these questions for your cross-exam, Mick? I kept them ten words or less, just how you said."

"Mick, will the jury respond better to a red tie or a blue tie?"

The man's blessing was as good an authority as a Supreme Court opinion. He was our general, our admiral, the captain of our ship.

And me? Well, I was his galley slave.

I turned the corner to walk down the long hallway to my office, noticing for the first time its narrowness. Twelve feet high but no more than half that across. The carpet footpath had worn down through the middle and smelled of musty paper mixed with the heat of burning plastic from an overworked copy machine. There was paper everywhere. Stacks of white papers piled on desks and left sitting in empty chairs, towers of court documents on office room floors, packed into overstuffed white binders, collecting dust inside manila file folders. Paper was currency. The more you had laying around your office, the more likely somebody might drop by your doorway to offer his services. Even I had a couple of bankers boxes filled with deposition transcripts.

But those belonged to Mick.

The voicemail light on my phone wasn't glowing and the inbound tray on my desk was empty. Weeks had passed since I last received mail. I hung up my suit jacket on the inside of my door and just stood there, wondering what action or thought might come next in my day. It turned out to be the sound of fingers tapping on a keyboard.

"Mornin'," came a voice across the hall.

I waved a hand through my doorway, but Russ Slaven didn't bother to look away from his computer monitors, fingers fluttering across the keyboard at his stand-up desk.

"Standing a little early this morning?"

He stopped typing and took a sip from a clear plastic tumbler, his coffee smelling like burned toast from all the way across the hall.

"I hit the stand-up for five hours every day, Walker. Did the math. I'm running one marathon for every month that I put in five hours per day at the stand-up, and that doesn't even include weekends. One full marathon every month, and I don't even have to leave the office. Think about that. Twenty-six point two miles and billing every second of it."

Russ pulled the trigger on the vertical mouse he held like a joystick, firing off an email with a sharp click. A punctuation on the mileage comment.

"Surprised a military guy like yourself hasn't gotten on board yet," he said.

I shrugged.

Six feet tall and not an ounce over a hundred and seventy pounds, Slaven had lean strands of muscle rippling inside the sleeves of his slim-cut shirts. He was a spy, keeping an eye on me from the office across the hall. I had to be cunning and watchful for the sake of a position I hardly wanted.

"Somebody was looking for you earlier but too bad you weren't here. Sorry, bud," he said, turning his shiny bald head back to the side-by-side computer screens above his keyboard tray.

The office was quiet this morning. Several of the rooms on the third floor had been assigned to the very senior partners, the "senior citizen" partners, a handful of attorneys in their midseventies who spent their winters playing golf in Palm Springs and their summers playing golf in River City. Sometimes they dropped by to collect their mail or thumb through old case files they kept inside their drawers, maybe even say hello to their secretaries. They came by to make sure the current bosses, especially Mick, knew they hadn't dried out completely in the California desert, that their pensions still needed paid.

"Eight thirty-two a.m. Jumping on a call at ten. Topic? Width of the wheelchair ramp into the building. That is the south—no, strike that—the north entrance. Possible noncompliance with federal statute."

His narration muffled but still recognizable, old Mr. Quinn down the hall recorded his thoughts into a mini cassette tape. He showed up to the office each morning, head bent low over the mic of his Dictaphone, puttering about as he clocked every minute of time spent considering the few issues still in front of him, trying his best not to mourn too long for the clients and colleagues left behind. Mick and the other partners had long since "opened Quinn's book," helping to usher the older man into a twilight retirement by divvying up his clients among the next generation. The old feeding on the older. The only client they left him was an outfit called Home for Good LLC, an assisted living company that helped old folks stay in their homes for a few years more.

"Dear Bob—good chatting with you about…"

When the morning's recording was finished, Quinn would drop the cassette at his secretary's desk, change into his jersey and wool slacks, then slip out the back door for a two-mile walk down to the river and back. By the time he showered and got his corduroy trousers back on, there would be a two-page memorandum to the president of Home for Good awaiting his signature.

I stepped out of my office and into the hallway. The week was just beginning, so there was hope of accomplishing something. The door at the end of the hallway was partly open and the light was on inside. I knocked and waited.

No answer.

I knocked more forcefully, looking through the gap between the wall and open door to see Quinn standing next to the window at the very back of his office. He was staring down into the empty alleyway a few flights below.

"Good morning, Mr. Quinn."

Still no response.

"Hello, Mr. Quinn!" I yelled.

Mouth open, he spun around, his face looking like he had just awakened from a hypnotic trance. He rubbed his ear. "I was just thinking about something, young man. Come to think of it, I can't remember…."

I glanced at the bare walls. The office was remarkably clean save for the stacks of papers arranged on the floor next to the table. No diplomas, no bar licenses, just a wooden golf club leaning against the wall and a lone bowling pin perched atop the heavy bookcase. Quinn eased into his chair, Dictaphone still in the front breast pocket of his white shirt.

"You seem older," he said softly. His small, bony hands resembled a bed of twigs when he placed one hand over the other. "We generally hire a straight-line group. People who start in kindergarten and go straight through law school in a…straight line."

The room smelled of dust and paper. I struggled to pay attention, barely listening while he described a problem, something he wanted me to research.

"Terrier bit my grandbaby's Maltese. Now she wants her friend to pay the bills."

Before the risen partner class had opened Quinn's book and taken his clients, he had been one of the city's most sought-after attorneys. His reputation was so strong that just saying Quinn's name around town could get you places. There was something about his calm demeanor that rang authentic to people who heard the man speak. Clients paid a high price for the relentlessly combative style Mick brought to a lawsuit, but they trusted Quinn in a way Mick never replicated in his own dealings with the older man's clients.

He closed his mouth for a moment and raised an eyebrow. "Prefer she just take better care of that dog," he said, reclining. "To learn…" Quinn slowly turned toward the alley, searching for a lost word, his train of thought stalling.

"Responsibility."

"There, yes. I knew it was in there somewhere. Would you find some law to help my granddaughter learn responsibility?"

He could have asked me to copy down the Constitution on a legal pad and I would have said yes. If there were a hundred lawyers crammed into the building, Quinn was the second one to show interest in putting me to some kind of use. I didn't bother asking if the work would be paid.

"Memorandum will do fine."

He looked done speaking to me but I had a question.

"Do you miss it?" I asked. "The courtroom?"

He set down his gym bag on the carpeted floor and again leaned back in the leather chair. He scrunched his lips. "No. Never much liked talking to judges, always the smartest guys in the room."

"What about the clients," I asked. "Do you miss them?"

"Not really," Quinn admitted. "Awfully demanding lot."

He stretched his legs out in front of him, crossing them at the ankles and settling deeper into his chair. He seemed to enjoy being asked a question, eager for the attention that had long ago turned away from him and toward a younger generation.

"Then you don't miss anything?" I asked. Suddenly, I was wondering what about this new profession was worthwhile if someone like Quinn found none of it made him even a little wistful.

"Well. That's not true. Only thing I miss is the jury."

"I hear they can be unpredictable. Mick says half the time the jury is just too dumb to—"

Quinn cleared his throat. He raised one of those spindly fingers into the air. "With all due respect to Mr. Ward, the jury is the only friend a lawyer gets in his career. The client's your boss, the judge is bound by the code of ethics to keep his distance from you, and other lawyers, well, I suppose you've already seen how that turns out. But the jury's waiting for you to come along and take them by the hand. They want you to be someone they can believe in…"

He shook his head, his eyes glistening.

"I got a dog a couple years ago. A dog can be a pretty good friend so long as you take care of him. Have you got one?"

I nodded, and the old man smiled, rubbing the gray stubble on his rounded chin. He again reached down for the strap handle of his bag, preparing to resume the routine that I had somehow interrupted. I sensed by now Quinn's kindness was empty, that he no longer had the ability to help me, but I had no other prospects. At least with Quinn I knew that everything he said was superficial, that he was too old and too tired to hurt me the way Ward or Slaven would if they had the chance. The firm was full of traps, but this wasn't one of them.

I shuffled back to my desk, opened email, and scrolled through the messages. Nothing. I put my palms on the desk and looked at the four walls surrounding me, almost as naked as the day I walked in for the first time. The room was quiet. People were always around at the law firm and it should have been impossible to be lonely. I stared at the few pictures mounted on my big wall and let my thoughts drift.

"No window means more space for decoration," Slaven had said when I moved in a year ago. "Make sure you put your law degree where clients can see it. Seriously, it's firm policy."

Firm protocol required a framed diploma hang on the wall, but I had a better idea. One night after everyone left, I hoisted a heavy, steel framed-print of a soldier in dress uniform holding a rifle with bayonet at his shoulder on a blue-sky day. The soldier was walking midstride in front of a marble box, the Tomb of the Unknown Soldier. The picture was not a window, but it drew eyeballs.

"That you in the picture?" Slaven said once, unironically.

Not everybody recognized the monument, but it made sense to them that this picture would hang in my office.

"I hear you're, like, the Chuck Norris of first-years," one of the filers had said to me at last year's firm Christmas party. The filers took their social cues from the rich clients they served, and there were enough rich people in town, people who loved the military and praised veterans, to communicate there was something to be gained in having an American flag flying outside your door. Only a couple more drinks and he asked what was really on his mind.

"Did you see anything over there? Did you see the real stuff?"

"You mean did I kill anyone?" I said.

He shrugged and glanced around the room, then nodded eagerly. I felt like a climber asked to explain the mountain to someone who never scaled a hill, so I played along with him, inhaling deeply, picking a spot on the wall and staring at it so hard my vision blurred.

"Yeah," I said, air passing out of my nose like steam from a kettle. "I saw the pink mist."

The filer blinked hard.

"So sorry, man. I knew I shouldn't have asked it. But I knew. I could tell you had seen shit. Let me get you another. What will you have? Can I get you a beer?"

I put a finger to my lips. "How about a chardonnay?"

The man blinked so hard you would have thought I hit him.

"You are an actor, man!" Dan had gushed when I relayed the story. "Did you tell him that you 'lost a lot of good men out there,' or did you save that chestnut for another hungry squirrel?" Dan cracked up laughing. "They can't help themselves. They want that secondhand glory. 'Tell me you're a hero.' 'I'd be really freaked out if you killed somebody, but please, please tell me that you killed somebody.'"

It was performance. The entire wall facing the open doorway was covered, sanctified, by pictures of war dead, two faces on either side of the burial photo. The left was a clean-faced young man wearing his dress blue uniform and glowering into the camera. He came from Indiana to be a rifleman in my platoon. Just a boy carrying the radio on his back, the thin green reed of an antenna sticking up over the top of his Kevlar helmet, the straps of his weighted-down pack digging grooves into his narrow shoulders. He spent more time talking into a handset than he did behind the gun that deployment.

"America wants to see me kill, sir. Not talk!" He was gone a month into the tour. A crack of the rifle and everybody was face-first into the dirt. I looked up to find him in a seated position, reclining with his back against the bulk of his pack and holding a hand to the side of his neck, red and slippery. On the other side of my wall was a picture of Sergeant West. Same face, same uniform, but a chest full of ribbons.

The phone rang and I picked it up. *"Hey, John. Wanted to let you know I'm leaving early today for an appointment."*

Office rules required that secretaries called their attorneys whenever they left early, came in late, or needed time off during the day.

"I've just had massive gas all weekend," she said.

I was used to this by now.

"Bloating. Gas. The works. Some diarrhea's involved, that sorta thing, and I don't know if it's gonna clear up on its own or if there's something he can give me that'll settle it down. My husband said 'Don't go in there if all's you're gonna do is stink up the place,' but I haven't missed a day of work in thirty years, John, not one. So, I'll be clearin' outta here at 'round three p.m. if that's okay by you?" she said, unashamed.

After less than a year together I could name every one of her kids and her brother and sisters, including the ones she refused to speak to.

"*Don't forget you got the meeting with that gang-banger type coming up. Oh, and remember you gotta keep after those summaries, John. Viv says Ward's hot for those sooner rather than later. And I'm told to ask if you'll be attending the Silver Beaver today?*"

"The what?"

"*One of these business jamborees. Somebody puttin' on the dog. Park ranger hat and raisin' his two fingers to get an award from the community for good works. You know, John, you should put yourself out there, at least get a free lunch out of it. Twenty-dollar plates and Ward himself is puttin' on the hat this year. God knows he'll have somethin' to say.*"

I flipped on my computer monitor and found the invitation near the bottom of a short list of emails:

Join us to honor Michael "Mick" Ward as this year's awardee of our Silver Beaver. Mick has demonstrated a special devotion to Scout duty. A leader in the boardroom, the courtroom, and in other rooms large and small across our friendly business city.

The invitation included a picture of the award, a silver beaver the size of a quarter hanging from the end of a blue and white ribbon.

"I'll see how I feel." I hung up the phone and looked at the cardboard boxes on my floor.

For the past six months, my primary assignment had been reading and summarizing the transcripts from depositions Mick had taken of doctors and scientists, engineers and salesmen, anybody with the slightest connection to the faulty product that started the whole litigation. A medical device company had chosen hospitals to administer a groundbreaking new treatment for men experiencing what the brochures called "leakage and overflow incontinence" after treatment for prostate cancer. The Apollo Pride was a mechanical enhancement inserted at the base of the penis, employing a tiny clamp to help regulate the flow of urine through the man's urethra. The results were positive, generally.

"No more wet spots. Apollo Pride gave me back my piece of mind...my pride," said one satisfied client.

That the company had designed Pride only for men who had their prostates removed was somehow lost on the local surgeons who inserted the thing into every cancer survivor suffering incontinence, regardless if he had only been treated with radiation.

"I woke up one morning and felt like a spike belt was wrapped around the outside of my dick," said one of our plaintiffs.

The warning had not been on the package label or in the advertising materials. None of the company's representatives mentioned the possibility that men subjected to different treatment might react differently to the device. So, we sued everybody: the doctors and nurses who operated on patients, the hospitals, insurance companies, brokers, and the marketing firms who sold the products. There was a period of six months after we filed our first lawsuit that not a day went by without a phone call from a different man experiencing similar groin pain or leakage.

I took most of those phone calls.

"Sign 'em up," Mick said. "Every goddamn one of them. Just make sure they bring their own pens!"

We ended up with several dozen plaintiffs and enough depositions to fill the boxes that sat mostly untouched in my office.

I grabbed a few sheets of paper and laid them out on my desk, picking out quotations that sounded interesting to me but didn't have the slightest bearing on the outcome of the case. It took only a few minutes before the absurdity of my task set in, that I would be reading thousands of pages of testimony, the same facts restated by different people, highlighting the same portions, and then typing up summaries in preparation for a trial that wasn't even scheduled, rendering one transcript of another, making copies out of other copies like a human Xerox machine. District prosecutors across the street made less than one hundred dollars per hour calling up juries and proving murder charges at trial. I made more than triple that slouched in my chair, shamelessly transcribing lines from one summary to another.

"Inefficiency at its most lucrative, counselor," Mick told me when I pointed it out to him.

A few minutes in and already I could not stand the work. The questions Mick asked were incessant, his answers bewildering.

OPPOSING COUNSEL: How severe was the pain you felt in your penis?

WARD: Objection, he's not answering that question.

OPPOSING COUNSEL: Excuse me—why not?

WARD: Because, Counselor, he's not here to give his opinion about his penis, okay? He's here to testify about the facts. You agreed to the rules.

OPPOSING COUNSEL: But that's what I'm asking, Michael. I'm asking about his penis pain, which is a fact you have admitted.

WARD: No, Counselor—you're asking after an opinion about his penis. I restate my objection. For the record, the question is outside the scope of this—

OPPOSING COUNSEL: Wait a minute, wait. There's no difference—

WARD: You wanna scrap with me?

OPPOSING COUNSEL: No. I don't want to—I want the witness to answer my question, Michael.

WARD: Objection, that's flat-out argumentative. Look, Counselor, if you wanna dick with me, then let's walk up to the judge's chambers right now and see how the dollars stack up.

The scene was easy for me to imagine by now. Mick fidgeting in his oversize leather chair, opposing counsel exasperated by the little man who seemed to be making it up as he went along, disregarding the meaning of objections he misused over and over again, the big city lawyer's assiduous preparation coming apart at the hands of a small-town agitator. I set down the highlighter and rubbed my forehead, wondering how many more pages I might get through before lunch.

It didn't help my concentration that I could hear footsteps shuffling outside my door. Even the slightest noise was enough to distract me from work I didn't want to be doing.

"Ah, yes...." I heard from someone standing in the hallway.

"The *Wrapped Reichstag*. One of my absolute favorites of the firm's collection. Pronounced rye-shtock. And to think it was only the preparatory collage made in shades of gray, only a grisaille, if you will. The actual work, all the wrapping and cover and all else, has been gone for decades. The artists created something they knew would not last, that time would erase their handiwork, and they did it for only one reason."

There was a pause before he finished his thought.

"To see what it would look like," he said, with gusto.

I could hear a young woman purr.

"Let me ask you something personal, miss. How does it make you feel to look at it; what do you have going on inside yourself, this very minute?"

I pushed the chair to the side of my desk and peered out of the open doorway to find Ned, the firm's self-appointed docent, staring at a young woman wearing a ponytail with a hopeful look on her face. I recognized her as a student recruited from a nearby law school. She was interviewing for a summer internship.

"The art makes me feel, well, it makes me feel, like..."

She looked hard into the black and blue sketching on the wall, her shoulder touching Ned's.

"Grateful."

He craned his head toward her.

"Grateful?"

She smiled.

"Grateful. I feel so much gratitude that this beautiful art, such a beautiful piece, is hanging here for me to appreciate. Right?"

Ned straightened his shoulders and took a step back.

"Very astute observation, Miss. Thank you for sharing. Thank you very much."

He pulled a pen from his pants pocket and tucked it neatly into the left breast pocket of his shirt. "That will be all the time we have for today," he added abruptly, raising a hand toward the elevators and leading her down the long hallway.

After a few minutes, I got up from my desk and walked to Ned's office. He was adjusting the blinds on his slim rectangular window, twisting a plastic stick until light spilled in at an angle.

"Something casual, Lieutenant," he said. "The woman wanted something casual."

He took a seat in the leather desk chair and draped one leg over the other, a look of fatigue on his clean-shaven face. There was barely a paper on the big wooden desk.

"The applications—dating apps and so forth. I knew that young woman. Had a very long conversation with her a couple months ago, actually, and neither one of us acknowledged this was a challenge because I could not stop thinking that she only wanted *something casual*, that she is a *something casual* kind of woman. I know of women in Chicago wanting something casual, and women in New York probably want nothing but something casual…but here? Can you believe she said that to me, this local woman? The brazenness of it. No, we cannot hire her. My God—I think I went to grade school with one of her cousins."

Ned's eyes widened. He had the habit of glancing over his shoulder whenever he was excited, eyeballs swiveling inside their sockets.

"Why the ring?" I asked, pointing to my left-hand ring finger.

Ned twirled the fingers in front of him, admiring the gold band on his ring finger.

"This old thing? Why, I picked this up over the weekend at the second-chance store downtown. I like it very much, it's just so matrimonial, don't you think?"

He raised the hand above his head to inspect the ring. He laughed, stuck the whole finger into his mouth, and pulled on the ring until it came off. He delicately placed it at the center of a small stack of pages on his desk.

"You're not going to declare war on costumes now, are you, Walker?" He tightened the knot on his green and purple silk tie. Ned dressed old but acted infectiously youthful.

"You wore the ring so the girl would think you were married, right? Couldn't let her think you'd been scared away by the 'something casual' so you got yourself married as a way to outdo her?"

He swung his chair away from me and began clicking pointlessly at the computer, the cursor snapping to no effect against a blank screen, then turned again.

"She seemed curious, which is just about the best you can hope for in a woman. But I'm bored talking about this. How was your weekend?"

I waited for the long whistle of a train outside to fade, then told him about the gun range and about Dan, a subject he enjoyed discussing.

"Man's history of violence revisited. I'd like to hear you develop that, you know, tell me more of the shooting period instead of the, er, death-worship period you entered into more recently," he said, nodding toward my office down the hall.

"Beats what everybody else puts on their walls," I said.

"I suppose you've taken the phrase 'begin with the end in mind' literally, haven't you? Anyway, this shooter, Dan. He's the good-looking friend who always fucks everything up, do I have that right?"

"*Was* fucking up," I said. "Everything is much better since the divorce."

Ned plucked the wedding band from the table and placed it into the plastic tray inside his drawer. Every woman at the law firm seemed to have a sister or a college friend, someone who "should have been perfect" for him. Women were always trying to set him up with someone who had gone to nice schools and had good hygiene and friendly manners. Ned turned them all away.

"Is there anything more American than divorce? Emancipation, I call it," he said. "Shedding something stale and old, something depleted of all…sensuousness. I commend your friend and wish him godspeed on his new walk of freedom. Send him the blessings of a fellow traveler."

I took Ned in, watching him sit so comfortably in his big, cavernous office, amusing himself with observations of the world outside this safe cocoon. He seemed content to be a bystander but his aloneness worried people, especially married women.

"What could he possibly be doing by himself?" They would ask. "By himself all the time. Taking walks by himself, listening to music by himself. Is he trying to walk off a midlife crisis?"

The thought of a man, particularly a man who washed his own clothes and could cook his own meals—a commodity, in other words—withholding himself from the marketplace offended them, for fear that perceiving Ned's aloneness as normal might call into question the virtue of their own busy and partnered lives.

"First there's the marital twilight phase," he said, settling in for one of his trademark discussions.

Whenever a male attorney at the firm filed for divorce, Ned followed the man's transformation like the British tabloids follow the royal family, keeping an eye on every facial expression, every change of clothes, commenting obsessively from a safe distance away.

"It begins when the husband notices he's being lightly oppressed at home, that his wife has made a tightening of the 'angle of oppression,'" he said, shaping his hand into a V and squeezing it like a vise. "First he's out for only an hour past curfew and she calls him to come home. The next time he's out for an hour and she doesn't call him, he feels like he's running a tab that needs paying. Anxiety builds. At work, the husband begins complaining about his wife more frequently, so he starts staying late at the office until soon he's coming in on Saturdays just to get out from under her. He justifies it by saying, 'Well, I've got no choice but to work double for that bonus so I can pay for everything. Memberships and private schools.' I call this the alienation phase, when the husband stops seeing himself as a member of the team, but instead as the general manager, a front-office type whose contractual obligation is to provide a certain experience to the players on the field. This goes on for a while until another realization dawns: I deserve a reward.'"

Turned fully toward the window, it was not clear if Ned was still talking to me or himself.

"He says, 'I'm going to happy hour tonight!' He shuts off his phone. Then comes time for the guys' trip to Vegas or a weekend golf tournament to wherever. 'I haven't seen the guys in years, babe. I need this...'"

Ned was giggling now.

As much as I enjoyed watching Ned tease out the subtleties of marriage and divorce, I began to wonder just how many pages of depositions I might clear before lunch, whether it was still possible to redeem myself for another day wasted on daydreams and self-pity.

"Ned, I'd better be getting back to—"

"And there she is," he went on. "Waiting beside the kitchen table to chap his ass about the nine holes on Sunday morning. Kid's been awake for only three hours by the time he walks in the door and still she is as hot as an oven mitt. The man needed a round of golf with his buddies. Where is the harm?"

"Sorry to cut you off, Ned, but I have to run to this local—"

He stopped suddenly. "The Scouts, is it?"

Ned pulled back the white cuff of his sleeve and glanced down at his watch. Though he was done speaking, I knew the morning's disquisition on divorce would continue inside his head for much of the afternoon.

I nodded.

"You do realize that if you're late, the grand-marshal Scout or whoever will conscript you into standing at the front of the room and leading the whole group in the Pledge of Allegiance?"

"You could join me," I said teasingly as I turned to leave.

Ned waved me off. "Not me, Lieutenant. We'll pick this up another time."

CHAPTER FOUR

I jogged through the sliding doors that opened to the hotel ballroom, where a couple hundred middle-aged men stood around tables covered with white tablecloths. Milk-vase centerpieces held arrangements of artificial flowers and purple balloons clustered against the ceiling. Slaven was standing at the firm's table near the center of the room, tapping his fingers against the back of his chair as people chattered all around.

"Whatever happened to ten minutes early is five minutes late, Walker?"

For the second time today, he caught me off guard.

"I saved you a seat next to the judge." He smirked, pointing to a small chair next to the large man whose back was turned.

When I was seated, I picked up the stationery card on my plate and read the menu: salad, prime rib with peppered gravy, German chocolate cake or strawberry cheesecake for dessert. The salad and dessert had already been laid out at the table.

"That's your punishment for showing up late." The judge moved a slice of cheesecake from his plate to mine.

"I meant to be early, Your Honor, but—"

"I'm detaining this fine slice of German chocolate as punishment for your tardiness, young man."

The judge smiled as I wrapped my fingers around his thick, square hand. He stood a head taller than me and was twice as large. His leather belt was cinched tight around his waist, dividing his body into two oversized zones of abdomen. A wide plaid tie stopped halfway down his blue shirt.

"And none of that 'Your Honor' business out here, young man. That's courtroom talk. Socially, I expect you to call me Judge, or, if we're familiar from the bar, 'Hoss' is appropriate." He clapped me hard on the back. "I think Judge will be fine for you."

These business luncheons were always uncomfortable. Hotel ballrooms stuffed with managers and salesmen, some older man I'd never heard of receiving an award for public service or lifetime success in one business endeavor or another. Service and success meant the same thing to people in the room. It was hard for me to stomach, both the awards and the meal, but I thought it important to make an effort to meet people, to be seen by others.

The lights dimmed and a man and boy stepped onto the wooden stage at the front of the room. They were dressed the same. Tan khaki shirts with kerchiefs tied jauntily around their necks, various ribbons and medallions swinging from their chests.

"Let us begin by Scout tradition as we recite our national pledge of allegiance."

Seated closest to the stage was today's honoree, Micky Ward. He popped to his feet, while the judge next to me raised himself in one long, wheezing breath, hands bracing the arms of the chair. While men around the room placed a palm flat over their chests and recited the words slowly and with reverence, I cast my eyes to the carpet floor and put my hands in my pockets. Whatever honor I'd won overseas made me exempt from public displays of patriotism, I figured. I stared awkwardly at my shoes until the group finished.

"It is now my distinct honor to invite to the stage last year's honoree, Mr. P. Allen Graybar, the fourth-generation president of Graybar Incorporated," the Scout leader continued. "He will now execute the official handover to our newest Silver Beaver. Sir, would you please come forward?"

A white-haired man from Ward's table stood. The crowd clapped. Slowly, he made his way through the crowd, a silver cufflink gleaming under the ballroom's chandelier.

"Did you know we're acquainted?" the judge said, speaking loudly to someone seated across our table. "I met him this past New Year at the home of a mutual friend. He was exceptionally generous that evening, and if you haven't met Mr. Graybar, you should, oh you really should! Indeed, he is a great man, a terrific gentleman, and I don't say that about any man. In fact, you would love him."

Graybar's posture was elegant. He wore a royal blue suit tailored closely to his slender frame, a red tie tucked inside his buttoned suit jacket, and black leather shoes, lending a touch of formality to the ensemble. The white collar of his shirt was fastened as tightly as two hands wrapped around his neck. He was a man who looked comfortable being in charge, at ease with himself in the center of attention. He ran a hand gently, casually, through the tuft of hair combed back from his wide forehead. He wore glasses, the frames so thin it looked like two milky halos covered his eyes.

"On my honor," he said, raising his chin toward the crowd and speaking into the microphone. "I will do my best to do my duty to God and my country and to obey the Scout Law."

His voice was low, right hand raised to his forehead in a three-finger Scout salute. While most men raised their hands and chanted in unison, I clasped mine in front of my belt buckle, feeling excluded from a group that never asked for my participation.

"To help other people at all times. To keep myself physically strong, mentally awake, and morally straight."

Graybar was one of the city's wealthiest men, the chief executive of its largest company. He was a man of causes and his money was everywhere. When I was a child, he'd helped to build our first modern concert hall, a venue that brought in headline entertainers. Big-city talent, he called it. "Like Kansas City and St. Louis."

His portfolio touched every industry, from real estate to entertainment, even agriculture. When the city condemned the old granary building that hosted downtown's farmers market, Graybar came to the rescue. He paid cash for a half-mile stretch of abandoned parking lot along the river and donated the property to a co-op that continued to host the market on Saturday mornings. He said his father had taught him there's nothing better "than hittin' a home run for the community," that his father loved getting a big W for the community. The man bankrolled ballfields for Little Leaguers, commissioned glass sculptures for the city hospital. He supported all the causes and campaigns one city could muster. When Graybar got involved in your cause, it was never just about the checks he wrote or the publicity he brought: it was the name he put behind you. The whole Graybar brand that got every law firm, accounting shop, and community bank to put their name behind you too.

His hand cut sharply from his forehead and gripped the outside of the podium. He stood there in perfect silence for several passing seconds, unmoved to smile or speak. I felt the white tablecloth moving above my thigh and noticed Slaven's leg jiggling back and forth, one pants leg swooshing.

"Let's eat," Graybar finally said, and the room again broke into motion.

The men at my table looked as happy as any attorneys I had seen since I joined the firm, their heads bobbing up and down as they swallowed morsels of prime rib, dabbing at the corners of their mouths with white napkins. They laughed and smiled, talked about their children's graduation parties and summer vacations to Europe, comparing handicaps and golf courses they planned to play once the weather turned. They relished being here, joining forces with other local titans to attend the same benefit luncheons and community galas year after year.

Surrounded by people who did not interest me, celebrating an award I had never heard of until this morning, I stared at the food on my plate and wondered why I had come. I preferred eating by myself, someplace I could be around people but not a part of any group. I avoided people, and not because I was a loner. I avoided people because being alone alleviated the pressure of fitting into someone else's conversation, telling the lies required to gain acceptance, to assimilate into a new group inferior to the one left behind.

The judge ogled his plate, the two-finger mustache above his thin upper lip bristling. Delicately, he slipped the ribbon off his cake with his left hand, pinched the plastic wrapping, and flicked it toward the flower arrangement at the center of the table. I pushed the food around to the outer edges of my plate the way a child does when he wants to convince his mother he's eaten enough of it to get up from the table.

As the noise of eating lowered, attention returned to the stage, where Graybar now rested his arms on the lectern. Having cleaned three plates of food, the judge delicately placed the sharp end of his knife between the tines of his fork and turned to face the stage.

"The Silver Beaver is a man of substance," said Graybar. "He has all the great qualities, the patriotism and thriftiness, and the grit, because a Beaver has American grit. He combines this grit with an indomitable will, a relentless desire for success. But success is never given, gentlemen. No, success follows one thing—hard work. Beavers have always worked harder than needed."

He spoke haltingly, stopping every few words and pulling back from the podium, as if to keep himself from saying more than he should.

"Such a man is here among us today. Please welcome my friend, my defender..." Graybar paused for the crowd's laughter.

Ward himself laughed so hard he doubled over in his chair, catching the tablecloth between his knees and nearly pulling his plate and glass of water to the floor before straightening up to take the stage.

"Get up here, Mick. Lemme put this Beaver on you," Graybar exclaimed. He slipped the ribbon holding the silver pendant around Ward's neck then lowered the microphone to the smaller man's height.

"Give me a break with the clapping. It's just me here. Just Micky!"

The judge tapped my shoulder, leaning close. "He's the best trial lawyer of his generation, young man. You would do well to pay attention. Also, ahem, that man was a groomsman in my wedding," he whispered. "So, soak up every word."

"What a beautiful meal, right?" said Mick. "I tell ya, this being the Scouts, I expected they'd have us foraging for lunch. But let's cut to the chase—the title here is 'How I Became Me.'"

I groaned. Another day was half gone with nothing billed on the transcripts piled around my desk. Another wasted afternoon. Another day I fell further behind.

"My first trial and I'm defending a guy in a two-bit car accident. I'd been workin' up that case for months and it was finally time to put the plaintiff on the stand. A middle-aged lady—just a regular, middle-aged lady—and I start to feel it. Like a hunter stumbled on the tracks of a big animal. I was picking up her scent. I'm pacing the courtroom, hittin' this lady with every punch I got. About two-thirds into this and I start feelin' it even more, so I put on the plaintiff's husband. Now, I hear what you're saying. 'Micky, what's the husband got to do with this?' Well, he's up there because he brings along this sexy claim, you know. Fella says he hasn't had sex with his wife since the accident. Big fella, too."

Ward shrugged. The audience, whose curiosity seemed to have overtaken questions about the appropriateness of whatever Mick was talking about, fell silent. Their attention was all that mattered to him.

"This husband, he's sitting in that box rubbing his hands like he's trying to wring water out of a dry towel. Sweating through the armpits of his brown suit, just panting like an animal. When he reaches for a tall glass of water, the glass slips though his fingers. I watch the thing fall to the floor and it shatters. I mean absolutely *shatters*, and we got water everywhere. The husband can't take it. He starts crying, a grown man, right there on the stand, right in front of the judge, the ladies and gentlemen of the jury, the whole courthouse. He's bawling like a bald-headed baby and so I stop. I stop and I begin to…think.

"This man is teetering on the edge of somethin' I can't see, and I got the power right then to push him over that edge with the right question, to sorta put my hand into his chest and knock him ass over teakettle down the mountainside.

"But the point of my story is I didn't. I coulda done it. I *wanted* to do it. I might just regret not doing it to this very day because Micky coulda dropped that man down a deep hole, dropped that man so low I'd have buried him eight feet in the ground. But I stopped. I dismissed the witness. Sent him home and just read his testimony to the jury. It probably cost me my verdict. I could have humiliated a man in public, but something inside said no. Something told me it was wrong to break a man down in public.

"My verdict comes back and I'm sitting in the gallery by myself and second-guessin', telling myself that next time I'll do what's necessary, next time I'll finish the job, when the judge calls me to the bench. He's lookin' down from on high. Judge says to me, 'Son, you are a *chain-swinger*.' I never heard the word in all my life! 'Ward, you are a *chain-swinger*,' he says again. He says, 'You're a bigger son-of-a-bitch than you give yourself credit for to risk your case and do the right thing like that. You have sensitivity, son.

"I never knew it could be a compliment to tell a man that he was sensitive. Always seemed kinda chickenshit, honestly, but the judge made me think. Think about the right thing. Judge is still sittin' tall on that bench, lookin' down at me from on high. 'But son," he says, 'remember that discretion is the better part of valor.' And so that's where I leave you folks today. It has been this Scout's honor."

The applause came and went as quickly as the doors to the exit flew open, nearly the entire crowd thundering out of the room like cattle before Ward had stepped off the stage. I turned my own chair around to an empty table, disoriented by Mick's story but expecting to at least shake hands with people before heading to the door. Piles of plastic wrappers and dirty dishes were all that was left of lunch.

As I pushed back from the table, I noticed a business card placed on the tablecloth in front of me, a simple white card with black lettering that spelled out the name of the judge. I flipped it over to the back, and read a note he'd left in red ink:

Young man, Benefit for the opera company at my house tomorrow evening. You'd be wise to come. Address on front. Yours, Hoss.

CHAPTER FIVE

*B*ack at the office, I squinted at the two computer screens propped up on my desk. I kept one tilted away from my door, out of view from the hallway in case anyone happened to peer into my office as they walked by. Something different was always up, a picture or image that offered a few minutes of relief before turning back to the empty email box on the other. Today it was Neil Armstrong. I pulled the edge of the monitor toward me.

I could just hear Slaven in my head, poking his face through the door to call me careless, inattentive, some kind of daydreaming Johnny not pulling his weight in billable hours.

The photograph was black-and-white, father and son. It wasn't Armstrong locking his helmet onto the white spacesuit or posing for the press corps in front of the shuttle. The picture was something simpler, a fantasy I kept for myself. It was Armstrong hunched over at the waist in a grassy field. No houses or buildings, just wide-open field. He was young, wearing a collared shirt and metal aviator sunglasses. He held a model airplane in one hand and his son stood beside him. They had the same haircut, the same style of glasses. The boy was listening to his father explain something, both staring at the tiny jet plane in total solitude. I could almost picture myself in his shoes, showing something to Charlie when—

"Ever wondered if the world is a machine?"

I clicked out of the picture, embarrassed. I turned to the doorway and saw Ned leaning casually against the doorframe, a wry smile on his face.

"You think it understands how we interact with each other? Keeps records of our preferences? Writes a line of code? Analyzes how often we interact with our preferences only to feed us more of the same, nudging us toward the same thing but slightly different? In other words... something 'new.'"

Goddamn interruptions. I was trying to hold something in my head, something pleasant for once, before Ned barged in on me.

"Have you chatted with Mr. Quinn yet?" he asked.

"Yeah," I said, wishing he would leave me alone. "Something about a dog. I'm not interested."

"Might he have the same thing to say about you, Walker? You've never shown any interest in him."

There was no interest to show. I had no respect for older men, older lawyers who hadn't done anything noteworthy to earn respect. Armstrong was in a different class. He got old, sure, but he probably never let himself go the way the old-timers did around here, and Armstrong packed more action and purpose into his life than Mick or any of the other flabby old filers who roamed the halls like the walking dead.

The light on my phone flashed and the ringer sounded. Ned stepped away as I lunged across my desk to pick up the receiver. It was a collect call. I accepted charges as the sound of a coin dropped into the register.

"*Gibney here,*" said a voice on the other end. The sound was tinny and distant, like the man was talking through a metal soup can, a thin strand of twine between us. Gibney was my only client and he was calling from jail.

"Mr. Gibney, this is John Walker, thank you for reaching out," I said.

Silence.

"I've been assigned to your file by an attorney at the public defender's office. Do you understand?"

I pulled the handset away from my mouth so he wouldn't hear me take a gulp of air as I tried to slow my breathing. Heavy breaths came through the thin reception of the jailhouse payphone.

"*File?*" he said.

"There are two charges against you. One for possession of a controlled substance with intent to distribute, the other for possession of a firearm by a convicted felon. You are a convicted felon, sir, correct?"

The "sir" sounded patronizing. I should have met him at the jail.

"I'm talking about your case," I added.

"*Call it a case then,*" he said. "*Don't got a file. Don't need another pretender 'workin' my file.'*"

I pulled the phone away from face again, still trying to take in enough air to slow down my breathing, to sound calm on the telephone. The man stood to lose a decade in a case called *United States of America v. Clayton Gibney,* as if the whole country was against him. I owed him something better than the jargon of a bureaucrat.

"This is absolutely a case, Mr. Gibney. You have a case. Actually, *we* have a case. Your liberty is at stake and I'm ready to fight this with—"

"*Just bring the tape,*" he cut in. "*I wanna see that bitch's video.*"

"Okay. So I'll be seeing you tomorrow morning. Let's see. Just a moment..."

I grabbed at pieces of paper on my desk, sheets of yellow legal pad with phone numbers and names scribbled in different directions, trying to find....

"The schedule. Here we are. We're meeting at 10 a.m. at the correctional facility," I said. "Does that still work for you?"

Click.

I gaped at the blank caller identification screen on my telephone. Gibney had dropped the phone back on the hook. I pulled his picture out of the mess of paper and laid it on top of the pile in front of me. He was my first client, roughly my age, with a pale complexion, gray eyes, and a long, crooked nose. According to the records forwarded to me by the public defender, he had been arrested a dozen times, doing years in prison on drug and gun charges. I folded back the pages of his arrest record. He got his start stealing power tools from hardware stores, mostly electric drills and handsaws. The notes scribbled onto his record said he had stolen the tools and dealt them wholesale to buyers all over the state. The law came down hard on someone dealing drugs or guns but had little to say about trading power tools for cash. Gibney got off easy, for a while.

He had been out less than a year when they chased him down last fall in a cornfield. He'd bailed from the driver's side of a moving car and rolled into a ditch, before he took off running into fields still thick with corn. When the police couldn't find him, they set up a cordon and released a German shepherd to track him down.

Sifting through the papers I found a picture. It showed Gibney's hands bound behind his bleeding back, red streaking down the seat of his jeans, a fist-sized flap of skin ripped out of his neck. The dog sat obediently in the corner of the photograph. Gibney's clothes were torn and stained, his body covered in dirt and blood, but his hair was clean—two long blond braids tightly woven and tied off with rubber bands. I clipped this picture to the file and collected up the loose papers, shoving the documents into a briefcase. This was the only case I cared about enough to take home.

Outside, the evening air was cool. The sun had fallen behind distant trees, orange and yellow marbling in the dark blue sky. The parking lot was empty. Attorneys had all gone back to their families by now and downtown was quiet. Slamming shut the door of my car, I thought about Grace and Charlie having their dinner together, my wife's school books and computer spread out over the kitchen table as she fed our son the food she'd made special for him. *Do they still set a place for me*, I wondered, running my hands over the steering wheel. They probably knew better than to wait up, that it was pointless to call and ask about my schedule. Grace knew I wouldn't have bothered to answer anyway; staying late at the office was an excuse when I didn't want to be home. I twisted the key in the ignition. Feeling the car shudder and start, I sat completely still in my seat and closed my eyes. It would be several more minutes before I was ready to move.

CHAPTER SIX

J ail was busy the next morning.

Lawyers and clergy lined up at reception, fluorescent lights bathing the crowded room in a yellowish hue. I rubbed my nose as the odor of Lysol and mildew rose up from the charcoal-colored floormats. The first floor was for intake or security, whatever new phrase the guards decided to use.

"Name?" a security guard demanded from behind plexiglass, not lifting her eyes from the computer. "Name and purpose," she prompted before I could stutter a response. The guard reached across an open bag of potato chips to buzz me through the steel door that led through a metal detector to the elevator at the end of the hall.

The whole place was falling apart. Tiles were missing from the hallway and lights blinkered off and on. The elevator didn't even have buttons. I examined slips of paper ripped out of blue-lined notepad and Scotch taped over the button holes. Second floor was the infirmary. Third was for women. The fourth floor was labeled "psych."

Finally, when the number five lit up, I stepped into a narrow corridor and followed a sheriff's deputy into a small room marked "conference." I took a seat in the chair closest to the door. A metal table sat in the center of the room, welded to the floor. A plastic clock hung crooked on the wall. I waited impatiently, listening for the sounds of keys jangling, a hand knocking on the door three times.

"Clayton Gibney for attorney," the deputy announced. "Got thirty minutes."

The door opened to a middle-aged man, his face long and thin like the broad side of a knife. Gibney's hands were cuffed together at the heels of his palms and chained to a belt that ran along his waist. He shuffled forward, reached for the back of the metal chair, and pulled on it, lowering himself into the seat. The metal bracelets around his wrist clinked against the table as he laid out his hands, squinting under the bright light overhead. Lines of ink, dark green and faded, spiraled across his wrists and forearms. I looked at the letters *SSV* on the back of his right hand.

"What does it mean?" I asked.

His eyes searched the room. He cleared his throat. "Sex. Speed. Violence."

The long, dirty-blond hair had been parted down the center and separated into thin braids that fell over his shoulders, the same style he wore on the day of his arrest. Pockmarks from acne were covered over by tufts of blond hair that grew long and curly around his mouth. So long were the whiskers that grew outward from his jaw that it gave the impression Gibney was sticking his chin out, pointing his chin at me like a challenge to authority. His body language was an invitation to either fight or back down.

"You bring the video?" he said. The chains around his wrists and ankles clanked against the metal table and legs of the metal chair.

I turned the laptop and moved it toward him. Gibney touched the play button and the scene came to life. The picture was grainy, the body-worn camera wobbling whenever the informant moved or took a breath. The conversation was barely audible against the noise of a fire engine's siren somewhere on the street outside. I recognized Gibney, kneeling on the floor of his garage wearing a Confederate flag bandanna wrapped around his forehead, turning a wrench on the front wheel of his purple and black motorcycle. He was the same man today as when he wore the wifebeater tank and baggy blue jeans in the video, but the orange prison jumpsuit, the white socks and slides, made this large man look smaller than he had on the outside.

I was talking to someone dressed for bed.

"Woulda set me up for the summer. Knew he was gonna test drive me. Punk bitch motherfucker," Gibney mumbled.

The word "fucker" sounded more like "fegger" coming through his teeth.

It was useless to get worked up over the informant or the heap of evidence prosecutors had against him. The videotape wouldn't get nervous under questioning on the witness stand. We watched the camera as it followed Gibney into his house, through a wood-paneled living room, and into a small, tidy kitchen.

"Off. Turn it off."

I hit the button and the screen froze on Gibney standing over the kitchen counter, a dozen tiny plastic bags filled with white crystal laid out neatly in front of him.

"We have some options here," I started. "One is that we argue these drugs were only for personal consumption. I have friends who buy wine in bulk because it saves them money, not because they intend to turn around and sell that wine to me or you or anyone else. There's no reason we can't tell the jury you were trying to cut down on costs by buying in bulk."

Gibney rubbed his face.

"Personal use, you know what I'm saying."

His nails were thick, curling over the tips of his fingers like the shells on a pistachio.

"Ain't sayin' goofy shit," he grumbled. "I wanted to see my bike again. Don't need the video for nothin' else."

"Let's go through the case against you and see what we can come up with for strategy," I suggested. "Sound good?"

Silence.

"You're looking at five to seven years, less with good behavior, maybe even less if we cut a deal. We know Hossler is by the book, so there won't be any freelancing. What I'm saying is we should consider doing a deal."

I didn't know any of that for a fact. Actually, I had never said this to anyone before, but I had overheard Mick say this into his phone while I stood in the hallway, and now seemed like the right time to repeat it.

"You follow, Mr. Gibney? I'm talking about a plea deal."

"Brother, I appreciate you wanna help, but I'm pleadin' guilty."

He wasn't supposed to say that. In the books I read, characters never said, "I'm guilty, so please send me away for five to seven years."

"But what about a deal?" I asked "We're talking years saved if you just do the deal."

"No deals," he said. "Don't talk to cops. Sold drugs to pay for my bike, man. My place. Puts cash in my pocket, but my place ain't a crack-house shithole. Ain't no needles on the floor. You saw the place—ain't no pregnant bitches walkin' round my livin' room and kids with shit diapers crawlin' round some junkies laid out on the floor. I got books, man. Piles of 'em. Financial literacy and shit."

Gibney sold drugs and stole motorcycle parts off the street. He'd never held an honest job and had spent enough time in prison to understand there was nothing to be gained by going back, yet still he sat there, wrapping a hand around the long whiskers of his chin and pulling gently.

I glanced at the *SSV* tattooed on his hand, the "*SS*" lightning bolts styled after the Nazi Schutzstaffel. His hands were plump and calloused, tendons thickened by hours spent gripping and working metal tools.

"You won't do a deal because of your gang?"

"Club," he shot back.

I shook my head.

"No feggin' dumbass gangbangers. Club's got a code. Code of conduct."

He wanted to explain himself, so I kept quiet. Slaven had warned me not to listen. "Guy is a no-shit, white-supremacist gang member," he told me before I took the case. "Lifelong criminal with a piss-poor record, a violent record." I'd listened to Slaven, but Gibney seemed familiar. There was the way he looked. The combination of youth and roughness in the lines on his face, the cracked and ruddy skin. I could tell he had spent most of his life outside, and he reminded me of other men I knew, in the physicality, but also his eagerness to explain the choices he made and what they meant. The credentials I sought and valued were meaningless to him.

"The code ain't got fuck all to do with the law. It says that if I want somethin', I take it. I rip a guy off for his wheels and if his shit should be mine and he don't think so, then I'll beat his feggin' ass for it. If I can't take it, then I might trade for it, but if some dumb bitch in this joint cuts a rail out on the back of a toilet tank and tells me to puff, I crack his feggin' head because I ain't a junkie either."

Gibney was sitting up straight now. The future had no meaning. Five years or seven years in prison, it made no difference, but how he had chosen to live out the past still excited him. He didn't care whether I advocated for him in the courtroom, only that he advocated for himself to me.

"You should see 'em in here. You know about die-ver-ticulitis?" Gibney asked.

I shook my head. "No."

"Die-verticulitis. Gets in your gut from the withdrawals, like polyps in your colon. Shit gets in there; peanuts and popcorn gets infected in there and—whoohee! You never been so sick in your goddamn life. I seen a dude in here, man, he ain't slept in a week. How come you don't know about die-verticulitis?"

I paused to think.

"It's wrong to be anybody's bitch in here is what I'm sayin'," he went on without waiting for my response. "Wrong to live like a nigger, like these feggin' niggers in here that act like they can't get shit on their hands else— can't do a motherfuckin' minute like a grown ass…"

Gibney took one of the braids in his hand and fingered the tightly woven grooves. He stared hard at me then broke into a big, open-mouthed laugh.

"You should see your face, man!" he howled, mouth wide enough for me to see the two gold caps on his incisors. "I ain't racist, man!" He stretched out his arms on the table so the sleeves of his orange jumpsuit rode up high onto his forearms, revealing tattoos of red flames that licked up both his wrists. "I say nigger cuz your rules say I can't. I say it every goddamn time, and you should see the looks on people's faces, like my big mouth just slapped 'em 'side the feggin' head. White or black? Don't matter. Man or woman? Fuck, my goddamn best friend in here is a nigger." Gibney hooked a thumb toward the door. "Only dude who can carry on a feggin' conversation about something other than titties or the block or whatever stupid shit. Check it out—anybody wanna do shit in here, wanna fly a goddamn kite in this motherfucker, they gotta come through me or him."

"You're not a racist; you just like getting people mad."

Gibney shrugged and continued petting his braids. "Guess so."

"It makes you excited to get people riled up, agitating them? Gives you a reason to fight?"

"It's that or a shovel to the face, man. 'Cuz I ain't nobody's bitch."

I glanced over my shoulder at the clock hanging on the wall. We had only a few minutes until the deputy came back to end our session. I pulled a picture from the folder and slid it across the metal table. "Recognize this?"

He snorted, running his fingers over the photograph. It was the picture of Gibney covered in blood and surrounded by cornstalks taller than the crown of his head.

"I can't figure out why you told the cops about the gun," I said. "It was mashed in the dirt when they found it, buried."

He cackled. "Well damn, brother, thought that woulda been easy for ya."

"Like you always tell the truth or something? Club rules?"

"Shiiit!" He started laughing again.

"You said there's a code of—"

"Code don't say I gotta help the cops, man. Who you workin' for anyway, little brother? Come on now and try again, lemme hear it…" He waved his cuffed hands to invite another explanation. "…and don't blow it out your ass this time either."

I set the pen down on the table and looked at him. First at the crooked notch of bone halfway down his long, thin nose, and then at his gray eyes. There was a quality of indifference in his gaze that made it easier than expected to look at him without being judged.

"I think…I think you probably knew it wouldn't matter."

"I never fuck with kids," he barked. "That's the line."

"But there weren't any kids."

"After that dog bit my friggin' neck, fat fuck cop comes over and puts his arm around me, says all sweet, 'We have kids coming into these fields to help with the harvest, son. They'll be all over this here silt loam soil. You know about the silt loam cause you're a local boy, and so God forbid one of these schoolkids happens to pick up that pistol.' After he said that shit, I told him. Seemed like the right thing to do, man. Not interested in analyzin' it."

"But that was a tactic," I said. "You must have known the officer was goading you, and so maybe we make the argument he hadn't read you your rights and—"

"Nah. Don't matter. Rule is I don't fuck with kids. Period. Simple as that."

Gibney reached his arms across his body and fingered the buzzer, raising his long frame from the chair and leaning against the wall. The white paint of the doorframe was covered with fingerprint smudge marks. There were no windows or vents into the room, and the air had turned sour with the smell of our breath.

"I'll run this place 'til they move me," he said in a low tone.

I collected my computer and documents, hastily cramming the blank legal pad back into my briefcase.

"This shit is mine," Gibney said in a whisper, looking at the floor. "My world."

The lock turned from the outside and the door swung open. Gibney lowered his chin and looked at me from the corner of his eye. "See ya Monday and don't worry about bringin' nothin' this time," he said, tipping his head toward my overstuffed briefcase. "Should be an easy day."

I stopped at the elevator and turned around, watching him shuffle his chained feet across the linoleum floor, his long head bowed forward, until he disappeared inside a locked door at the other end of the hallway.

❏ ❏ ❏

Outside on the sidewalk, I buttoned my jacket tight across my chest and rolled up the collar to shield my neck from the wind. The Graybar building towered over a low-slung skyline of office towers and apartments that surrounded Power and Light. There had been nothing in the file to document the marks and tattoos Gibney had made on his body. Maybe others had forgotten to make a note of them. Maybe they never noticed the marks at all. I glanced down at my own pale hands and remembered how eagerly the men had taken their deployment paychecks to the tattoo parlor, covering themselves in the images of things they did not want to forget. Images of death, mostly, but also names of friends written on tombstones and dog tags, the kinds of images nineteen- and twenty-year-old boys either dreamed up or heard about from an older brother.

For all the expectation and excitement we had going to war, death was personal for only a couple of us. It was personal for me and West.

The task I had given them was surveillance. I sent West and his spotter to dig into a desert ridgeline and told them to watch. Watching was all we had done the few months we had been in country. The team spent days studying their subject from nearly a mile away, squinting into a piece of glass while their shoulders, pressed hard into the stocks of their rifles, went numb. They watched him like he was the lead actor in a movie, taking note of his face and how it changed, his style of dress, who he spoke to or smoked with. They narrated the scenes as the man shambled from one end of the mud-brick courtyard to another, rode his motorbike to the market, drank his chai, checked his phone.

West called back to base to let me know nothing had happened. He whispered storylines to his spotter just to keep each other awake. West favored the lyrics to country music songs, lending down home character to his ordinary routine. I can remember the sound of his drawl coming through the crackle of the radio. He was singing Dolly Parton's "9 to 5." That was his report at the start of the third day on observation, the day the subject touched something. It was before noon when West and his spotter saw a rifle's rusted barrel slip out from inside a burlap bag.

"Cleared," I said into the handset.

The word floated across the miles between us. I waited while the minutes passed without a report. West came from the country—I knew he could spend hours there, lying motionless, eyes burning with fatigue but unable or unwilling to stop watching. But this was no longer enough. I spoke again and louder this time.

"Cleared to engage, over."

West knew not to waste his chance. He relaxed his breath and pulled. The man fell to the ground for the last time, the movie suddenly over.

Back at the office, I dropped the briefcase on my desk and fell into the seat, my mind churning through memories a decade in the past. I had seen Gibney's flames before, just as I had seen the little green skulls wrapped around his wrist like a string of pearls, a man's demons stitched into his skin. I spent that afternoon slumped in my office chair and not wanting to move. There had been times I wished the walls around me would fall away and open up to another place. I craved freedom to walk back into the club on base where we used to gather, and to step out of the office into an open field were fantasies that occupied my afternoons. Not today, though. I turned off the lights and closed the door, unplugged the phone, and then the computer.

Alone, I thought about the accident that had left me here, wandering from one day to the next like a fool who had nothing to look forward to. I had become a captive to memory, measuring today against what no longer existed, living and feeling less and less with each passing week. I pulled a drawer out from the desk and rested my feet on it, leaning further back in the chair while I listened to the low hum of the copy machine across the wall. The smell of ink and hot paper kept me company now and hours passed without anyone noticing me, wondering where I was or what I was doing.

Finally, I stood up, accepting another day had ended with nothing accomplished. I noticed the judge's business card still sitting on my desk. I ran my fingers over the raised letters of his name and title, then flipped it over and looked again at the invitation. "*A benefit for the opera company*," it said. The judge's house was only a few blocks away. The idea of being around people suddenly seemed okay. Maybe I'd meet someone I could talk to, someone who might understand how it felt to be alone.

What was it that Dan always said? All those summers ago, the first time I caught him looking over my shoulder at the way I folded my skivvy shirts and socks, how I tucked them neatly into my locker during basic training, easily passing the inspections that Dan failed time and again. It was the first time we really spoke. I wasn't sure what to think of him. "Life is like a bunch of pop quizzes," he said, offering a handshake. "Sooner or later, you find somebody better to cheat off. You know, to watch and copy how they do it. You might be the only way I get through this place."

I chuckled thinking about it, slipping the business card into my pocket and hustling for the door.

CHAPTER SEVEN

Ruth Ryan awoke early. It was the sound that had roused her from sleep, an awful sound of brass grommets clanging against a metal pole. She was staying on the fifteenth floor of the Residence Suites and the designers of this otherwise fine and historic four-star hotel had permitted an American flag to be planted directly outside her window. Every gust of wind caused the flag's metal grommets to slap against the flagpole.

"*Grande, tesoro, bravi tutti,*" she muttered, massaging her temples with both index fingers, trying to soothe away the ache inside her skull.

She pictured two men standing on a narrow scaffold, hammering the shaft into the brick wall less than ten feet from her bed. Was the flag her punishment? Punishment for taking residence in a country she loathed, for traveling to any American city and performing for any American audience that would have her? She was Irish, not American, had never wanted to make even a temporary home in the biggest, hungriest, loudest country on Earth. Yet here she was, the artist in residence, at the Residence, being tortured by the great yardarm of her country of residence.

She set her feet down on the carpet and sat up straight at the edge of the bed, lengthening her spine all the way from her seat through her neck. She pressed the palms of her hands together in a gesture like prayer and, with eyes still closed, began rubbing her hands together. She rubbed slowly at first then picked up speed, sliding her hands up and down, palm to fingers, until she could feel the surface of her skin warm with the heat of friction. She kept rubbing until the warmth began to burn, then she pressed both palms against her face so they covered her eyes, the swell of her cheekbones. It had been cold last night. The temperature gauge she kept on her bedside table read three degrees Celsius, and the heat entered her like warm sunlight. Palms together and a touch of warmth. Her full lips softened into a smile.

Wherever she spent a night on the road, the windows stayed open. She heard other actresses say the natural air was better for sleeping respiration, something about it being cleaner for the lungs than recirculated air from inside the building. But that was not the reason her windows were open. She took in a full breath and welcomed the chill inside her nose, filling up her chest and then letting it out through her mouth, her lungs clenched tight as fists. Ruth Ryan kept the windows open because she believed even the slightest sensation of pain, the scorch of cold air on bare skin, brought more details, more feeling.

No matter what city, hotel room, or state of mind in which she found herself, she counted on this ritual to be a reminder of her breath, the new day. Last year a colleague had introduced her to the technique during a one-woman performance she made off Broadway. The show was called *Axe*, starring Ruth as Lizzie Borden and accompanied only by an electric guitar. This was an experimental production based on letters the famed murderess wrote during a period of confinement, and Ruth had hoped the role would expand her repertoire beyond traditional opera, opening up new opportunities in singing theater and fill her calendar with steady work during the summer months. But the show had been a miss. The guitar amplifier was somehow not loud enough and audience members—there were more than she expected—complained on their blogs and social media that Ruth's vocals overpowered the guitarist's chord progressions. Instead of expanding the audience's expectations of opera, she had gotten in their way, drowning out the electrified sound of what she learned was their main attraction.

The feeling of failure had taken months to overcome, but it was not the audience's lack of appreciation that bothered Ruth. How many times at fundraisers and galas had she reassured whoever would listen that opera was not all "park and bark," "let me stand here in the center of the stage and sing my aria at you"? They called that outreach. Or was it called "reaching out?" She never could remember the difference.

What bothered Ruth was the repeated, incessant, frenzied attempts at relevance.

Relevance.

The word everyone seemed to be courting these days.

This word was what put her on the stage alongside that guitarist, writhing and jumping up and down like a rock and roll groupie. She grimaced just remembering the drivel promoters had printed on their posters and pamphlets, hoping this magic word might win them a share of the crowds that lined up to watch hip-hop musicals and orchestral adaptations of children's movies, entertainments for which immediate acceptance was the only measure of success. "One hundred years of timely and relevant opera," "one hundred relevant years of timely opera," "making timely operas relevant to the lived experiences of our modern lives." The combinations were endless.

For every year of "relevant" opera performed in the last one hundred years, she thought, *you are left with ninety-nine years of irrelevance, each performance so carefully written to its own time it loses the thread of transcendence, the greater wisdom of all the performances and performers that came before.*

She wanted to disappear from time, not become it. Ruth grasped the window with both hands and forced it shut. Her body felt cold but her mind was alive. The skin was taut and pale, fine hairs of her arms and shoulders standing on end as she ran a fingertip gently along the cool underside of her wrist. She wore only a loose-fitting tank top.

The hotel room was a mess: the bed was a tousled pile of sheets and pillows; paperback books were heaped on chairs; and pictures covered the floor. She could hardly walk from one end of the room to another without stepping on something, a photograph of Monet's butter-yellow dining room here, *The Artist's Garden at Vetheuil* over there. Ruth had a habit of holding onto things, pictures of herself in costume and clippings of newspaper articles about immigration and refugees, the crisis at the Mexican border. Everything that interested her lay strewn across the floor. The clutter had been curated for inspiration but also for comfort. She was traveling too much, spending her days on the same fifty feet of stage, dressed in someone else's clothes and exposed to a theater full of eyes, the hotel room became her only sanctuary.

She stood up from the bed and pushed hair out of her face. On the table next to the window a leather notebook and sharpened pencil beckoned her, demanding she commit twenty minutes to the stream-of-consciousness writing that helped to drain stray thoughts and memories onto the page.

She took a seat but pushed the notebook to the side of the table. Flipping open the silver laptop to her social media channels, she checked the status. Even a successful career like hers required plugging a few coins every so often into this new digital meter. Directors and agents had educated her about the importance of her "brand," about identifying her "touchstone," and whether that should be yoga or gardening. Even baking, if she could be careful about it. These experts all claimed it mattered less what the touchstone was and more that it was relatable to ticketholders, that it could be used over and over again as the unifying theme of what they called her "social message campaign." Ruth's touchstone was easy: her childhood home in Ireland. She filled the screens with photos of rolling green hills and limestone cottages, ocean waves exploding against a rocky beachhead.

She clicked on the latest post, a dramatic portrait of herself standing at the edge of towering rock cliffs wearing an emerald ball gown that floated behind her in a heavy wind, the sea heaving itself against rocks at the cliff's bottom. Ruth thought it shameless, but the photograph had more than one thousand likes and several comments beneath the heap of hashtags she dutifully added.

"Girl, you're f*cking GORGEOUS."

That was from @SnappleTree83, who had accompanied her on piano for their recital performance of Sondheim standards at a private fundraiser on the Upper East Side. She clicked the "like" button and kept scrolling to the other new comment.

"This girl made me the luckiest boy this side of the pond."

That one was her husband. His comments were the most over-the-top, mawkish praise that only an American could be comfortable giving. Bram was also a singer, a lush baritone renowned for his commitment to the acting craft. She clicked his icon and scrolled through his posts. There was a photograph that showed him wearing the police uniform of Scarpia in Puccini's *Tosca*. Another showed Bram rehearsing the titular role in Verdi's *Rigoletto* for a one-night-only performance in Milan. She sat back in the chair and looked out at the empty streets below her room, the rooftops of brick office plazas and vacant sidewalks, a city still asleep. It gratified her to watch Bram's career rise to heights that she may never see again.

Ten years earlier she had been the star lyric soprano at the Metropolitan Opera, hailed by the *Times* for her "fierce poise" and "breathtaking coloratura," what one writer had deemed her "diamantine presence." That review alone had earned her auditions with directors in New York and San Francisco, bringing in offers to sing cabaret, recital, modern, and traditional opera, filling her head with song and her calendar with more roles than she had the time to learn.

Now she was lucky to play the Beggar Woman at a show in Kansas City. The drop in prestige came when the strands of gray began appearing at the part of her hair and a bagginess set in along the lower jawline. The changes to her voice were hardest to tolerate. Singing the mezzo-soprano range was all the proof she needed that her instrument had withered, that she had spent a lifetime mastering her body and voice for both to betray her in middle age.

Still, she enjoyed seeing Bram play the world's biggest theaters. She was the one who knew about the Heinrich Gustaf competition, the tournament of American baritones that sponsored a European tour for the winner, and so she had entered his name into the draw while he was "too busy" rehearsing *Macbeth* for the twelfth time. It was Ruth who had completed his application and Ruth who signed Bram's name in the signature block. Ruth who dropped the package in the mail. The memory made her laugh, how he had insisted on two weeks of isolation at a cabin they rented upstate, trying to master that score's difficult elocution, marching through the woods with the libretto and loose sheets of music clutched in one hand, the other undulating up and down as he felt his way through each and every word.

"I can't stop Hispanicizing the double consonants! My Italian sounds like Tijuana Spanish! There just isn't enough goddamn time to get it right!"

When she told Bram she had entered him in the competition, he was surprised, angry even. But when he won that competition, his Italian sounding richer and more natural than ever before, his reward was a red-carpet tour of the best their world had to offer. Ruth liked to think it was her confidence in him that propelled both of them forward. As her career waned, his was just beginning.

And, Bram was a winner in private settings, a patron's pet whose deep baritone and boyish features played to the vanities of most audiences, particularly men.

"My God, a barrel of a voice for such a sweet-faced young man."

That was last fall. Bram had been invited to perform at the home of a Southern businessman. The pictures he sent showed a Greco-Italian revival mansion with some five floors and dozens of rooms. There were sprawling acres where the tycoon kept a stable of thoroughbreds. Ruth read about the place online in a home and garden magazine, how it was built in the early 2000s but "called to mind the heart and spirit of the antebellum South."

The guests had gathered for a reception in the mansion's ballroom, where a Steinway grand piano sat underneath the crystal chandelier, a scene made for a magazine photo shoot. The guests were older couples who thanked and applauded Bram after his performance, filing into the dining room for hors d'oeuvres and drinks. When their backs had turned, the old tycoon moved in close, cupping Bram's elbow and guiding him out of the light made by the chandelier and into the adjoining room.

"Will you meet me at my office tomorrow afternoon? Take the elevator. Tell the receptionist you have a private appointment. Your director has made necessary adjustments to your schedule."

When he walked into the man's sprawling downtown office the next afternoon, the blinds were closed. Bram would have been a fool to turn down the man's invitation, risking not only this job, but future roles with the company and conductor. Ruth knew he made relationships through every company in which he performed and every town he visited. *Our careers were stronger for them*, she told herself. Any wife suspicious that her husband was taking too great an interest in the traveling baritone was relieved once she noticed Bram's wedding ring.

Things were different for Ruth. Performing in private made her the object of investigation, not attraction.

"You're still young," they said.

"Settle down. Start a family with your husband."

She pushed down the lid of her laptop and gazed out the window. She heard it often, that particularly American anxiety over making a family.

"I bet your husband misses you. Can't be easy on a marriage."

The morning sky was iron gray, blending into the concrete buildings and paved streets freshly swept of debris. Behind the one tall building standing at the center of town was a brown river, and beyond that a green ridgeline of wooded hills. Everywhere else was farmland. Days before, as her plane descended toward the airport runway, Ruth had looked out the window and noticed how ordered the Earth looked from above, the ground cut into even squares of green and brown like the top of a vast checkerboard.

She stood up from the desk and stretched her arms, drifting over to the satchel that lay against the door. She opened it, taking inventory of the few items inside. Black leggings, black sweater, black cowboy boots, a black coat, and several sets of underwear. The only color she allowed herself was the lavender scarf that hung over the back of her chair, a cashmere/silk blend. She could afford a dress or a new blouse. Certainly, this weeks-long engagement in the blustery Midwest warranted more changes of clothes, a heavier coat at least. She had the money. But Ruth starved herself of luxuries for no other reason than it gave her pleasure to abstain. That, and it kept her backpack light. The weight of objects could only slow her down.

The telephone rang.

"Ruth speaking," she said.

There was a pause on the other end of the line. Her voice had that effect on Americans, as if they were surprised to hear their own words spoken in a different accent, their brains needing extra time to process the unexpected sounds.

"Oh. Good morning. This is the front desk calling to say that it's now 7:15 a.m. on Monday morning."

The man's voice cut away to silence.

"Very fine, sir," Ruth said dramatically. "Thank you for calling me and I do hope you have a lovely day."

She waited for him to respond, but all she heard was the *click* of the man hanging up his end of the phone. Nothing more than a routine exchange, yet Ruth somehow felt she had been impolite.

She set down the phone and returned to her satchel. She unzipped a small compartment on the side and reached into the pocket, her fingers finding a satin cloth. It was there underneath the cloth wrapping and only half the size of her palm, a piece of glass straight on two of its sides and broken into a jagged slash along the other, like a piece of paper that had been torn. She held it up to the morning sunlight that beamed reddish orange through the window. The glass was mostly clean but for smudges of fingerprints. She exhaled a fog of breath onto the flat surface and wiped at it with the satin cloth, admiring the sharp edges that stuck and pointed.

"Remember."

She had written this word into her journal one morning, her own subconscious rambling on about how the artist's existence was not on the smooth plane but always along the cutting edge. Her habit had been to avoid reading whatever came out of those journaling sessions, but this revelation had appeared during a period of frustration, when her judgment had gotten in the way of performance.

She couldn't help but decide whether she liked a character, whether she agreed with the woman's motivations. The characters she played seemed too eager for approval and too quick to mistrust themselves. These judgments leaked through into performances that critics found "safe" and "inhibited."

"If life was smooth, art was flat," she had written.

Then *Norma* came along. It was her first time performing the role of the priestess. Ruth had the usual reaction after reading the libretto, wondering why this prayerful woman had become the story's victim and doubting the sincerity of it. *"Another suffering woman,"* she thought, memorizing lines and trying not to let her own indifference affect the performance. Ruth planned and prepared and expected her performance to feel like the others, taking the stage and executing lines and emotions on cue, expecting to deliver a type of service to the audience but nothing more.

Then the orchestra joined. Decades of performing were behind her but she heard something elevated in this music, the luxuriousness of Bellini's endless melodies that drew out her energy, fluttering high notes exhausting breath and body in a way that suspended time.

"Everything is in the music."

Not the costumes or the characters. Only the sound. Music was not in service to the story. It was the other way around. As she stood on stage opening night, empty of conscious thought, it was like Ruth had pressed the cutting edge of the glass to a vein and closed her eyes, feeling the character take over and begin to play. From that point on, she stopped judging and became what she sang.

Ruth put down the glass and squinted at the clock. She grabbed one set of black clothes and tossed them into the bathroom, hurrying to slip out of her top. There were two productions premiering this week, and rehearsals started in thirty minutes.

CHAPTER EIGHT

The judge lived in Splendid Acres.

There were only a few places in town an ambitious person could choose from when deciding where to make his home. Midtown condominiums were fresh and modern. The suburbs on the far west side of town were large and spacious, but owning a home there failed to signal the kind of class awareness that mattered in a city where a prospective client might drive through your neighborhood just to size up your credentials.

Splendid Acres was different.

It was historic. Architecturally significant, even. Large plots on curvilinear roads, grand setbacks that made each one of the fifty or so homes look like its own private estate, with little copper plaques fixed to the exteriors and a community rulebook that kept all the homes preserved in their original style. There was never a question of which neighborhood was most prestigious.

The judge's house was among the most tasteful, a Tuscan revival with a red tile roof and a tan stucco exterior. A line of cars was already parked on one side of the wide street, and a man and woman were making their way across the stone path that led to his front door. I turned off the engine then switched the dial to the classical station.

Polish. Reserve. Taste.

These were the qualities I noticed in the music, and so I hid myself just inside the driver-side door, looking into the side mirror as I straightened my tie, preparing myself for the performance ahead.

"I was just telling someone about you...." the judge said as I approached. He was standing on his porch with an arm extended to welcome me inside his home.

The entryway was spacious and full of light, with potted succulents arrayed on a glass credenza. I could see a sliver of the kitchen beyond the foyer, and beyond that the parlor, crowded with guests. It was a beautiful home, but still it was a home, a place where the tinkling sound of liquid splashing into a toilet bowl could be heard from behind a wooden door off the entryway.

"Allow me to introduce you to Terrence."

He wore blue jeans pulled tight over cowboy boots. The small man's gray mustache was well trimmed, as if it had been drawn onto the upper edge of his top lip.

The judge put a hand on the man's shoulder.

"Terrence is general counsel at Grayb—"

"Oh, it's actually head of the law department," Terrence cut in. "That's what they're calling it over there. You know how they bureaucratize everything nowadays." He took a sip from the glass of red wine he held by the stem.

"But many years ago, Terrence was—"

The small man blushed.

"I was a squid, if you can believe that. Petty officer in the navy, at your service. Could barely put a Band-Aid on someone without getting queasy and there I was, didn't have the stomach to be a school nurse, much less a medic on patrol through the jungle! Now look at me. Forty years old with an ex-wife, two sons, and one helluva husband later, and—ta-da!"

"So, you were drafted—" I started to ask when another man touched the sleeve of my jacket.

"It's a wonderfully peculiar story, don't you think?" the other man said. "Terry and I are just exasperatingly busy right now. We're performing total reconstructive surgery on a Georgian revival just around the corner. Maybe you know it?"

I looked up and scanned the white plaster ceiling for a hint as to whether I should admit I knew nothing about this neighborhood or play along.

"Actually, is that the one—"

"That *is* the one! The remodel has become such an organic extension of my inner artistic vision. My—rather, *our*—goal is to rescue the whole darn thing and turn the basement into a sort of apart—"

"Excuse me, but haven't we met?" Terrence interrupted, squinting at me. "Silver Beaver! You were sitting with the judge? Mick mentioned you when we were sitting with Paul Graybar at the head table. He told us you'd joined his firm. 'We got a sniper with an eye for the truth,' is how Mick said it, and Mr. Graybar was very pleased to hear it because he does love veterans. My god, does he appreciate them. He owns that shooting place off the highway. The, umm, the Shoot Shop, is it?"

"Top-notch place," I said.

"Wonderful," said Terrence. "And I see you're single?"

Terrence and his husband wore graphite-colored wedding bands, tungsten or titanium, whatever metal broke apart when placed under heavy pressure. I looked at my own bare fingers, then pulled the keychain from my pocket to show them where I kept my wedding ring, next to the house key.

"And where do you two reside, if you don't mind the question?"

"Across the river," I replied.

He shot me a pitying look.

My neighborhood told him everything he needed to know. East of the river was the middle-class commuter suburbs, where houses were packed together like cigarettes in a carton, where nobody worked but everybody lived. Floor managers and schoolteachers crammed the bridge every morning on their way into the city and again every evening on their way back home.

Terrence knew that life. He'd traded it in years ago for everything he had now. He rubbed a finger across the thin mustache and looked past me, taking a long sip from the glass. Wine and power were his interests, not mine.

"My sons were so different," he said, changing the subject. "The eldest is very handsome, but he can be so proud and standoffish. It's something people sense when they're around him. Although not as handsome, his younger brother is so much warmer. Always hosting, you know? Just the most inviting and bright-spirited man. And *oh*, did that quality make his older brother jealous, what with all the goodwill he'd been building up."

I smiled and nodded along, trying to keep my disguise. The parlor was filling up with bald, round-bellied husbands standing beside their wives, everyone talking so excitedly I assumed they knew each another. Dan always said the only thing rich people loved more than other rich people was a war hero. I'd been invited to play a role for them.

"Well, do take care of yourself, young man." Terrence leaned forward to shake my hand, then disappeared into the parlor.

I wandered past the hors d'oeuvres table and through an arched doorway that opened to the private library. The wood floor was covered by a red and blue rug that faded to white in the middle, and the shelves were packed with books from floor to ceiling. The guests' laughter as they handled plates of cheese and bread sounded more distant than before. I held a hand to my forehead to shade my eyes from the glare of sunlight filtering in through a west-facing window. The evening light turned yellow and green as it passed through a panel of stained-glass squares built into the window frame, and I watched the colors play on a wooden chair. The room was quiet, prayerful. I wondered if anyone would notice me hiding in here. I was already exhausted, afraid of being exposed by men more cunning than I was, tired of calculating every step, every word, every smile and expression.

Clink. Clink. Clink.

After someone tapped a wine glass with a spoon, voices lowered and footsteps shuffled from the kitchen into the parlor. People took their seats on sofas and chairs. I moved aside a stack of coffee table books and made a place for myself on a thick plank of oak flooring with my back to a wall.

"Thank you all for being here," the judge announced. "If I weren't in the company of such discerning patrons, I would break into an impromptu aria!"

I pressed a smile to my face and scanned the room. On the chaise lounge, a woman in a thick red cardigan matched squares of cheese to crackers on her Bernardaud plate, while the man next to her dozed quietly, head slumped at his chest.

"This week marks the beginning of the inaugural River City Opera Festival. Nothing like it in St. Louis or Minneapolis. River City is the only city in its class to put up the funding and talent to bring New York–caliber performance to flyover country," the judge said to a sniggering crowd.

I could hear Terrence hissing in the back row. Nearby, a tall, slim man stepped closer to the front of the room, a red-haired woman by his side. They were a peculiar pair in this crowd of bulbous bellies and silver heads.

"To help me introduce this evening's guests, please welcome Mr. P. Allen Graybar."

I turned to watch the gray-haired titan make his way to the head of the room, commanding the crowd's attention like a master of ceremony preparing to make his address. He wore the same blue suit, the collar of his white shirt now open and a red silk square tucked into his breast pocket. Graybar walked straight to the red-haired woman and offered both his hands, which she took eagerly, pulling him in close and leaning forward to touch her cheek to his.

"I want to share one thought before I depart for another engagement." He spoke of resources and influence, how wealthy aficionados since the Medicis had found their fulfillment through patronage, making it possible for Brunelleschi and Donatello, Fra Angelico and Filippo Lippi to bless mankind with sculpture and painting. He pronounced their names in nearly perfect Italian, pressing the tip of his index finger to his thumb and waving his hand about like a conductor at the rostrum. There was something menacing about his presence. He faced us with his back straight and one hand resting easily inside his pocket, the bright steel band of a dive watch shining against the seam of his trousers.

"Did you know that Lorenzo was the patron of Michelangelo?" he posed.

"Ahhh," the fawning crowd responded.

The crowd welcomed him, a construction man rhapsodizing about art history. Whether he knew anything about opera was beside the point. The room was filled with retired bankers and attorneys, owners of car dealerships and life insurance companies, a group of men more concerned with the sponsors' names plastered to the back of the program than any name that might be inside its pages. Though I recognized few of them, I imagined these people were all the money and ideas that mattered to our city, and that if by some terrorist explosion or act of God the judge's house was leveled, the city would be left without an ounce of importance in the world.

When Graybar finally finished his remarks, the red-haired woman acknowledged him, holding her hands together and bowing while the crowd clapped for both of them. He blew her a kiss then walked out the front door.

"Why here?" the tall man said suddenly, not waiting for the door to close behind Graybar.

"Yes, I'm asking you. Why here?"

The man ran a hand through his blond pompadour then tapped his chin impatiently with the tips of his fingers, two gold bangles clinking lightly at his wrist. Confused by the silence, guests turned toward one another with empty looks on their faces.

He clapped his hands together.

"Picture your playground. The ones in your neighborhoods and outside your grandchildren's schools. Wood chips and painted swing sets and plastic slides. My playground is different. My playground is pure. My playground sparkles. My playground is one hundred percent metal. Recycled metal, all of it, from the shining swing seats to the tunnel slide, and even the soft cushion underfoot. Every inch, every corner, every link, bolt, and beam sparkles with the glint and shimmer of an old bottle cap, a barbecue grill, bicycle, a Little Leaguer's baseball bat. Every metal fragment spliced into your ordinary, conventional daily lives becomes a device of play."

The crowd watched the tall man step back and forth dramatically, strands of hair falling onto his forehead. He continued on like this for several minutes, gesturing wildly with his hands and stomping his boots for emphasis as he pitched his musical playground to the audience. He was the director, nodding in the direction of the red-haired woman who stood a few feet away, smiling only to acknowledge her role in the affair as his presentation neared climax.

"The playground is merely a prelude, a preface, barely even the opening act—an appetizer for the *plat principal*, if you will."

The director's thin fingers burst like fireworks from clenched fists. "First the playground, then…brother and sister. Trapped, locked in a room together, alone in a world of their own creation. We've chosen this festival for the world premiere of *Les Enfants Terribles*."

The crowd watched in silence.

He grabbed the lapels of his fitted jacket, tugging hard on the fabric to straighten himself up. "And, for your pleasure, these performances will be made by one of the finest voices of a generation, one of the most distinguished actresses, an absolutely magnetic, worldwide presence on the stage. She's chosen you. Let me introduce the star of this festival."

I noticed the studs first.

Diamond-shaped studs were fastened into the outline of a dragon on her blazer. She was small, a few inches over five feet, dressed in a black blouse and tights, rhinestones skimming the top and sides of her cowboy boots. She stepped toward the crowd.

"An incredible *ting* the director has orchestrated in the rehearsal room. Never in my life have I seen so many *ahr-tists* in one room. Our baritone sketches the most beautiful hand-drawn portraits of the dancers, who are bending and preparing their bodies in the most beguiling ways. The amount of creativity is something like *Parade*—has anyone seen it?"

The woman on the chaise lounge looked at her husband and shrugged. The rest of the crowd was silent.

"Never before have I seen this much energy pouring out from a group of artists."

She placed her hands to the sides of her face and held her mouth open in awe, or a close imitation of it. My legs and back were numb now. I shifted my weight and the wood floor beneath me groaned. She glanced at me, eyes flickering though she faced the crowd.

"When the lights dim for *Les Enfants*, and you hear the first flutters of the piano, when you hear that first arpeggio." She moaned. "It does something wicked to you."

She swept back her hair and held it down flat against the top of her head. The woman was more dramatic with her face than the director, but her voice was calm and deep. She lowered her hands and strands of cherry-colored hair fell back around her forehead and ears.

A man wearing a V-neck sweater and khaki pants raised his hand as if trying to get a schoolteacher's attention. "Wait a minute, Miss. Did you all just say the floor is made of metal? How's that safe for my granddaughter? She falls more than I do."

"The children's safety and comfort will be assured," the woman said. "Those metal filings are like sand, actually, so the little ones shouldn't be at risk, but I wouldn't recommend bringing your infants."

"You gonna sing something then? He said you're the singer." The man looked around, beckoning to the other blank faces in the room, rallying them to join. "You're a singer!" he jeered.

"If I start a song, then how about you all have to join me, how's that?" she teased.

The man shrugged. He knew the evening was paid for by him and others like him, that the director and singer were here for his pleasure, and that she would have to oblige him. The rest of the group stared at her expectantly. The singer stepped back to collect herself; she flexed her shoulders and chest, loosening her body. Splotches of red appeared on the skin above the collar of her shirt.

"*Oh, Danny boy, the pipes, the pipes are calling...*"

The sniveling started by the second verse, cheeks dabbed with handkerchiefs and tissue, tears collecting at the edges of eyelids and voices softly humming along out of tune. The woman in the red cardigan had taken to gazing out the window as, one by one, the singer disarmed us until even the catering people had left their posts in the kitchen to peep around the corner, their faces reverent.

I caught my mouth with the palm of my hand. It seemed like a joke.

I wanted to stand up and yell, "This is a parody, don't you get it?" The bona fide Irish singer delivered a moment, a manipulation, which tugged at the heartstrings of these bona fide Irish-American patrons.

"...*I'll be here in sunshine or in shadow*..."

I blinked fast as the singer's voice rose. I turned away from the waitstaff and the crowd in front of me. I looked hard at the sole of my shoe, snapping my eyes open and trying to stiffen my aching back against the wall in hopes the music would not work its charm on me. I was ready to cover my ears and close my eyes when finally, the song ended. I looked up from the floor and watched the singer's cheeks arch into a dimpled smile. She bowed to the crowd and turned to the table beside her, picked up her glass of chardonnay, and resumed her place in the corner of the room. The crowd stood and clapped.

It was getting late. Grace would be wondering when I would be back, reminding herself that I never came home on time, that I could not keep my word about coming home at a reasonable hour. But when I turned to face the open doorway, there she was.

The singer was standing in the center of the wide hallway looking at me, her lips moving. I could not hear her voice. She had worn glasses before, rectangular lenses that concealed some of her face and made her appear friendly and innocent. The glasses were gone now, revealing eyes clear and blue. She focused on my face as if it were the only thing in the room.

"You're Irish."

She moved a long finger back and forth over her eye. The fingernail was natural and unpolished, a plain gold wedding band the only jewelry on her hand.

"Those are Irish eyebrows you have."

Her face was pale, a coat of foundation that stopped midway down her neck, where she blushed in waves of red the same color as the crimson on her lips. She looked smaller up close. The size of her boots, the width of her shoulders.

"Um—okay." I stammered.

"Did it make you nervous to sing in front of the group?" I asked, recovering my composure.

"I hadn't warmed up my voice," she replied. "Could you tell? I was flushed up there in front of everyone."

"Maybe," I said.

"I should have sung the third verse. Though maybe better for a funeral than a fundraiser." She nodded over her shoulder at the small group in the kitchen, where the director was shaking hands with the judge.

"Or a parade," I said.

She was comfortable, it seemed. There was no sign of nervousness in the long pause between words. She scrutinized my face.

"You know it then?" She bit her lip.

I nodded.

"You're a soldier."

"Was," I said. "The band played it the day we left."

Ruth smiled. "You looked sort of dreamy there, for a moment. Lost in thought."

I felt my cheeks flush.

"It's a beautiful image, marching off to war. Operatic. Life should resemble a good opera—gratuitous with drama and just enough violence," she said.

I glanced out the window. The sky was dark outside. Through the glass I saw a guest shuffling head down along the stone pathway to the driver's side door of his car. There were only a few people left talking in the kitchen by now, but I was not ready to leave. She took a step toward me and blinked for the first time.

"There's a connection between soldiering and having the impulse. A good deal of innocence and an equal amount of greed. Now, do you know anything about innocence and greed, Mr....?"

She looked at me expectantly. Preoccupied with the sound of her voice, I was startled to speak.

"John," I whispered.

"Never mind all that, John. Why don't you tell me instead what you did in the army?"

There were years spent hunched under an eighty-pound pack, dirty, shitting in plastic bags on training assignments, when carrying around a pile of your own shit could not be justified by explanations of war. Where to begin?

"I was in the—"

Someone tapped Ruth's shoulder. She turned from me and patted the man's shoulder, beaming a full-wattage smile and thanking him for his compliments. She kept her eyes on him as he waved goodbye and walked out onto the porch, then whispered to me, "Keep going. I'm listening."

"Infantry," I said.

She blinked. "What a coincidence. My writing is about guns and the border. Migration into this country. I wonder if you would be willing to take a look at the text, given your background? Perhaps we could meet?"

I thought of coffee shops and a restaurant downtown. I waited for her to suggest someplace, but she stood there motionless and silent for long moments. I searched her face, following the sharp line of her cheekbones, the way her eyes had been set inside her face. Before I could respond, the director strode briskly into the foyer and swung one long arm around Ruth's lower back. He said it was time to leave and she nodded dutifully, breaking her trance. She set her wine glass on the coffee table, and I watched the hem of her black jacket lift as she bent.

"Do you have a card?" she asked.

I reached into my jacket and passed a card to her, the director looking on. She scratched a nail over the raised letters, then slid it into a pocket on her hip.

"Good night," Ruth said without smiling, then followed the director out the door.

Grace was running a wet dishrag over the counter when I came in the door. I stood in the hallway, my thoughts wandering back to the party, to Ruth, wondering where she stayed when she came to town. Surely somewhere exotic, a big four-story house that the artists rented and lived in together. Maybe even an entire warehouse downtown in the Market District, a building with outdoor space to really spread out. Perhaps an artists' colony, a campsite, an enclave in the middle of nature far away from the office plazas and parking garages that crowded out everything natural in the landscape. I pictured performers laying out their instruments and costumes in a grassy field, a woodland glade where artists saw and heard each other at all hours, feeding off each other, warming one another by the fire of their imaginations.

Grace tossed the wet dishrag into the sink and pushed up the sleeves of her oversized wool sweater, her blonde hair loose and unkempt.

"The star soprano was there," I said without further explanation. "Ruth Ryan. She's singing at the installation piece and then in the world premiere."

She stared at me.

"The star of the opera, Grace. You know—the playground. *Les Enfants Terribles*. We talked for thirty minutes, though it felt much longer."

"One of the guests was a singer?" she asked, walking over to the laptop computer at the kitchen table.

"She came to the judge's house and sang for us because some batty old man…"

I pulled my phone from my pocket and placed it on the table in front of her.

"There she is! A review of Ruth in the *New York Times*, Grace, and we were together earlier tonight, chatting in the judge's parlor. I didn't know someone like her came around. She wants to get together and talk about her writing."

"Sorry, who wants to meet?" Grace asked, and I explained it all over again.

There was bitterness in Grace's question. She rolled her head from side to side, yawning dramatically as I recounted how this incredible performer had wanted to ask me questions, to sit and talk about things. Grace was wearing pajamas and seemed ready for bed. Suddenly, she stood up from the table, stretched, and planted her hands on her hips. The cotton waistband of her old track pants was colored gray and fading. So many years of effecting this pose—gripping the sides of her waist, arms cocked out and elbows pointing—had taken a toll on the threads that frayed underneath her fingers. Whether she heard anything I told her didn't matter.

"Who knows," she said, letting her arms drop to her sides, "you might have something useful to tell her."

Grace kissed my cheek, then walked down the hallway toward our bedroom and turned out the lights.

CHAPTER NINE

Alone at the coffee shop, Ruth leaned her head to the side to convey what looked like curiosity, judging her portrait in the screen as it beamed across ocean and continents.

"How's Venice?" she asked.

"Ugh," Bram spat into the camera. "God is it humid in this town. I'm not acclimatized, *bambina*."

Ruth hated when he called her that. It didn't matter which language he said it in.

"Did you know that someone coming from a place outside of Venice will lose *three times* as much through perspiration as a native of this city? I'm absolutely guzzling fluids and still I'm sweating like a farm animal, *bambina*."

Bram stopped to take a swig of sports drink, the crinkling sound of its plastic label sending an unpleasant static sensation through her earphones. She winced and turned down the volume. The drink had turned his mouth the color of red fruit punch. Bram was sitting in a makeup chair preparing to appear on television and promote that evening's show. He never told her these things in advance, no matter how many times she asked him for an itinerary or a schedule, just a taste of all that wondrous attention he was being served. Foundation and powder had already been applied, his straight hair slicked back atop his high forehead. Ruth thought he looked like a campy vampire character from a teenage romance movie. Red lips, white face, and clumpy black eyelashes. His eyeballs bulged out from dark eye shadow.

Bram loved drawing contrasts. The inharmoniousness of sight and sound. He would cower on the stage, shoulders forward, hanging his head, making himself small and meek as if to tempt the audience into reading him only by his soft, boyish face. *What a sweet young man*, the audience would think. Bram had done it so many times by now he could almost feel them tremble when he thrust out his chest and opened his mouth, emitting the baritone voice, a steel cannonball of sound lobbed at the audience from the stage.

"Did you pay the rent, babe?" she asked. "It's coming due on Monday and we don't want to fall behind another month."

Bram was attentive and supportive. And yet, still a man. The simplest housekeeping chore was always too much to ask of him, somehow outside his range as a partner.

"Just focus on hamming it up as Malatesta, dear. Such a delicious role. More in the vein of true theater than—"

Bram's face jerked away from the screen. He was talking excitedly with someone out of the camera's field of view.

"Yes, yes, yes, okay! Huh? No, absolutely not, *señor*. *Comprendo*? Do you understand Spanish, sir? I *comprendo*!"

He was flustered when he turned back to look at her. "Gotta go or I'm late for the television program. Oh, it's exhausting, and you understand. When will we ever be able to rest again together in the same city, *amore*? Just a walk with you, my love, and my spirit is rejuvenated one thousand times."

Ruth hated when Bram postured like this. But channeling lines from whatever character he played in the last production energized him. That was the problem. He never stopped acting, flexing this one strength whenever she wanted him to be honest, or to say nothing. He was a poor author of his own feelings, whatever they were.

"*Toi, toi*, my love."

Ruth blew kisses to the digital hologram of her husband. "I love—"

He disappeared from the screen.

She set down the phone and picked up the warm cup, cradling it in both hands until the heat scalded her skin. Ruth had asked the barista to pop her coffee "just a bit" longer into the microwave, until the clouds of steam rose out of the cup like smoke from a fire. She pressed a bare palm to the window and looked outside at the brick buildings along the river. The brick streets were empty and all the restaurants were closed except the coffee shop. Did everyone go to bed this early? She took in the empty storefronts and darkened windows, metal chains tied across the door handles of a bookshop, a florist, and a secondhand clothing store. There were no apartments, no row houses. This city wasn't at all like New York, where people could make their whole lives in a single neighborhood and not feel constrained by their surroundings.

She had first noticed the children at the airport. Big families with four and five kids running up and down the escalator in the terminal, laughing, crying, playing, and fighting. They overwhelmed her coming off the airplane, and so she expected to see them everywhere in this city, and she did that first weekend, unloading out of an over-sized pickup and following their parents to a restaurant, walking slowly to take in the window decorations in the Market District. That was days ago. She'd seen only adults since then. Office workers and merchants, the kinds of people who locked their stores and drove away at five o'clock in the evening because school was closed and they needed to be home with their children.

Ruth looked around at the empty coffee shop. The barista was touching up a display of white cups arrayed in impeccable formation on a shelf behind the counter, standing steadfast next to the brassy red espresso machine adorned with an operatic winged cap. Several flyers were taped to the inside of the glass door, among them an adver-tisement for that week's installation piece, a picture of two children floating blissfully on a swing set.

"Bring your children and make the playground a fam-ily affair."

How happy the children looked in the picture. Ruth pictured herself in their place, in the denim jumpsuit and Converse shoes the director had made her wear, singing and swinging like a clumsy, overgrown schoolgirl. She squirmed a little in her chair and placed a hand to the side of her abdomen, groaning not because the thought of the playground embarrassed her, which it did, but because her side ached in a way that made it hard to take in a full breath without feeling pain. A stabbing sensation lanced her ribcage each time before her lungs could fully inflate. She stooped over the table.

The pain was only a reminder of what she already knew, that she was too old for this. She was too old to be dancing on stage with women ten years younger, too old to hold her own alongside their lean and finely tuned bodies, stronger and more agile than she'd been even in her prime. Ruth was a singer, yes, and an actress when the role demanded, but she'd never been a dancer. Standing on the same stage as these women felt like swimming alone in open water, crawling facedown into a heavy current. Soon enough she would have to answer the questions she'd been putting off. When would the hands of time finally drag her so far out to sea the only way back would be to wash up, to acknowledge her withering instrument for what it was, to move on to whatever was left for her to do?

Part of her wanted to concede defeat, give up performing in new shows put on by adolescent directors who cared little for whatever it was the *Times* had said about her all those years ago. She could settle down far away from any city, someplace lush where she could tend a fenced-in garden of her own. A real vegetable or flower garden, not just a couple of pots on a patio. All the time she was wasting on lines and steps and makeup and godawful social media would become time spent with her hands sifting through soil, reaching down and touching the roots for once. New work would come. She'd figure it out in time. Maybe she could teach voice lessons. She could get a baby grand piano and build out her own studio and...

Ruth shook her head. It took only a moment for the idiocy of that idea to show itself. She'd never even taught a dog to sit, let alone a child to sing. There was one job she'd had her entire life. There was nothing else she knew how to do.

Ruth reached under the table and grabbed her bag. She pulled open the pocket and peeled back the cloth covering, laying it flat on the wooden table. She'd carried it with her since she was sixteen, the memory of where it came from buried deep enough in her mind to avoid but never forget. She stared into the bottom of her empty coffee cup, turning it so the last bead of cold brown liquid slid from one edge to the other.

How smell loosened the knot of memory.

Coffee brewing in the kitchen...She thought of her mother wearing a plain apron over a yellow dress, standing like a stone rolled in front of their kitchen door, her heavy frame blocking his exit.

"Don't leave," she said to him that day.

She had pleaded with Ruth's father before, panic rising in her voice, her round face glistening with tears. Ruth stood beside her mother, chest heaving and eyes watchful, too focused on seeing to blink. He stood in front of them both, his fists clenched at his sides in silent anger or frustration—she could never tell which. Her father was bound for another city. Some other country maybe, walking out for the family he'd kept hidden from them, the brother and sister she wouldn't learn about until they telephoned years later after seeing Ruth's name printed in an international newspaper.

Days before, her father had promised to take her to a singing competition in Europe, just the two of them, to the biggest audition of her career. He'd been the first adult to tell her that singing was important. When her mother scolded her for not washing the dishes, for not doing her homework after school, it had been her father who said, "Singing is more than frivolity, dear." Ruth never felt more loved than when she sang and her father was in the audience, that out there in a dark sea of people was the only person who mattered.

Now he would disappear, again, out the door too early on a Monday morning, not even a note on their kitchen table to explain himself. Her father was a poet of no fame and little output, a baffling man who never worked a job, yet somehow covered his own expenses on a pension he'd secured for a disability she couldn't see.

"Sing and struggle," he'd told her one of their final evenings together, listening closely for her voice to vibrate below pitch, to slip off key. He made her start over again, made her sing until she performed without flaw three times in a row. He wasn't a musician but he had a decent enough ear. Her father had been the one to remind Ruth to practice, to never stop practicing.

"If you practice the right way when you least want to, you'll perform the right way when you least expect to."

His advice made her laugh when she thought about it now. It was never technical, but it hadn't needed to be. She was a singer from the country, more athlete than artist, and she had hundreds of miles to cover, as many miles as auditions, before arriving on a stage as big as Dublin, let alone London or New York. Every artist needed someone to notice the potential she couldn't see, the potential she had not believed in. She had counted on her father always being there to see her more clearly than she could see herself.

Ruth poured out the last drips of coffee, rubbing a wet circle onto the table with her index finger. More than smell, it was the sound that lingered, that high, shattering pitch when his fist broke through the glass pane over her mother's shoulder, exploding the rectangular window into a puff of glass that cut her mother's ear so badly she fainted at the sight of blood dripping red on the yellow cotton fabric. Looking out the open door at the taillights on her father's hatchback, dimming and then disappearing against a blue horizon, Ruth had felt nothing. She had reached for a dish towel and applied pressure, holding the back of her mother's head with one hand until her eyelashes fluttered open again.

The next day, everything was new. How easy it had been to carry on without him, how naturally resilient people were as children, buoyed by competitions and birthdays, all the things they had to look forward to.

There was a local man who taught voice at the public school. One morning, Ruth hugged Mother goodbye and started for the door leading out to the front lawn, dragging behind her a heavy travel bag packed full of sandwiches and homemade snacks, books, and trinkets from home. She was one foot out the door when she noticed it, the fragment of glass wedged between the doorjamb and a cabinet, light glinting off the sharp edge of the jagged side. It was the part he'd smashed with his bare fist, the last thing in her life he bothered to touch. The floor had been swept and mopped clean. She picked it up and slipped the glass into her overstuffed bag, then shuffled to the car.

She took first prize in the competition, beating hundreds of conservatory-trained singers from the best schools in Europe, each singer better dressed and better schooled than she had been. Ruth performed her best that day, just like her father said. She sang the rage aria "*Der Hölle Rache*" with the broken piece of glass tucked underneath the sleeve of her dress, hidden so that no one saw what she could feel.

She'd carried the glass with her from then until now, backstage of every performance, each audition, and along for the trips she'd taken across this country and others. The competition launched her career at a speed she never expected, without a father to welcome her backstage or wait for her outside an audition room. She posed for the cover of a Christmas album before the end of that first year. Alone in a dark room, wearing a strapless white ball gown with her back toward the camera, she looked over her shoulder into the barrel of a stranger's lens. She'd never worn such a dress before the photographer presented it to her in the dressing room, sliding the zipper up her back and gently sweeping her long auburn hair off the unblemished skin of her neck.

"Closing in five minutes," the wait girl announced to an empty shop.

Ruth ran a finger underneath the collar of her black sweater and pulled the wool fabric over the edge of her shoulder, bracing herself for the cold. The once pale, unblemished skin was long since covered over with a thousand tiny freckles. She pushed aside the cup and shut her bag, then looked at the flyer for the playground taped to the front door. She peeled it off the door and inspected it one last time.

She thought it was funny how little we changed through the years. So long as there was a role and a stage, an audience waiting for her, Ruth could remain forever a child at play.

CHAPTER TEN

shoved my feet into my boots and pulled tight on the laces. Forty pounds of sand were crammed into a rubber bag at the bottom of my old rucksack. I bounced at the knees to let the weight settle against my body. The wind swayed the branches of a maple tree in the yard and the morning air was cold enough that my neck tensed when the wind blew underneath the bottom of my sweatshirt.

"Let's see if I can warm up," I whispered to no one. Grace and Charlie were still fast asleep.

First steps on the road were always uncomfortable. The shoulder straps were working their way into my back and the metal frame poked at my sides and tailbone, each step jostling the pack in unexpected and uncomfortable ways. The pain was stronger than I remembered, but the trick was to stop thinking, to shut off my mind and count time instead. That was how we managed it in country, counting seconds with each new footprint on the trail, forgetting the pack's weight and the currents of pain shooting down our backs, our arms swollen and numb. There was always enough pain to distract us from worrying about what might lie buried underneath us.

My thoughts skipped back years into the past and landed on West again. He hadn't planned to be on that deployment. He told me as much before we left.

"Already got my share, sir—already seen the white elephant. These old bones finally had enough playin' cowboys and infidels."

There was nothing left for him to prove by the time we met, just a couple of months before the battalion left for Afghanistan. The bonus for reenlisting was not what it had been earlier in the war, a paltry ten grand to sign on for four more years, and that was before taxes. I knew enough to realize I needed him. Standing a few feet back from the row of shooters on the firing line, his thumbs hooked into his web belt and a clump of Copenhagen stuck along the inside of his bulging bottom lip, West took the time to explain to me, his new lieutenant, how the system worked.

"Way I see it, sir, higher-ups wanna push out all the combat vets by givin' 'em a shit bonus. Got a buddy up there at headquarters, said he seen a buncha generals and higher-ups were sittin' around the table and no shit, they wanna kick out all the combat dudes 'cuz we're used up. They wanna send us to Wounded Warrior or out-process us to the VA, don't wanna deal with the shit we brought back from the old war. I shit you not, sir, got it all down on a fuckin' Power Point."

West turned his head to the side and let a stream of nut-brown liquid spurt from his mouth, then rocked his weight onto his back hip and nudged the front of his Kevlar helmet with one finger, tipping his helmet just high enough that I could see the tan line in the middle of his forehead. He was a young man dressed as a soldier striking the pose of a cowboy from a Hollywood Western.

"Time for the private sector. That's where I'm headed. Time to get my hands on that peace dividend over in the private sector."

Guys talked like that sometimes, speaking of the private sector as if it were a physical place, like a church or the gym, a place of open admission to any man who knew what he was looking for.

"Cha-ching," he said.

I'd asked him what exactly he had in mind. He shot another stream of dip spit then rubbed his lips with the back of his hand, metal cuff bracelet shining in the full afternoon sun.

"Underwater welding."

"You know many underwater welders back home in Indiana?"

West flinched.

A shooter on the firing line had dropped rounds out of the black center of the paper target, fingers fumbling over the rifle's charging handle. West knelt beside the man, eyes scanning the length of the barrel. He tapped the man's helmet with one hand, directing him to move over. He laid belly-down in the grass, easing his shoulder into the back end of the long gun and resting his chin on the top of the buttstock. His face slid down the side of the butt-stock until it sealed into the black rubber like a cheek in a pillow. One eye was behind the scope lens, his body an extension of the gun. He pushed up from the ground and took one step back, making room for the shooter to mimic his routine.

"Got a buddy in Biloxi," he said. "One of the seniors on my first pump and he's pullin' that good money, well over six figures, and his crew is chill. Absolutely no fuck-fuck games. Those dudes don't give a fuck about admin shit like here, 'cuz if you know your shit they're cool as fuck, but if you're a bag of ass down there, well, you're gone and don't expect a warning either. But they love snipers 'cuz they know we can operate independently."

West fished out the wad of tobacco from his lip and flung it onto the ground, wiping his finger on his pants. It sounded like the private sector was dying for a young man like him, a young man with an armful of tattoos, no education, and a tobacco habit. A young man who knew how to operate independently.

"Sounds like you have a plan, Sergeant. Are you good in the water?"

"Nah, sir. Rock in the water on account of my body fat bein' so low. Too much muscle and shit," he said, rolling his eyes.

"Ever thought about sticking around for one more deployment?"

He dragged a finger across his brow then pulled a pack of Marlboro Reds from his cargo pocket. "No offense, sir, but my bootlaces seen more combat than all these green-as-grass knuckle draggers you got here. Nah, I'm good. Don't feel like riskin' my ass one more time waitin' on some haji to turn my nuts into jelly."

He sucked hard on the end of his cigarette. His head shook and smoke clouds spewed from the corner of his mouth.

"What if I put you in charge of all the teams? I hear Afghanistan is a turkey shoot compared to Iraq. I could use someone like you, someone with skills."

I knew what I was doing. Tell a man he was needed and he couldn't help but show up for whatever you asked. It was only a few days later that West swaggered up to the platoon's morning formation with his reenlistment contract in hand, pinning the single sheet of paper against the back of the man he'd instructed on the firing line, then signed his name.

I limped into the office later that morning and tossed my keys into a drawer. My knees and back ached from the miles I carried the rucksack through the neighborhood, but my head felt clear. Although the boxes of deposition transcripts were beginning to collect dust, I still could not bring myself to work on the summaries. At least not this morning. I knocked on Ned's door, finding him seated in his chair and looking out the window, fidgeting with a plant on the windowsill. That work was not on his mind was one reason I sought Ned's company. He shared a wall but nothing else with Slaven.

"I met a woman last night."

"Good for you," he said. "I hear they're everywhere nowadays. Women, I mean. As a matter of fact, I encountered one myself. We matched months ago and went out once."

Slaven was talking loudly into his speakerphone from the office next door, his voice crackling and pulsing through the air around my head.

"Have you noticed there doesn't seem to be any decorum left?"

Ned yanked apart the lapels of his jacket, flattening his chin against his neck to get a better look at something on the front of his clean white shirt.

"Right along here is where it was," he said, a hand hovering over the side of his chest. "I'm talking about a young lady who fails to acknowledge me in the grocery. That a young woman refuses to look at my eyes but offers me two whole eyefuls of—how do I say it, delicately—side boob."

A tray of folders was arranged in a metal organizer on his spotless desk. There was no way of knowing what the folders held or even to whom they belonged. I had never seen Ned work. According to the biography he authored for the firm website, Ned "focused his practice on delivering comprehensive corporate counsel to complex international clients." To my knowledge, it was not something the firm had ever done.

His was the only office attorneys cared to drop by for a leisure visit, burning precious minutes of billable time to leach off Ned's style, his sophistication, picking Ned's pocket for something to say about the menu of a new restaurant or an order to make at the trendy cocktail lounge. He was older, a brush of gray on both sideburns and around his ears, with a well-guarded private life no one had ever seen but assumed was just as cosmopolitan as his manners. Ned was a tastemaker. Ned was a person who made choices, and in the choice between sexless work and doing nothing, Ned preferred to do absolutely nothing.

"I saw her near the entrance to the store and she was with a gentleman, if that's what you call a man who wears a stocking cap inside of a building. I pass from the fruits toward the vegetables and the young lady and I make brief eye contact, so there's recognition, and she simply looks away. Who knows what interested her? It was as if my eyes had been magnetized to repel. So, I tell you, there's no decorum left since the applications commandeered our dating lives."

"You could have greeted her."

"Well, no, actually," he thrust his arms in front of himself. "My arms were full, John! I had two armfuls of fruits I was carrying. Just think about how this unfolds. 'Oh! Hello. Good to see you, and who is this?' prompting her to introduce Brooks or Brock or whatever his bros call him, and so he shifts his groceries to her and extends a newly freed hand to greet me."

"Could have just put your apples in a basket..."

"You wouldn't understand, John, how hard it is being alone sometimes," Ned sighed. "This world is made for two."

He sniffled, then reached toward the back corner between his desk and the window, retrieving a long plastic grasping tool, the kind with gripping handle and a plastic trigger that activates a pinching motion in the three-pronged claw. He stuck the tool in the small space between his desk and the wall and pulled up a scrap of yellow paper, depositing it in the wastebasket.

"We matched and met only once. Whomever said women are inferior to men in their capacity for love was onto something."

"Nobody said that, Ned."

Noise from across the paper-thin wall was buzzing inside my ears, sounds of Slaven squawking like a rooster into his speakerphone. But Ned did not seem bothered.

"What if all recorded history is just women competing against each other for a prize they never even wanted?" he said.

"How could history be made without men competing too?"

He stopped grasping at trash and brought his hands together, tenting his fingers. "Have you ever noticed how women prefer *The Bachelor* to *The Bachelorette*?"

"I don't have time to watch television," I said.

"Women become more feminine through competition—acquiring a man or producing children or taking care of their parents. My point is, the man is never her prize. You don't see what I mean?"

There was more I wanted to say, but the sound of Slaven's voice hammering through the wall had knocked loose my train of thought.

"They want to be objects," he continued, but the noise had become unbearable.

I wanted to tell Ned about dinner, about the woman I met and how she listened to me. Instead, I walked back to my own office and closed the door, propping the back of the chair underneath the door handle and hoping to block the sound of Slaven's voice from penetrating my own walls. I opened my email and found one new message in the inbox. As I held the cursor over the subject line and traced the letters with the pointy end of the arrow, my heart beat faster.

The subject said "From Ruth."

Dear John, Lovely visiting with you last night. It's rare to have a conversation quite that "real" at a fundraiser. I've been thinking about you, my new pen pal, and I want to recommend you look into Translations *by Brian Friel if my idea on borders and guns did anything for you. Worth a read.*

Cheers, Ruth

I read it a second time, then a third. I kept reading Ruth's message until the thrill of reading her words finally moved me to consider a response. Or, I wondered, should I let this message sit for a day or so, treat it like an email from anyone else and wait to tender my reply? I stood up from my desk and walked down the empty hallway, heading into the bathroom. At the sink, I filled my hands with cold water and splashed my face. I could hear the rustling sound of a newspaper coming from the bathroom stalls, one or another of the old filers down from five probably, maybe Mr. Quinn. I grabbed a paper towel and dried my forehead and cheeks, then walked back to my office and opened a blank reply.

Dear Ruth, I am planning a trip now to our used bookstore downtown, which you should visit if you have time.

I'd like it if you went there with me, I thought to myself, but had enough sense not to write.

Be in touch if you want to discuss your idea about guns and borders—it sounds fascinating. Best, John

I clicked send without thinking, pulling my hands back from the keyboard as if it were hot to touch, then reopening the email from my sent messages and reading her note and mine, again and again, the chain of correspondence we had begun. The message could mean whatever she wanted, whatever might be found between what little I wrote and what more I wanted to say. I opened my drawer and pulled a tin of Copenhagen from where it lay hidden beneath a stack of yellow legal pads, slipped a pinch into my mouth, and let the tobacco massage into my gum.

There was more I wanted to know also.

I typed her name into the search bar and watched the light blink before retrieving articles and photographs, video clippings cascading down the length of my screen. I clicked her personal website and a new page unfolded, an anthology of other people's words jamming into the center of the screen, italicized quotes about the intensity of her voice, how it was "agile" and "breathtaking." Long before I discovered Ruth singing kitsch to a roomful of stodgy patrons, the *Times* had recognized her as a "rising star of singing theater; a beguiling soprano; a polyglot chanteuse with the silvery, rich tone of a clarion songbird." There were dozens of photographs on her website, her hair changing from red to blonde, her appearance mutable as one role morphed into the next. I studied the images closely, comparing her expressions and how much her face changed with color and costume; a peasant, a mother, a renaissance courtesan, even a man. I watched her face disappear inside each character she played, hair and mouth and body all out on loan to the different roles she played through the years. Everything changed—everything except the eyes, which were unmistakably her own.

"You've not lived until you've heard Bram in the role of…"

This was a role I never heard of in a show I had never seen, but the man whose picture was embedded in the post, blowing kisses to the camera, his face glowing like white phosphorous, eyeballs bulging like two Ping-Pong balls— appeared frequently. I flicked the mouse and scrolled down the rest of her social media pages. There he was wearing a costume in the makeup chair; there he was leaning on the railing of a bridge looking at a body of water; and there he was again, this time standing onstage with his mouth open wide. I could see something unexpected about him, something in the way his plump lips flattened shut when he put an arm around Ruth's shoulder and kissed her cheek. She had worn a wedding ring the previous night, and still I expected a different man in the role of husband. Someone older, someone more commanding.

I pushed back from the computer. Another afternoon was nearing its completion with nothing to show. Staying late at the office held no promise of the productivity that eluded me thus far. I buried the tobacco tin under the legal pads and shuffled a few papers, but before getting up from the desk, I saw something that made me stop. The video at the top of my screen and the time stamp that read a few minutes after ten o'clock last night. It was a social media post made shortly after we met. The frame was Ruth standing alone on stage, her face bathed red by floodlights mounted to the ceiling, arms reaching forward into the camera. I hit play and she came to life, singing.

"...*and the road led to Redhead / all five feet nothin' / from the moment I saw him, I could see it all! / Everything I wanted, and everything he wanted / stretching into the future...*"

The music stopped. Redhead, she said. Was she singing about me? She posted the song less than an hour after we left the judge's house. I turned off the screen and walked into Ned's office, finding him sitting on his window ledge, holding a binder of papers and looking down at the street below.

"What's the first thing you notice about me?" I asked.

He turned slowly to face me, inspecting me up and down.

"Well, your tie is too long," he said. "The tie is sup-posed to be worn to the top of the—"

"Not my clothes—me."

He straightened up and squinted.

"Copper, a few shades up on the value scale I suppose, but, colloquially, your hair is what I notice about you, Lieutenant. Your hair is red."

Red, he'd said. I'm her Redhead. I smiled and backed into the hallway.

"Say, I wanted to ask you..."

Before Ned could finish his sentence, my feet were moving, floating across the carpet and leading me out the door to the parking lot.

CHAPTER ELEVEN

The voicemail was brief.

"Charlie purposefully kicked a friend in the head while they were waiting in line to go down the slide," Grace said in the voicemail, her tone flat. *"The school director said they're not talking about kicking him out yet, but they need to get him on a program. I'll see you tonight at home after your grief meeting."*

I played it again.

Grace relayed the news without a word as to why our son had kicked a kid in the head, how he managed to kick another kid in the head.

"Can she have her own opinion?" I shouted in the car, tossing my phone onto the passenger seat and watching it bounce onto the floorboard below.

"Did the kick happen while they were playing?"

Were a couple of three-year-olds going too rough and knocking each other around, or did my son walk up to another child and a put a shoe to his head? By the way, Grace, how did he manage to kick a child in the head? I searched my imagination to find action-film kickboxers dealing knockout blows, the snap of a leg and flick of the tennis shoe to an attacker's temple. Had someone trained Charlie for this? How did these teachers know that Charlie did it all with *purpose*? Some person told

Grace our son was guilty of a purposeful head kick and she never thought to ask a simple question?

Pay the fuck attention, I thought.

The car rocked when a concrete mixer screamed by me on the interstate. I tried focusing on the road, then reached for the knob of my radio dial, twisting until the volume rose on the chamber music thrumming through my speakers, still shaking my head at Grace's stupid message.

The car slowed.

I pulled off the interstate and started down Birch Road then turned onto Dogwood, which turned into a street named Sequoia. This was a neighborhood divided up by trees that grew naturally in other parts of the country. The house I was looking for sat on the edge of an excavated lake. The greatest compliment you could give something in this town was that it seemed like someplace else.

I had just put my finger to the bell when the door swung open.

"Come right in!" said Mary, the white-haired woman wearing a bright cardigan and floral pants. She grabbed my hands and pulled me inside. Her head reached the knot of my tie. "So, so good to have you here tonight."

She showed me the way to the living room where a handful of guests sat on sofas.

The home was spacious on the inside, an open concept with the carpeted living space running alongside the tile floor of the dining area, a straight line that divided one big room into two. I had heard about this group at church via a coupon-sized advertisement for "Grief Ministry" on the back page of the weekly parish bulletin. The law firm wanted new associates to get involved, to find a cause, and then "put yourself out there," so I ripped out the page and wrote my name and number into the blank space, dropping the stub into a basket. Mary called back before the end of the week.

"*Who did you lose?*" she asked over the phone.

"Nobody."

"*Sorry for asking, but why are you interested if you haven't lost someone? Everyone in my ministry will have lost someone, most of them much older than you.*"

"I want to help people.... I knew people who died when I was in the war."

I heard sighing into the phone before she asked, "*And are you also suffering?*"

"I'm perfectly fine."

A white candle burned on a coffee table in the center of the room, a thick cylinder with at least a hundred tiny seashells sticking out of its pearl-colored wax. I took a cup of tea in both hands and sat down.

"Beautiful piece, isn't it?" Mary said from high on a barstool she positioned at the head of the room. Her hair had the texture of cotton candy and glowed in the sunlight pouring in from the window behind her. She sat upright, at least a couple of heads taller than the rest of us in the room. I figured it was cancer and dementia that left these people, mostly women, stranded in her living room. A husband's long bout with illness, a car teetering off the road and into a tree. Women were always the ones left behind, and maybe they liked it that way. I nodded without paying attention to what she was saying, distracted by the big picture window behind her. A man jogged along the sidewalk that skimmed the outer edge of the lake.

"Thanks, everyone, for walking together in grief. I'm so blessed to be tagging along with you on your grief walks. However long those walks might be, however tired we might feel, know I will be with you for every step." Mary balled her hands into knobby fists and shook them.

"Everyone, take a moment and look at that candle right there on the table. Do you know who that is? Why, it's Jesus—Jesus is here with us tonight, in this very room, and he's inside that candle burning so bright and warm in the center of everything that's going on for us. Think of it as His room, the Lord's room, and we'll start every week by looking at that candle and acknowledging His presence, and then saying a centering prayer. Now, can anyone tell the group what that means?"

The woman next to me reached up slowly from the handle of her walker and touched the back of my hand. "Young man," she whispered, "what did she just say?"

"I said a CENTERING PRAYER—Marianne, please listen," Mary barked.

"I think I have it," said the only other man in the group, a widower who raised his hand sheepishly in front of his chest. "Where we use our imaginations and such. For example, you imagine yourself taking a walk along the beach with Jesus, and then you—"

"That's right, Skip," Mary said encouragingly. "Did everyone hear what he said?"

Heads nodded, everyone in agreement. The man look-ed puzzled.

"My name's Ted," he said.

A stereo speaker piped in the sounds of birds chirping and flows of water through a rocky brook, drowning out the man's response.

"Can everyone hear Skip?" Mary waved an arm in the man's direction and heads bobbed along agreeably. "We're taking a journey with the Lord by our side, and it's my job to show everybody how it's done. So, take a big, nourishing breath into your nose." She paused to demonstrate. "Let it out slowly through your mouth." She demonstrated again, more loudly. "Let new air cycle into our bodies and refresh our spirits."

Eyes closed, I listened to the raspy sounds of people taking their calming breaths, air moving together through the room.

Mary described the scene. We were walking along a beach early in the morning. Temperatures were warm. A gentle mist fell on our faces and necks. The sun was rising behind a distant and watery horizon.

"Now, a second set of footprints is forming behind you..." she said, and there I was in the place Mary des-cribed, looking back to find someone following me along the seashore. I looked closer at the person coming up behind me, wiping the ocean water from my eyes.

What a surprise. It was Ruth in a cover-up, walking barefoot at low tide, wearing a Panama hat and thick black sunglasses to protect her eyes. Ruth was looking out over the ocean with her hair swept back over bare shoulders. I stopped and looked more closely. There was Bram nearby, the cuffs of his pants rolled high on his pale legs. He was stumbling through deeper sand farther up shore and away from Ruth.

"You can see Him, smiling at you in that calming way..." Mary continued, but I did not see Bram smiling at all, actually, and his presence was not calming. Not to me, at least. If only I could pick Bram up and drop him somewhere away from this part of the beach, somewhere else, perhaps somewhere far out to sea...

"—John, come back. John, we're centering ourselves—"

Mary snapped her fingers in front of me and my eyes opened. I had fallen asleep.

"Okay," she said, kicking one short, floral-printed leg over the other. She tightened her lips. "Do you know what a mantra is, John?"

"A statement you recite over and over again," I offered, my jaw stiffening.

"Mm. Not quite. Whatever helps you get in touch with something. The mantra is Jesus for me, and I will sit here and just say Jesus, Jesus, Jesus. When I say His name over and over again, I actually feel my body relax, and so what I want us to do this evening is first to tell our grief stories, and then to come up with our very own personal mantras, something we can take home with us and use whenever we want. How does that sound?"

The group was silent. Marianne rested her chin on the metal crossbar of her walker, eyelids fluttering. I looked away and into my cup of tea, tilting my head to one side and imagining the tendons and muscles running through the base of my neck stretching, pulling, lengthening under the skin.

"Marianne, can you tell the group your grief story?"

The older woman lifted her head from the walker, still stooped forward on the couch, her small body taking up half of the seat cushion. She pulled a tissue from the breast pocket of her blouse and rubbed her nose.

"I suppose I'm here because..." Her voice gargled into a cough, what sounded like phlegm breaking clear inside her throat. She patted lightly on her chest. "My daughter. She was fifteen. Been years now, decades. She was walkin' with a boy in the middle of a dirt road. Told her not to. She never listened to a word, my girl. It was late and summertime. Suppose it was so dark you couldn't see nothin' but what was in front of your headlights. Car come up on her from behind and, well, all the rest."

Marianne wiped along the inside of her bifocals with a finger like a windshield wiper on the wrong side of the glass, then pressed the glasses back on the bridge of her nose. "I've been livin' in a home for a few years now. Since my late husband passed. Couple days ago, somebody new, just moved in I guess, he come 'round and ask if I had kids. I tell him about my daughter." She moved her hands to grip the sides of her walker.

"Man gets a 'sorry-for-your-trouble' look and says to me he guessed God must've needed another rose for his heavenly garden."

Mary reached for a box of Kleenex from the end table and thrust it toward me, but Marianne put one hand on my wrist and waved the other toward Mary.

"People say the dumbest things, don't they? All, don't they?" Mary said, her lips pressed into a frown. She reached underneath the seat of her stool and pulled a lever to lower its height a few inches.

"Who knows where my daughter is?" Marianne said. "I don't."

"Now, Marianne, of course we know where your daughter is."

"What are we doin' here if we know where she went? She ain't in any garden; I know that much. I looked at my daughter's face when we got to the hospital. Her whole face was crooked. It wasn't her. No. Face was yellow, purple down the back. Doctors said she looked that way because her neck was broke. I told 'em that one wasn't my daughter. I couldn't recognize what they were showin' me."

The room was quiet. I kept my eyes away from Marianne. She was close enough that I could have touched her on the shoulder, could have reached for her hand the same way she had reached for mine, but the woman was composed, not crying, not even a catch in her voice as she spoke. I sat still and listened to the grind of my teeth sliding back and forth inside my mouth and kept my eyes away from Mary for fear that she might put me through whatever she was doing to Marianne.

"If I have something black and ugly inside me, Marianne, the first thing I do is pray. I close my eyes, I ball up my fists, and I pray. Dear Lord, we pray for the soul of Marianne's daughter, and we ask that you give her mother strength. Our loved ones might be gone from your earthly kingdom, but we know they're in a better place now. Your heavenly kingdom, with your son Jesus, and so we pray for the repose of all their souls. Amen."

Mary opened her eyes and started thumbing through the stack of papers she held in her lap, grief worksheets and inspirational quotations she had compiled. The room remained silent. We depended on the church to make sense of our suffering, but all we had to offer each other was silence.

"Jesus doesn't want us to be sad!" Mary said, breaking the pall. "Jesus wants you, me, all of us, to be happy and holy, and the reason we grieve is because the memories of our loved ones are still alive on the inside."

Mary shook her head vigorously now, willing herself to believe what she was saying. God had never promised happiness but made sure of our suffering, and still this foolish woman sought an explanation. It was pathetic, her need to seek reasons for things that were beyond explanation. She gave others the impression she was above grief because she understood it, had accepted it as part of some larger blessing. Prayer was no different from knocking on wood or crossing your fingers, something used to ward off misfortune. I had no need for it. I tucked my hands under my legs to wipe the sweat from my palms and looked up to find Mary staring at me.

"The group would like you tell everyone your grief story, John. It's time for you to tell us why you're here."

The room was quiet. Heat rose in my chest and neck. Explanations led nowhere. Talking had become painful. The room smelled suddenly of powder and wax, of death, and I wondered why Mary had needed to rise up and challenge me, why she could not leave me to the privacy of my own thoughts. I'd kept my ghosts with me for this long and would not reveal them to her.

Marianne reached over from her walker and patted me on the arm again. The other man shook his head from across the table.

"You saw some bad things, son?"

There was friendliness in his face. In fact, everyone's face seemed to hold an abundance of compassion and pity.

"Losing a buddy can be just as bad as losing a spouse...."

It was kind of him, acknowledging what he assumed was my trauma. Kind of him to decide that my loss of a buddy could come in the same magnitude, the same size and weight as the loss he had suffered, as if the man were telling me, "I have compared your loss to mine and decided it is significant enough to qualify for inclusion in this group." My face twisted into the same frown he was making at me.

"Never knew what all of it was for," he said, shaking his head in exasperation. "War. Senseless war. What we were even doing over there, puttin' young guys like you and your buddies in harm's way?"

I heard a whisper of my own voice rising out of my throat, but the man could not stop talking, first about buddies, then about war, about death and who can talk about it. He was gaining momentum on the topic, the women in the room sighing and nodding in agreement.

"...can only imagine what you saw. We're all old. Young guys are not supposed to be here."

What had I seen anyway? I wondered. I hardly knew anymore.

"Senseless," he repeated, reaching for his cup of tea.

My memories were filled with life, more life than whatever passed for living out here, where sharks hunted for every last feeling of pride or confidence, where nothing was yours to keep. I took a deep breath and noticed my palms were dry and my leg had stopped twitching. Though my nerves were jangled, I let myself sink deeper into the couch cushion and prepared to speak.

"You don't have to share if you don't want to," Mary offered, but there was no turning back.

"I want to talk about my friend," I said. "Sergeant West."

Mary leaned forward and so did the man. It was simple enough to me. They were eager to hear a story and so I told one.

West was twenty-five when we left home, and handsome in a recruiting poster way, the type of soldier incapable of flinching when bullets splashed in the sand at our feet.

"The guy everybody wanted to make proud," I said. "The guy everyone wanted to be. It happened our last day. Just one day before we were scheduled to fly home. We thought it was over. We left the patrol base and the shot-up plywood boards we'd stacked to wall off the area where we put our sleeping bags. We made it through the IEDs. We were at the big base waiting to catch a flight out of the combat zone and the air smelled clean. No more piles of black ash where we burned plastic and cardboard from the stale rations we'd eaten. The platoon was spending the night on the big base and everybody was happy because there was a coffee shop and a pizza restaurant. It was the kind of base where everyone slept on a mattress, everybody got an AC unit that blew freezing cold air, the kind of base where somebody else stood guard so you could sleep.

"We were restless that last night, so West and me took a walk. You know, take a look around the big base, see all the things we'd been deprived of and enjoy the freedom of stretching our legs without fear. West wanted to pick up something at the store, a tin of Copenhagen or something like that. I can't remember what he wanted so bad it couldn't wait until we got home."

I sat back on the couch and took in the man's face across from me. He looked like a child listening to a bedtime story, his eyes wide and mouth hanging open, listening with anticipation.

"We walk into the tent and it looks like any convenience store on the inside, the kind of place we hadn't seen in months, and the two of us are just wandering the aisles, staring at the stacks of beef jerky and canned soup, holding candy bars in our hands like they were made of gold. I spot a rack of glossy magazines near the front of the tent. I tell West, 'Hey, man. I'll be up there waiting for you.' He kind of flicked his head, tipped his forehead up to say he understood. I watched him long enough to see his back. Then it happened. The mechanical voice sounded calm on the base's transmission system. *'Incoming. Incoming. Take cover.'* There wasn't time to take a step. I learned later it was an artillery round, a 120-millimeter rocket, the one-in-a-billion rocket that hits its mark. This one landed just beyond the store. There's a flash of light then darkness. I lose consciousness for a few seconds. When I come to, I'm on my back. The world is all red and brown around me. Dust so thick the insides of my mouth were coated in it. I scramble to my feet and there's a light bulb flickering inside my head, eyes blinking open and shut, a high-pitched sound like a dial tone ringing from inside my ears. I couldn't hear myself scream.

"I found him. West was on the ground, on his back. His face was peaceful, his eyes closed and his arms out to his sides. He looked normal, as if he'd laid down to take a nap in the middle of the aisle. Everything was so normal." I touched myself on the cheek. "His face was smooth. A piece of metal was stuck into the side of his neck."

I reached toward the candle and fingered the outer rim of a seashell bulging from the side of the wax cylinder.

"That piece of metal was aluminum. Funny, isn't it? The rocket turned a soda can into a projectile. The can was still fizzing brown soda in West's dead hand."

I looked out the window, setting my gaze on a woman pushing a stroller on the path and trying not to blink.

"And I find myself wondering, some days more than others, does it count? West's death. His sacrifice. Does it even count because of the way he died? We were done by then and had survived the gunfire and explosions. We'd already finished fighting the enemy. Or is it just friendly fire when your buddy is killed by a piece of shrapnel from your own case of soda?"

Marianne raised a hand to her mouth. The man closed his eyes.

"I never heard a story like that in my whole life," Mary said. "It's devastating."

For the first time tonight, Mary was right. Come to think of it, I had never heard a story like it either. In fact, no one had ever heard such a story like this because I made it up. I invented the story right there in Mary's living room.

"Son, God bless you and God bless your sergeant because that is just the most senseless thing I ever heard," the man said.

"God loves you."

Mary put out her hands and closed her eyes for a second time this evening. Everyone bowed their heads, hands joined with one another.

"We pray for John, that he may keep the faith through this senseless loss of his friend, Sergeant West, and for the repose of Mr. West's soul, which we pray is in heaven, and that John knows his friend died so that we may gather here peaceably in your name. Amen."

Truth was irrelevant. The arousal of a good story was all that mattered. They accepted mine like a drug and suddenly there was nothing left for me to say.

"May I be excused?" I asked.

"Yes. Go. John, take all the time you need," said Mary.

I hurried out the door to my car, laughing at my own audacity, the creativity it took to invent the story without any preparation and to tell it so flawlessly. I could hardly suppress the laughter as I jogged to the street, trying to remember the looks on people's faces as I piled one lie on top of another, reminding myself to call Dan and unload the whole hilarious drama on him as soon as I could. Finding my phone still resting on the passenger floormat, I swiped eagerly at the screen and found what I had hoped for, "From Ruth" written in bold letters:

> *Dear John, your suggestion of the bookstore was perfect. I went there this afternoon. Combing through the stacks always gives me chills, like I'm looking through the private collection of someone deceased. I will certainly drop you a line once tech week is through and I have a bit more time to myself. I'm eager to hear your opinion on my idea. Thinking of you.*
>
> *Cheers, Ruth.*

I fiddled with the picture to make the words bigger, then smaller, reading the message both ways before setting the phone on the empty seat beside me. I didn't know what "tech week" entailed but I wished it were already over.

I looked back through the window inside Mary's house one last time, noticing the lights were bright and warm and the silhouettes of people still talking. I had been gone only a few minutes, short enough that no one would think twice if I opened the door and sat back down, rejoining them for more stories and prayer. I thought of Grace and Charlie going about their bedtime routine, taking care of themselves and not waiting for me, not even wanting me around. I turned on the engine and pulled out into the empty street, letting myself drift away to the sound of classical music still playing on the radio.

CHAPTER TWELVE

Another week sped by and nothing was accomplished. The only improvement to my routine came in the mornings when I dropped down to the floor, chest bumping the hardwood and arms cranking like pistons. One. Two. Ticking push-ups off in cadence with the second hand of my watch, pulling my knees underneath my chest and letting my jellied arms swing lifelessly by my sides. Something had gotten into me. I hadn't done push-ups like this in years.

"I want my blue shirt!" Charlie was yelling downstairs at the breakfast table.

Retrieving my phone from the bedside table, I walked into the bathroom and tapped the passcode into the locked screen. It took three times before I remembered I had changed the code. I swiped to one page and then the next, scanning top lines of Ruth's social media profiles. More than a day had passed since the last time she posted a new picture, a couple of days since she emailed me. I switched off the phone and dropped it onto the bathroom counter. I turned on the faucet and ran cool water over my hands, splashing it onto my face.

"I barely know her," I muttered to myself.

"Who?"

I whirled around to find Grace standing a few feet back from the doorway, pulling the shirt Charlie wanted from the dryer.

"Who do you barely know?" she asked.

"Nobody," I said, hurrying into the closet. I wondered how much she had heard and what else I had said.

"Why don't I ride along with you and Charlie today?" I suggested to change the subject.

"Could you grab his shoes then? We're already running behind."

In Charlie's room I scoured the mess of toys and yesterday's clothes piled around, tossing teddy bears and flashing rubber balls into a basket, picking up each shirt or hat in hopes of finding the pair of shoes underneath. Sifting through the mess that covered the floor, I decided winter boots would do, the only thing I found to put on his feet.

"Do we have any idea where the shoes are?" I asked Grace.

"He likes to hide them behind the toilet, but don't worry about it. He's already put on a pair."

I tossed the boots back into the pile of clothes and kicked it into the corner. I couldn't even beat my son at finding his shoes.

"Sure you're okay to come along?" she asked.

"He's got his shoes on the wrong feet. Let me fix that for you, buddy," I said, starting toward him, but they looked at me as if I were the one confused. Charlie screamed and jumped into his mother's arms.

"He puts his shoes on every day all by himself. Right, Charlie?" Grace wiped a tear from his eye while he scowled at me.

"His teacher says it's important to allow him to do these small things for himself. Everything we do for him, we take away from him," Grace instructed.

The way she looked at me told me I had intruded on their morning routine. By the time we were on the road I still didn't feel like letting it go.

"I don't know what's more ridiculous. My son wearing his shoes like a clown, or his day care calling itself a school. It's a day care. If it were a school, then I'd expect one of its first lessons would be putting your shoes on the right feet. 'Hey, kid, you wanna put your underwear on your head? That's no problem here at Montessori, just as long as you're the one putting the underwear on your head. What's that, kid? Wanna put your shit underwear on your head instead, wear it around the playground for your friends to see? Fine by us!'"

Grace had stopped listening. "Old Macdonald had a farm. E-I-E-I-O. And on that farm he had a…"

She and Charlie were singing now, oblivious to anyone but themselves, belting nursery rhymes out of tune, reminding me of a couple of dogs howling at the moon.

I looked out the window. Buildings and signs floated past. There were coffee shops, a strip mall, gas stations, and supermarkets attached to vast, empty parking lots. The waste of it all. The absolute mess of concrete and stupidity that made up this pointless town.

"These people razed a fucking cornfield to build things nobody needed," I remarked.

In fact, they built two of something nobody needed, all our land processed and developed by a company in Houston or wherever, a made-to-order city. No wonder these people flocked to the military. They already had the taste for standard issue. Local people were happy so long as they got their choice between two familiars—a Starbucks or a Dunkin' Donuts, a McDonalds or a Burger King—so long as they never had to risk their comfort on something unproven at delivering bland satisfaction. How ironic it was that Grace had blamed the bases for making her want to leave the military. "The sameness," she once moaned. She moved us all the way back to the smack middle of the country to feed on the same coffees and conveniences she could not stand while we were—

"JOHN!"

I blinked.

The car was parked. Grace and Charlie were standing by the front door of the day care, holding hands and staring at me. I shook my head in confusion. I was still buckled into my seat.

I was nearly an hour late; Slaven was waiting for me when I stepped into the bathroom at work.

"Invest your time, Walker, don't spend it."

He was bent over the sink, wearing a green checked shirt with his bright teal tie flipped over his shoulder, diamond designs running from tip to knot. He looked like a M. C. Escher print in riotous technicolor.

"Attorneys don't have one single ounce of respect. Look at this mess!" He was dabbing the granite countertop with a paper towel. "Can you believe how wet this counter is? Disgusting. I can't believe I'm wasting billable time doing janitor work because we've got attorneys taking baths in the sink. Baths. Like...birds!"

He tossed the wad of wet towels into the wastebasket, then grabbed one dry paper towel, which he used to grip the handle of the bathroom door. He held it open and looked at me. "There's something I need to run by you, Walker, but not right now, no time. I'm interested in getting your opinion on something, and it's personal. We'll talk when there's time."

That was rich. Slaven having a personal topic to discuss.

The office was quiet that morning and I didn't feel like sitting down. The thought of burying my face into the trough of overdue work piled up around my desk seemed even less appealing than usual, so I tucked a yellow legal pad under my arm and started marching the halls instead, puffing my chest in a look of authority. I walked pointlessly from one end of the building to the other for no reason except that it felt good to be on my feet, looking every bit the part of a guy going someplace. I said *good morning* as I passed mail clerks on my way to nowhere.

At least twenty minutes into the routine, I noticed both of my shoes were untied and I started to laugh. It was funny to see my shoelaces undone and dragging across the carpet. Years earlier I couldn't have walked ten steps without a stern-faced person in uniform calling me out, pointing a finger at my feet and telling me to "fix those laces," as if there were a tool I could use to keep my shoes permanently tied. People were always minding each other in the military, policing one another's behavior according to a list of rules. Here, nobody cared. Nobody bothered me about my shoes or my appearance, which gave me the feeling of freedom, a freedom to come undone, to walk around with shoes unlaced until I smashed my nose into the carpet, if that was what I wanted.

By lunchtime I decided to take my walking outside.

The Graybar building was towering compared to the rest of downtown's corporate buildings, but inside it was a hollow shaft, office rooms built into either side of the building like honeycombs clustered neatly against the walls. I stood alone in the middle of the ground floor with my head pointed up, spotting the back of a working person in an office near the center of the east wall. She was sitting at her desk, huddled into the computer monitor in her private office chamber. All she had to do was swivel around in her chair and look through the window into an identical glass office across the building on the west side. Each worker was always part of a team, always visible to at least one other person but always out of reach. Everybody was paired up, except when one of the workers stepped out, of course.

Standing on the escalator, I watched a herd of employees pushing through the metal turnstiles and surging for the door, ID badges dangling from lanyards attached to their belt loops. Some wore backpacks. Others had duffel bags slung over their shoulders, moving more quickly than the competition as they hustled to squeeze in lunch-hour exercise at the Graybar gym. Still others were already coming back with lunch in hand, holding white sandwich bags and charging through the same turnstiles but in the opposite direction of their colleagues, fighting against the current of moving bodies like salmon swimming upstream.

I stopped near the turnstiles and noticed the digital ticker built into a slab of industrial concrete just above our heads, red block numbers flashing the price per share of Graybar stock. I wondered how many would-be trips out of the office had ended right here, an employee on his way out the door when he glanced over his shoulder at the ticker, noticed the stock price was down, and thought better of his decision to leave.

"Best not be seen leaving my desk today," he might say to himself, turning back for his glass office chamber.

I made up a salad and claimed a chair in the corner. Most of the tables sat only one or two people, and they scrolled silently through their phones, eyes scanning a video, maybe an email. No one seemed bothered that I was looking up from my own plate to watch how they ate and what they looked at. I stared at a group of men who had pushed their tables into a long column running the length of the dining area. They were seated close together, holding cards in their hands and playing a game, gnaw-ing on sandwiches, slices of pizza. The purpose of their gathering was not to eat but to play the game. I finished my salad and set aside the plate, looking more closely at the insides of a handful of cards held by a bearded man whose back was turned. Pictures of wizards and monsters, a big-breasted woman holding a long, sharp sword. The bearded man was quiet, whispering to a man sitting in the next seat over who studied a handful of cards lying faceup on the table. The bearded man put one of his cards into the pile facedown, then drew another. People all around came and went but no one from this group seemed in a hurry to leave. How silly they looked to me, grown men wasting time playing a child's game, and doing it in a public place. They bothered me, how small and feeble they looked. I walked past them to place my empty salad bowl on the belt and it disappeared through a black rubber flap into the wall. I had decided they were an embarrassment to themselves when my phone vibrated inside my pocket.

> *Dear John, No need to buy it. I've gotten the last Friel copy for you, the only one they had. You just let me know when you're going to the playground and I'll have it for you after the show.*
>
> *Cheers, Ruth.*

She'd attached a photograph of herself holding the book at the bookstore, a glossy pink paperback at the end of a black sleeve. I never would have found this book buried under a stack at the end of a poorly lit aisle, never finding on my own what Ruth had shown to me. I wanted to reach across that table and grab one of the men by that dangling ID badge and shout to him, "You would not believe the woman I have met! I met her right here." I puckered my lips together with knowledge of the secret treasure I had found.

I walked slower than usual that day.

The sunlight was shining on me in a way I had not felt in months.

I was always sitting in one chair or another, taking a seat somewhere, getting seated. I stood anonymously at an intersection downtown waiting for the light to change, standing alongside strangers who never stopped to notice those around them, the type of person they might find if only they looked around. How these downtown people all pulled out phones or looked at their shoes or stared blankly at the cars driving past. People would look any-where to avoid looking at each other.

Walking the sidewalk that led back to my building, I got stuck behind an older man dressed in a gray uniform. He was in his late sixties, I guessed, and there seemed to be something lame about his left foot, the way it hung limply from the ankle each time he raised his knee, moved it forward, then dropped it on the pavement one step in front of his body. Because we were still a yard or two from the door to our building, I cut ahead of him, then held the door open to let him enter first.

"Thanks, sir," he said, looking into my eyes.

He shifted the bag of potato chips into the crook of his elbow, a can of Coke in his other hand.

"About time to post the watch."

The man staggered through a service door off the main entryway and into a small room the size of a coat closet.

Lawyers wrote off their Friday afternoons.

For those who made it to the senior ranks of the firm, the weekend officially began sometime late Thursday. That was when Quinn and the others would leave town for lake houses in Iowa and Minnesota, a horse ranch in the country. There would still be conference calls to join and documents to redline, but their weekends had the power to stretch into mid-Tuesday, when they would drop in for just a couple of hours to pick up their mail, catch up on correspondence. If he didn't have court on Friday, Mick spent the weekend at his condo in Chicago or joined Graybar on a private jet to one of the great man's cabins in Jackson Hole or Sun Valley. The long weekend was the payoff for wringing every last minute of billable time from the best years of your life.

The younger attorneys had their fun too. The first call went out around noon.

"Lunch?"

Then the first reply.

"How about a place we can walk to?"

They weighed the merits of a sushi bar and a brasserie, talking over the distances and comparing expectations of how busy the place was going to be and whether they needed a reservation. They talked through all these things, as thorough and even-handed as law school trained them, knowing deep down that none of it mattered. They were after booze, and they would have been happy with a box of cold chicken nuggets if the place served pints of beer and bottomless margaritas. They needed to drink, and nothing satisfied their thirst like the taste of workday alcohol. The grand prize was two or three drinks over a long lunch, shambling back to the office half-dazed to knock around a couple hours of phone calls and emails. The more seasoned attorneys taught new hires to save for Friday afternoon whatever deadhead work we could accumulate during the week. The goal was to pile up a few hours calling a client you hadn't checked in with for a while or phoning in half-dazed to a status hearing about a trial still years away, anything that let you burn minutes of billable time without exposing yourself to too much thinking or prolonged conversation. Around 3:30, just as your tongue started to feel dry and your head a little foggy, somebody would send out the call: "Ready for happy hour?"

A few more drinks and you were home free.

Lawyers drank to forget.

It was their way of numbing up, taking a short break from the anxiety that came with welcoming somebody else's problems into their lives, bound to deadlines and court dates that amounted to a lifetime preoccupied with unintended consequences. Anybody who had clients knew the feeling. How a problem eating away at you when you lay down to sleep spawned three new problems when you woke up the next morning.

Clients gave you a task simple enough: preoccupy yourself with everything that might go wrong; invent the problems before they materialize; answer one question by asking another. Doing this right meant walking a tight-rope, which was why the client hired you. They hired you to walk the tightrope ahead of them, stepping carefully along a narrow string while looking straight down into the pit of their own personal, financial, or marital ruin. You did it so you could report back on how to avoid falling in, but there was never time to stop or turn around, no way of stepping off for a minute to catch your breath. You were stuck up there, and the better you proved to be at keeping your balance, the more you would be asked to do it again, even as you noticed the string getting longer while the pit only got deeper. With any luck, if you held your nerve against the self-doubt and uncertainty, the fear that this case would be the one to knock you down and bury you under so much shit you would never find your way back, if you could manage all that anxiety and keep your mind fixed on finding a solution to the client's problem, well, eventually, the client's problems became your problems too. You started speaking in the first person.

"We must...."

and

"Our options are..."

You would stay late and come in early, dreaming up new ways to bail yourself out of what should have been unsolvable problems. That feeling was the goal, the thing you worked toward, because no lawyer will ever be craftier or more stubborn, more effective, than the one convinced it is his ass that might be left hanging in midair.

And if you needed a break, there was always booze.

Slaven poked his bald head into my office. "It's time. You in?"

It was less a question than a command.

Tranche was our rallying place.

Just across the street from our Power and Light building, it was packed most days after work with young professionals coming off a ten-hour run at the law firm or the bank, maybe the Graybar Building next door. The place was big and open with a concrete floor that glowed white from the track lights and split into three spaces by sliding glass dividers. There was a coffeehouse on one side, then the bicycle store in the middle, and the bar, our bar, on the other side.

The flat white countertop was low enough that patrons could rest their elbows on its surface while seated in the armless Eames chairs. Several feet back from the bar were a cluster of plywood coffee tables in the shapes of boomerangs, each finished with a sleek black lacquer and curved at just the right angle to trick the viewer's eye into seeing his drink sliding right off the tabletop, though it never did. The bartender kept the lights dim enough that the plastic stars pasted on the ceiling glowed to reveal sprawling constellations.

We always sat in the back.

"Tell me about your water selection, please."

Ned adjusted the silk square of fabric folded into his sport coat's breast pocket while the waitress scratched her head.

"Not tap. I'm talking about pH levels. Do you have something over eight? Seven and a half, even—Miss, do you have any alkaline options whatsoever?"

"We've got, umm, Dasani and it comes in a...bottle," she said with sarcasm.

"Just give me a cup of tap then with two lemon slices, please, and no ice, if it's not too much to ask."

She scribbled into her notebook and turned toward Slaven, who asked for scotch.

"And lemme order an apology for my friend, the water guy. Excuse me, water boy."

When it came to his right to drink on a Friday afternoon, Slaven was a citizen policeman, issuing citations to anyone who deviated from what he decided was normal behavior.

"Should I be concerned about your mental health, Ned?" he asked.

"Wait a second," the waitress said, biting her bottom lip. Her brown hair was thick and swept back into a messy bun perched on top of her head, a yellow pencil sticking through it at an angle. "It's cool your friend is into water. It's very on trend with what people are doing right now, being mindful, mindful drinking, et cetera. Like, it's totally a good thing to know when you need to cleanse," she said. "Mindfulness."

She was looking at Ned, who was looking out the window.

"Mindfulness?" Ned repeated.

"You know, mindfulness, like meditation," the waitress replied. "Clearing your energy, gently bringing breath back into focus. It helps me get clear in my intentions. Keep things nice and slow," she said.

Of course. We understood, men slowly pouring our lives away at the playground and on the commute, lounging around our living rooms as life unfolded around us like the slow, tinkling song from a music box. Everything nice and slow, please.

"We have some slow blinkers here," Ned said. "All of us. Midwesterners, I mean. The idea of trying to slow down even more seems ludicrous to me."

"It's like a practice, that's all," she said, flustered. "You're the one who came to a bar for a glass of water."

"But I'm already in a practice that gives me great peace," Ned replied.

"What's that—loneliness?" Slaven snickered.

"I practice something called mindlessness. Have you heard of mindlessness before?"

"Look, if you're done ordering, then I'm—"

"I may be the only practitioner in River City. The goal of mindlessness is not to think, but to become more sensate, to be more chemical, if you will, to make as much money as I possibly can. Actually, more even than you probably can imagine, and without any concern for how it's made, what I spend it on, or why I spend it. Money is mindlessness, one of our purest motivations. Mindlessness is a discipline and one must practice it all the way to perfection. So once per week I drink wine until my face becomes as numb as a corkboard, then I go out, either to a

bar or a restaurant, it doesn't really matter, and find someone nice to talk to. I'll be talking to some nice dentist or
marketing woman, asking how she's managing to satisfy
the demanding and ungrateful boss while still protecting
her time to take care of herself and so on, but instead
of listening, instead of being mindful in that moment, I
picture white noise coming out of her mouth and let the
sound of her voice buzz inside my ears like tinnitus until
the pain becomes so distracting that I have no choice but
to abandon the conversation I started and run away."

The waitress scowled at Ned, her bottom lip curled in
as if she had tasted something foul. She slapped her palms
against her thighs. "Let me take care of these orders."

"The hell's wrong with you, man!" Slaven said. "That
chick was into you and you blew it!"

"I have a very full Friday evening planned for myself,
and I did not need that young lady, or you, interfering."

Slaven smirked. "Dinner for one, I bet," he said, laughing at his joke.

His necktie was snug against the top button of his
shirt, and his insulated lunch box sat at his feet, its woodland camouflage pattern in odd contrast to the muted
industrial colors and smooth lines of the concrete floor,
the metal legs of the chair.

"Excuse me? Why, of course, Slaven. I would like to
tell you about my plans this evening. I'm seeing a new
outdoor sculptural exhibit in the Market District, then
I'm returning to my condo to enjoy tagliatelle al ragù alla
Bolognese which, I'll have you know, includes a healthful

splash of white wine in the ragù. After which I will transition into my Friday evening purification ritual."

"Wait," Slaven said, shifting uncomfortably. "Never mind. Don't want to know."

Ned smiled and went on. "After dinner, I'll strip naked, scoop handfuls of Vaseline, and apply a thin coat over every inch of bare skin, from forehead down to my toes, Slaven. I'll do the dishes like this and I'll tidy up the kitchen, then I'll spend no less than one half hour soaking in a scalding-hot bath as the jelly melts off my skin. By the time I tuck myself into bed tonight, my skin will be pure as sunlight."

Slaven choked down a mouthful of scotch.

"I'd invite you to join, but I assume…" Ned teased.

Slaven pounded his chest with a closed fist, wagging a finger. "No, no—absolutely no. You do your naked thing by yourself. I got work, buddy. Dinner at home with Chris and the boys, then back to the office. Keeping my face… err, to the grindstone, as they say."

I wondered if she answered to that name, Slaven's wife. He called her Chris but she'd introduced herself at the Christmas party as Christine. Slaven had always preferred the nickname. "Chris is picking me up from work," "Chris is getting dinner," "Chris spent my whole bonus on a new Subaru." It was a boy's name, a buddy name, and from what I gathered, Christine had dedicated a life to making a home for her husband, taking care of the household and managing the children's schedules, treating Slaven like a man when all he wanted was to be a boy again. Slaven was the breadwinner in the family and he liked it that way, once calling his wife a "reserve player" he could put back on the field if the game situation ever demanded, if ever he lost his job or did not bring home the big bonus he had been banking on.

"Why not take a night off? Files can wait," I said, sipping as little as possible of the IPA I ordered and hoping Slaven wouldn't notice.

"Can't spare a night off. We got two trials scheduled for next month and—"

"Come on! You know they always settle." I spun my finger in the air like an imaginary record player. "Each one the same as the next."

Ned frowned.

"That's your problem. You're not hungry enough. Wanna be successful? Get hungry. Wanna have a big career in front of the judge? You gotta show up every day ready to feed, you hear me? Ready to feast on these files. Stop wasting time thinking about whether they're gonna settle or whether the plaintiff's full of shit or whether you're billing too much time to some poor schlep or whatever else. Watch Mick. Stop complaining and start eating your hours. Start feasting on these hours, Walker."

"But isn't that the problem?" asked Ned.

"That you don't bill any hours? Yeah, I guess I'd say that's a problem..."

"Walker's point—his complaint, if you will, that the work is too boring to care about. Our work, the work of this midsized law firm in this midsized city. It's all just maintenance work, really, maintenance of the status quo.

Negative work. Like shoveling little bits of coal into a smoldering fire."

"More like you and Walker are just too lazy to dig your knuckles in, but that's just me," Slaven snorted, tossing back the last of his scotch.

"Don't much like complaining myself."

Ned had gone too far. To cast doubt on the work's importance might be received as a vote against summer barbecues and four-wheel drives, against children running barefoot across a green lawn, against everything that made middle America a fine place to live and raise a family. And work, according to Slaven.

"It does strike me as true that the quality of legal work is quite low here in River City, that the work will never be interesting here because the people, our people, are incapable of properly articulating their problems. Not people in general, mind you. I've no doubt that the storytelling people from the South can complain with great imagination, and that your average East Coaster complains with immense particularity, but these people? Slaven, really, the folks here simply can't bring themselves to put into words whatever bothers them. They've had no practice in it."

"Seems like you've gotten the hang of it," Slaven shot back. "Complaining I mean."

"It's in the name, isn't it? The plains. Plainspoken. Plain clothes. Plain meaning. There isn't the ambition to express much of anything that digs deeper than the plain Jane, plain and simple, plain old truth around here."

"What might that truth be in your opinion, oh wise one?" said Slaven.

"We don't like to complain. Don't know how. It's been frowned upon by generations all the way back to the Homestead Act. It's probably in our blood by now that just when you finally get up the nerve to really lay it on somebody, to let it all hang out there about how awful the boss has treated you or how your wife doesn't deserve a red cent in the divorce, you start feeling more than a hundred years of shame pulling back on your coattails, reminding you to stop complaining and...make yourself useful!"

A few cars drove by outside. The bar was busy but not yet full. Slaven shook his head and rubbed his eyes, disoriented. In one uneven motion, he hooked the strap of his lunch box over his shoulder and shot to his feet.

"Of course. Two of you, just a couple of...never mind."

"I agree with Ned," I said.

"Not even gonna go there about you two," Slaven said, exasperated. "Hard work is still a virtue how I see it. I'm teaching my boys about hard work, what that means."

"What does it mean?" Ned asked, crossing his legs at the knees and raising a finger to his lips.

"Money, for one," Slaven said. "You just went on a pretty good rant in favor of it."

"We should all make the money we need to properly indulge ourselves," Ned said with a shrug. "The joy of modern life is even a minimum wage entitles one to live like a Tudor king in this wonderful country. So I ask again,

Slaven, noting the quality of your tie, the style of your lunch pail, your whole aesthetic: What is it you want that makes you work so hard?"

The door chimed and a group of young women hurried inside toward the bar.

"Respect," Slaven said, looking down at both of us now, his bald head shining under the light canister. "I want people to see me, know that what I do is important. Doesn't matter if you say the work is boring or I'm boring or the whole damn world is boring—it's important, got it!? It's important because everybody sees it that way. Hell, it's better they don't have a damn clue what it is we do—makes it seem even more important!"

He put a ten-dollar bill underneath the empty glass and turned toward the door, shaking his head.

"Have a great weekend you two. Try not to hurt yourselves lounging around in a vat of Vaseline...or whatever."

He stomped out the door, not-so-secretly happy that his weekend was full of work and ours was not. The more time we spent not working, the more outstanding his performance would look to Ward. The bar and tables were crowded with young people in professional dress, smiling and laughing like their futures depended on it. Ned waved a hand toward them and pointed to his watch.

Outside, the sidewalks were busier than they had been an hour before. I followed Ned, weaving through the crowd of people pouring into Tranche and hustling to keep up as we made our way to his car. I tried to tell him about Ruth and the night at the judge's, to explain everything

I had learned just by reading about her online. Months, years even, had gone by since I had made a friendship with someone, and here she was, someone who asked questions but expected nothing of me in return. I knew Ned would understand what I was feeling, how friendship could not be forced, how it happened without warning or invitation. He appeared to listen, idly tossing his keys into the air and catching them in his hand. When we approached the parking lot, I told him about the playground tomorrow and the opera.

"Will you take your family?" he asked, tapping something on the pavement with the pointed toe of his leather shoe.

"Grace and Charlie can come," I said.

"Let's talk more after the weekend. Walker, you're not without charms yourself," he said, stepping into his car. He pulled a container from his glove compartment and carefully placed his sunglasses inside, snapping it shut and returning them to the compartment. "Be sure to introduce your friend to Charlie, by the way. She'll be glad to know him."

CHAPTER THIRTEEN

The bookstore was stacked to the rafters with paperbacks. Alone at the end of a long aisle, I pulled a thin volume of stories from the wooden shelf and flipped through, finding a white notecard stuck in the back pages. I pulled a pen from my pocket and scribbled out a note on the lines of the card.

> *Dear Ruth, Try these stories. "Without sin there would be no art."*

"Are you ready yet?"

Grace was standing with Charlie a few feet behind me.

I kept my eyes on her as I tapped the top of the notecard into the pages of the book.

The weather was cold but the sun shone through the glass wall of the museum building, illuminating a thousand colorful balloons sculpted in blown glass that lifted up from floor to ceiling, curves and curls of glass woven together as if floating upward from the museum's marble floors, a frozen plumage of light and color.

There were no visitors in the hallways of the museum that morning, but noise filled the rooms. On our way to the second-floor gallery, I heard the sounds. Chains clanked;

metal rattled; a woman's voice warbled through empty space. This was not music. I rounded the final corner to find a crowd gathered along the perimeter of a large, rectangular room. Mothers with children packed in their strollers stood next to young women wearing billowy black dresses or white tank tops, their hair dyed pink and purple. The playground had attracted all types. Graybar sat coolly in a chair smack in the middle of the room and in front of the stage. Nearby, wearing a chambray shirt over denim jeans rolled up at the ankles, the director was swaying his head from side to side at the sound reverberating off the heavy museum walls.

Everyone's attention was focused on the center of the room, where a complete children's playground sat atop a raised platform. The equipment was made of bright metal that resembled the shape and structure of a playground in any schoolyard or park. Wearing matching denim ensembles, four performers "played" the equipment. One man beat the slide with drumsticks and long metal chains. Another ran back and forth on a clatter bridge. A woman dragged a hand along a series of metal windchimes that hung from a swing set. People watching the performance looked uneasy, even confused. Many were drawn by descriptions of the installation as a "space for imagination and musical play," but the scene before us was odd, a clash of sound, heavy objects struck over and over in an otherwise quiet and cavernous room. Ruth sat on the titanium swing and moaned long, unintelligible phrases in repetition, her voice nearly drowned out by the rattling and thrashing of metal objects.

The performance lasted only a few minutes before the sound stopped altogether. I glanced back at Grace and Charlie, who looked stunned as the performers walked slowly off the platform and through a door. The crowd did not clap at first, unsure if they had witnessed the end of something or nothing at all, waiting until the director shouted "Bravi tutti!" to begin clapping.

"That's about right," grumbled a man next to me, planting his wooden cane on the floor to brace himself. "People'd give a standing ovation to a dogfight 'round here."

Children rushed onto the platform, dragging their parents, clambering onto the swings and banging against the big drum, filling the room with noise. I watched from the entryway while Grace and Charlie climbed the metal ladder to take their place in line for the slide. I looked back to the doorway and saw the performers reemerge, first the men and then the other woman, and finally Ruth, who stood alone until Graybar approached. He cupped a hand around Ruth's ear and said something that made her nod politely and smile.

"Did you know the playground is made of one hundred percent recycled yard and household waste?" said a girl next to me.

"Like soda cans and bicycles and water pipes, literally all the stuff that's in your garage," her friend replied.

Both wore oversized gray sweatshirts with the name of their school scrawled across the chest. Steam, along with the smell of hot chocolate, rose from the Styrofoam cups in their hands.

Ruth hugged one of the musicians next before moving toward the director, who embraced her with both arms. Her eyes were looking at the faces of people nearby, scanning from one to the next.

"God, was it frightening, you know what I mean?" asked one of the girls. "Too many, like, knives and forks banging together, like, a million coats zipping and unzipping…"

I felt her eyes from across the room.

Her white canvas shoes were spotless. The denim suit she wore had been stretched thin across her hips and breasts, the buttons on her shirt undone to midchest. The director had conceived this costume to render her and the others nameless, to strip away identities and conceal her body inside a shapeless uniform, a television commercial for a jeans company.

"Oh God, like, you must be exhausted. I can't imagine how hard it must be to sing and swing in real time like that!?"

Ruth shifted her gaze to the girls. "I'm much looser on the move."

I reached into the back of my waistband and pulled out the book I had been keeping for her. She took it in both hands and studied it, feeling the barely worn soft cover. She turned a shoulder to the two girls, giving us a few feet of space to feel alone in the center of the gallery

"I left you a note," I said.

Ruth was silent, still looking over the book. She had done this before, giving me silence when I wanted a nod or glance, anything that told me what she was thinking. She turned away and pushed through the doorway near us, disappearing down a flight of stairs.

I looked back at the playground where Grace and Charlie were flying down the slide together, hands thrown high over their heads as Charlie squealed with laughter. I tried to smile when they walked toward me, but the whole room, all the people and noise, had become an intrusion.

The door swung open and Ruth emerged.

Charlie scowled and pointed a tiny finger at Ruth's hair.

"It's the same gorgeous color as your shirt. Is red your favorite too?"

Her face spread into a wide grin and Charlie nodded. She stuck out her tongue and ran a long finger against his cheek.

"That was metal as fuck!" said a man walking up from behind Ruth. Yet another interruption. "You annihilated that set!"

He wore a sleeve tattoo underneath a V-neck shirt, holding his hand up in the air to give her a high-five, as if she had just come off the playing field. He made a bottle out of his thumb and pinky and tipped it toward his mouth, his tattooed arm draped around the neck of a woman from their group. He was flaunting himself, how easily he took what he wanted.

"You coming?"

I watched Grace take Charlie back to the playground and stood there stupidly while the man whispered something into Ruth's ear. I imagined what he was saying.

"Have you picked up another face in the crowd?" He came to humiliate me, the tip of his nose burrowing into her thick, tousled hair. She touched him on the shoulder and turned easily, released the younger man with the grace of a schoolteacher sending a child home at the end of the afternoon, waving politely as the small crowd of performers walked toward the exit and disappeared from view.

"I still want to talk with you," she whispered, standing next to me, both of us watching Grace and Charlie still playing. I gave her a time and place and she nodded. She inhaled deeply and raised her arms, as if wanting to reach toward me, before dropping them to her sides and following the crowd out the door.

Later that night I leashed Rex and walked outside.

The neighborhood was quiet. Lights were on through windows, but no people were outside. We walked alone for minutes before I heard another sound, the metal chains of a swing set swaying in the wind. Something hard and dense crashed against the insides of a metal trash can still upright at the end of an empty driveway. Sounds were everywhere, each one piercing and unnatural. Was it always like this, I wondered, a concert of metal and trash, playgrounds without footsteps or human voices, not even music blaring from a car speaker? I thought of Ruth's friend, how he taunted me in the doorway, knowing I would not go with them, that I was not free to go where I pleased. It was foolish to think I had anything in common with her, that this was anything but a performance piece—Ruth and the book exchange, the invitation to talk. I was the bored man, an easy mark, just another piece of equipment on a playground built for her amusement.

Had she come here to play with me?

Maybe there was nothing left to prove in New York, other places where none of them were born but all of them had chosen to live. Like me, the artists were sons and daughters of somewhere else, quiet places where the only examples of success had been working people, the kind who married young and obligated themselves by the same ruling principle as their parents. Their hometowns had no place for them, the kinds of people who wanted to perform life, not preserve it. What the performers conspired to make was different from snark, more than a clenched fist raised high above their heads. This was an assault. They were the new anticulture, transgressing whatever habits of conventional behavior had escaped the attention of a previous generation. Their playground was a front-line piece, an act of aggression against all the people—schoolteachers and coaches, Mom and Dad, husbands and wives—who rejected them in the first place.

I buried my fists in the pockets of my coat. *I hate it, too,* I thought. *Attack. Eviscerate these people for all I care.*

I preferred the rebellion, however vain and offensive, to the boredom that had enveloped my life. Ruth didn't want to be ordinary. Her rebelliousness, her defiance of rules and expectations, had ignited the impulse to finally reject what I never respected. I could feel my face flush and I gripped tighter on the leash in my hands. My only fear was to appear uninteresting in Ruth's eyes and, for the first time in years, I began to see a new purpose for living.

CHAPTER FOURTEEN

T he next morning, I stood at the end of the pew.
Early spring light filtered red and purple through the
stained-glass windows. Grace had Charlie propped
on her hip, a bow tie fastened at the collar of his but-
ton-down shirt.

She wasn't raised Catholic, so she had been spared the
years of scratchy uniform pants and daily prayers, initia-
tion into a culture of fear.

"We understand that Hell's punishment is the eternal
separation from God," the priests taught us, "and being in
Hell is like drowning in a lake of unquenchable fire."

Because she'd avoided the education, Grace loved the
choir and candles, the smell of incense wafting through
the air. She loved it all with the zeal of a convert. When the
congregation held hands in prayer, she grabbed hold of
Charlie and me. When the congregation joined together in
song, she lifted her voice. And when I stayed silent while
the chorus of voices recited the Lord's Prayer, Grace joined
in. I passed the time looking around the room, scanning
faces and bodies to imagine what people did for a living
based on how they dressed. Most looked like professional
sports fans, wearing football jerseys and tennis shoes,
men and sons dressed to match, everything done in unison. Opening and closing their books, sitting and stand-

ing on cue. They sang and blessed themselves, keeping their eyes pointed toward the altar, toward the sculpted cement statue of Christ with his head slumped forward, the enormous body bolted to an invisible cross floating above the priest.

The body was what impressed me: the sheer size of him. Mass had become an exercise in discomfort. How I let my mind go into my lower back as I sat upright, then sink into my feet when I stood up. When we knelt, my mind was alive not to readings from the altar, but to the aching of a knee joint that creaked. Not until the short, sandy-haired priest slid off his thick wooden chair and ambled up to the center of the altar did I put my mind back inside my head and begin to listen.

"Some weather around here," the priest opened. "Not like that beautiful stretch of Bermuda turf grass with that yellow pin flag flapping in the distance."

He had just returned from a vacation, somewhere he could indulge his love of golf in the early spring months. He was a golfing priest, and people appreciated hearing about his trips. It was harmless, the long-winded homilies about the dogleg left in Scottsdale or the par five at Pebble. This priest had never abused anyone, and there had never been stories in our parish of a priest stealing away at odd hours to take a nip, muffling a yeasty belch in the confessional box, the secret alcoholic, the "whiskey priest." Those stories were for the magazine exposés and television programs from other places.

"...for forty days Satan tempted and tested Jesus in the desert..."

Here, we were left with a leisure priest, a semiretiree who whiled away his ample free time petitioning the God of the Old Sod for a favorable lie off a biffed tee shot, and it bothered me. At least those other priests, the ones exposed in newspaper investigations and movies, had lusted for something they could not be so proud of to talk about at Mass, at least they felt enough shame to keep quiet about private vices that could not be explained. The boredom of our priest stuck to him like a damp perfume, and still he showed up at the altar each weekend to lecture us on life's petty vanities.

He was walking through the aisles now, entering the climax of a sermon I did not care to hear.

"You will be tested by the sweetness of temptation, which pours into your life in energizing waves. For when you feel your heart pounding through your chest, and your breath quick with the pleasure of anticipation, and you find yourself alone in the privacy of your own room, your own mind," the priest paused to catch his breath, pressing his hands together—

"Stop."

The congregation was silent.

The priest said it again, this time with a harsher tone, balling his hands into fists.

"Stop!"

He looked across the silent crowd and lowered his head, climbing into the thick wooden chair beneath the long foot of the Christ sculpture.

"Let us pray," he said, and I closed my mouth.

We stood in rhythm, the entire congregation.

But I had forgotten the words. The language was the same as last week, each Mass a rehearsal for the one next Sunday, demanding little more than a commitment to indulge each other as witnesses to our own piety. Words mumbled. Hands held. People around me stood together like statues.

I focused on a middle-aged man standing in the front row nearest the altar. He rested his hand in the small of his wife's back, rubbing gently where her shirt clung with static to her skin, revealing the edges around the clasp of her bra. He had the right idea; keep going. Slip a hand underneath that sheer fabric and unclip. Let her tits swing out into the open, bend her over the pew and fuck her right now, rocking and thrusting in front of the congregation, right in front of that priest, having his fun while everyone else stood around oblivious and uninterested, hypnotized by the sound of their own voices. Some of us would notice. Some of us had been waiting for it, here in the room filled with stained glass and crucifixes, packed in by people singing with one voice to a cold image of Christ rising toward the ceiling, where one man had finally made a display of his desire, his own passion. The harlots and prostitutes went into heaven while these people stood around dreaming a melancholy faith, avoiding flesh and pleasure, the only life that surrounded them. Before he could move any further, the low murmur of prayer ended and the priest again retreated to his chair. The man pulled his hand away from his wife. He grabbed the back of the pew, light glinting off his wedding band, bracing himself to take a seat.

That evening at home, Grace passed me the day's newspaper. "Did you read that?"

I glanced at the photograph of a man holding two M4 assault rifles, one in each arm, the type of picture everybody posted after basic training, a recruit's way of telling his family and friends that he was different than before.

"Police said he was known to have an infatuation with guns and violent acts," Grace read from the article.

How foolish, I thought.

It sounded like the description of any soldier who ever wore a uniform, for whom an infatuation with guns and violence were a competitive advantage in the hiring process.

"Are you still seeing that woman tomorrow?"

"Yes."

"You have a lot to tell her, about guns and so on," she said, turning off the water and spinning around, grabbing a white towel off the countertop.

"Exciting, isn't it?" I said, sensing the weakness she couldn't let herself reveal.

"What?"

"Her perspective. An artist's point of view. She wants me to be part of her process."

"Great," Grace said.

"I'm happy to talk to her."

"Yeah, I said great."

"I really think she'll get what happened. She'll under-stand what—"

"Do you hear yourself? If you need somebody to 'understand,' then we get a specialist, a professional, a therapist at a hospital will 'understand,' okay? A therapist will 'understand' what happens when you watch a guy split in half, not some opera singer you met at a fund-raiser!" Grace exclaimed. "You can admit you need more than me to help you."

Grace had heard the story so many times it bored her. There was the explosion—the flash and smoke—the sand flooding up and stinging my eyes when I regained con-sciousness, staring at the watch on my wrist, its glass face cracked and the hands frozen in place. Of everything she heard, it was the watch that captured her attention.

"I don't get it," she said the first time I told her the story. "Why did the watch stop? The blast overpressure would crack the screen, but the mechanism is battery powered. The explosives were only, what, a few pounds? That watch should have kept telling time. Did you change the battery afterward to test whether it was the power source?"

We were sitting on the edge of our bed in the house we rented off base. Her eyes were earnest as she fixated on that one detail, a mechanical detail that was trivial but somehow intelligible to her. Grace had always been the midwife for my most difficult thoughts and, after years of listening to what I could never explain to myself, this was all she could deliver, that I should find someone new to tell.

"She's not your friend. Friends don't appear out of no-where. They develop over time, like, a long time, a lot lon-ger than one week. Do you understand what I'm saying?"

I looked away.

"Do you understand what I said?"

She looked exhausted, rubbing the front of her wrinkl-ed brow.

"I got it."

"Just promise me you'll see her this time and then that's it. Can you promise me?"

She stepped toward me with arms outstretched and closed her eyes, pressing the side of her face into my neck. I kissed her cheek and held on tightly, remembering for an instant how good it had felt to come home to Grace, how safe I felt in her embrace. Whatever I had been through, whatever I was feeling now, she could never know.

"I promise."

CHAPTER FIFTEEN

*T*he courthouse was empty Monday morning.

The echo of my footsteps kept me company on my march toward the core of the building. I read the words scrolling across a television monitor mounted to the wall outside the courtroom: *United States of America v. Clayton Gibney.*

"You picked right, son. Guilty."

The prosecutor was wearing a plain black suit with a white shirt and red tie. His hair was cropped short on the sides.

"No, General," I said, following the prosecutor into the courtroom and making my way past the front of the empty gallery seats. "That's the client's decision, how he pleads. You know that."

The prosecutor dropped a thick manila folder onto the table, pulling out stacks of white papers clipped together and sliding them around the table like a dealer passing out playing cards. Today he was a prosecutor, but he was also a brigadier general in the national guard, and he wanted everyone to know. Once the paper stacks had been arranged in formation he dropped into his chair and fitted a pair of reading glasses across the bridge of his bony nose.

"Thirty-five years of trial experience in federal and state courts. Drugs, guns, organized crime, not to mention another thirty-three years prosecuting in uniform and arguing law of war with those morons at the United Nations, comin' within a cunt hair of a Geneva Convention violation in the first Iraq War. You heard right, son, the first one just around the time you were still shittin' in your drawers. I guess that shitload of experience might happen to include what you're telling me, son. You realize these fellas are all guilty, don't you?"

I laid out a few pages on the table, character letters that attested to Gibney's good qualities, his sense of loyalty, his honesty. The letters were written by friends as well as a probation officer and chaplain from an old case. I expected the letters would not matter. The judge never read them.

"Son, do you understand how many shithead dope dealers I been through in my career? I'm talkin' from here to Baghdad. Hell, I prosecuted a ring of shit-dealers on TQ back in the summer of '08. Crooked fucks looting amphetamines off dead hajis and selling them for surplus dough back on base. Don't think I haven't seen ol' boy's kind before."

He had served one full tour overseas, spending a year on a large staff at an even larger base, giving legal advice to a part-time general nobody had heard from since that deployment. The prosecutor never left base, never fired a shot, never laid eyes on a local who didn't work in the base chow hall or laundry tent. The enemy of his tour would have been a finicky air conditioning unit, maybe a spotty internet connection that gave him an excuse to bitch at some soldiers about the importance of his work. To him, my presence in this courtroom was a type of insubordination.

He still outranked me, after all.

A door carved inside a wall next to the jury box slowly opened and Gibney emerged, flanked by two U.S. marshals, dressed in the orange jumpsuit and black slides, handcuffs jingling at his wrists and ankles. The marshals showed the emotionless stare of soldiers, eyes opened wide and pointed straight ahead. They had bald heads and bushy beards that made their jawlines look twice as strong. One gripped the underside of Gibney's upper arm as if he were finishing a bicep curl.

The handcuffs kept Gibney from reaching the arms of the chair behind him, so he grasped the underside of the table, arched his back, and poked out his behind, hoping to land it blindly onto the seat of his rolling chair.

He caught his breath and glanced my way.

"Today's like New Year's 'cept the resolution I'm fixin' to make is gonna last me seven years instead of one," he said.

"All rise," the bailiff announced from behind a computer screen in front of the judge's bench, and another concealed door behind the tall leather chair opened.

The heat was rising inside my suit jacket and a bead of sweat slid down my ribcage.

"Please be seated," the judge said, the flowing fabric of his robe accentuating the great melon head, making the stubbly mustache above his upper lip seem even smaller.

"Now hearing *United States v. Gibney*. Mr. Gibney, how do you plead, sir?"

The judge was looking down at a computer screen beneath the edge of his dais. The blue light of his desktop monitor reflected off the lenses of his glasses.

"Guilty, Your Honor."

"And have you reached a settlement, counsel?"

"The United States accepts this defendant's plea of guilty," the prosecutor announced. "However, counsel petitions this court to deliver its argument. May it please the court."

The prosecutor stood and buttoned his suit coat, then grabbed hold of his lapels.

"I submit to Your Honor that this defendant is an offense to justice and decency, good order, and honest living. He has two prior criminal convictions, both for possession of controlled substances with the intent to distribute. Further, this man," the prosecutor's head swung from the judge to our table, and he pointed a finger at Gibney, "brings with him into this courtroom a conviction for possession of a firearm by a twice-convicted felon. At the time of his arrest, this man..." The general knocked his knuckles against the table, again pointing at Gibney, "... was dealing in sizeable quantities of methamphetamines, multiple methamphetamines, the scourge of this community. He was in possession of a motorcycle, Your Honor, a chopper in street parlance, that was not licensed to him but to his lady, if you can believe that. Because a man who hides behind his lady ain't got no honor left."

Gibney was quiet.

"Here it is—" The prosecutor peeled one of the papers off his desk and slid a photograph of the motorcycle onto the court's overhead projector, beaming the picture onto a screen for the benefit of the few people in the courtroom.

"Thought I wouldn't see her again," Gibney whispered.

"But these facts are merely incidental to such heinousness, the hellaciousness, such goddamn—"

"Language, General," the judge cut in, eyeglasses still blue from the light of his computer.

"My apologies, Your Honor—as I was. Mr. Gibney brought with him a loaded gun."

The general slapped a picture of a gun onto the projector.

"Lest I remind this court of Check-off's gun. Yes, Check-off's gun comes to us from thee-ater and holds that a criminal will not bring along a weapon unless said criminal has intent to use said firearm in commission of a crime. The parallel here is uncanny, Your Honor."

The prosecutor rested a hand on the wood-paneled jury box.

"Defend-ant knew officers of the law would hunt, find, interdict, and detain him. Defend-ant knew he could not escape, evade, or scheme his way out of the law's reach. Yet he brought that firearm. Such a man of utmost violence, a man derelict in the sacred duties of civilian relations, must be duly punished. I humbly pray this court order a sentence of ten years, the maximum provided under the sentencing manual, Your Honor."

"Thank you, General."

He collected his papers from the projector screen and turned out the light.

"The floor is yours, Lieutenant," the prosecutor smirked.

I reached across the table for a glass of water and drank, wiping my lips with the back of my hand. There were only a handful of people around but I could feel their eyes on me.

"M-My client is a twice-convicted f-felon," I stuttered, rising nervously to my feet. "He served his time…"

The judge waved a hand at his ear, as if brushing away a fly.

"He served his time…"

Again, the judge waved his hand.

"I said my client has served his—"

"Your microphone, young man. Move closer to your microphone because all I'm hearing up here is a tiny whisper."

I reached again for the glass of water on the table and gulped, noticing the two marshals scrolling their phones. The prosecutor was doing the same. The room felt hot. I had once performed my job calmly under threat of danger. Violence had not made me afraid. Now, in this courtroom, I found myself paralyzed by the pressure of speaking in public, my heart pounding heavy beats inside my chest.

"He served his time…for b-both offenses, he served his t-time," I stuttered. "He accepts responsibility. You can see from his character letters. My client is, uh, a man of his word. He asks only that you take him…at his word."

"Is that all, counsel?" the judge asked.

"Uh, and there was a firearm at the scene," I started, going off my script of prepared remarks, "but not on Mr. Gibney's person. The weapon was not anywhere near my client at the time of his arres—"

"Excuse me, counsel, but are you suggesting the weapon did not belong to the defendant? He's on record admitting it was his gun." The judge straightened up in his chair. "Why do you raise this now?"

I stuttered but could not respond. The right word, any word, escaped me. Gibney was looking down at the floor, the prosecutor was already shuffling papers back into his envelope, and still I could not fix my thoughts on what needed to be said. It felt as if I was on trial, and at the same time invisible to those around me. Why had I lost my will to fight?

"I...nothing further."

"Good. Does the defendant have anything he would like to say?"

Gibney didn't move. I leaned across my chair to whisper into his ear and tell him this was his last chance to speak, but he brushed me off, pulling the microphone toward him with both hands.

"I'm not innocent. I do not seek forgiveness for what I have done."

"That all?"

The judge had the side of his face propped against his fist, watching Gibney lean in to the microphone

"That's all."

"I see these character statements and it looks like there's a few of them," the judge said, quickly leafing through the papers, skimming the top of each page before setting the stack aside. "This court accepts your plea of guilty to the charge and sentences you to ten years in prison. You will receive a credit of one hundred twenty days served toward your sentence. You will have the right to appeal this sentence if you so choose. Marshals, please take this man into custody. This hearing is adjourned."

Crack.

Gibney stood and stuck out his chin. He looked at me without turning his head.

"I'm sorry I didn't have more," I said. "I wish we could have fought."

Gibney shook his head. "Won't do no good. I got shit left to prove on the inside, man. Might come outta this better yet, at least better than some other limp dick swingin' on the sidewalk. I see how useful folks end up out there. Come by jail. I need a good conversation every now and again. So do you."

Gibney reached out with clasped hands and shook mine. He was a liar, a criminal who used violence to accomplish his ends. But today, he seemed not to care what happened to him. His wildness seduced me, how defiant he had been under accusations of the prosecutor and the glare of the judge. Unlike me, Gibney wanted nothing from them, and so he took their blows without complaint, prepared to absorb all the punishment and nastiness they could deliver. Whether this was true only in my mind hardly mattered. He was the same man today as the first time we met.

When the marshals came back to lead him away, he cracked a smile.

"You bald motherfuckers know I'd drop both y'all. They still teach you bitches how to roll, man?"

The marshals cracked a grin and shook their heads, then disappeared into the wall.

I parked the car around the corner from the coffee shop and took my time walking to the front door.

Ruth was standing up from her chair and waving a hand through the air. She wore black leggings, the same kind she wore at the judge's house, and a sleeveless cotton shirt that showed the strap of a black bra. She opened her arms wide and I stepped in, holding onto her ribcage, noticing how much smaller she felt than I imagined. The book I gave her was facedown on the coffee table.

"I've read every story," she said, sliding into her chair. Freckles dotted her cheeks and nose. Her cobalt-blue eyes bore into me, as bright as if they'd been cut from the sky.

She complimented my family and called Charlie a "charmer."

While Ruth spoke, I realized she was older than I'd noticed at first, with creases forming at the corners of her eyes and on her forehead. I hadn't come to talk about my family, so I remained silent. She reached into a bag for her phone and introduced the opera she told me about nights ago. I took her phone from across the table and began to read.

The audience enters a large theater. A man in uniform walks onto the stage. A pipe organ sounds and the man instructs the audience to stand before directing half of the theater to leave their seats, and companions, and enter the hallway, where another man in uniform provides further instructions.

The aim was shock and terror, separating families and friends then spreading them across the theater, groups spilling over into hallways nearby, bombarding them with commands shouted in foreign languages. Sixty minutes of chaos at America's southern border. I told her it was nicely written.

"What do you think of the story?" she asked.

"Might benefit from an introduction, maybe a roadmap or…"

Ruth shook her head, frustrated. She sat back in her chair and snatched the phone from the table, flipping the off switch and pitching it into her bag in one movement. I apologized, afraid she might dismiss me. I was curious why she wanted to inflict pain, whether this was the artist getting off on the audience or something more.

"Why not let them watch it on stage?"

She laughed. "I want to push these little boats into the storm, not offer them safe harbor. It's what they come for. What it feels like crawling over sand. Heat off the canister's spotlight."

Splotches of red showed on her neck as she writhed and moved in the chair, acting out the words as she spoke. The audience was the drum to beat upon.

"If you're not protesting, you're entertaining, and I won't be their entertainment."

"You said there were guns in the story?" I asked.

She cocked her head to the side in a look of confusion, red lips pursing as if she herself hadn't mentioned the idea only days before. Ruth pulled away from the table, tossing back the last drops of black coffee. She set the cup down and looked through the glass door at the sunlight outside.

"Shall we have a walk?"

I set my cup, still hot, on a tray of dirty dishes and followed her out the door. The air was crisp, the sky exploding around us like waves of cold blue water. The streets were mostly empty by late afternoon and we were the only pair strolling that part of downtown, striding together in lock-step, both wearing glasses to protect our blue eyes from sunlight. I chuckled to myself over it, our connection, how even the red of her hair matched the rich burgundy shade of my cordovan shoes.

Her pace was quick.

Ruth pointed toward the theater a few blocks away, where Graybar and the Power and Light buildings were visible in the distance. She talked about the history of our downtown, famous people who had come here a century earlier to perform. It was embarrassing how much more she knew about the city than I did. Ruth waved a hand in the direction of a woman clutching a black handbag, who did not seem to notice.

"Reminds me of a home," she said.

"Dublin?"

She shook her head. "I grew up in the west. Barren and windswept. Did you know there are twenty-three kinds of orchids growing out of a three hundred-million-year-old limestone slab? We had a cottage on the edge of a plain where goats and chickens roamed in the yard. Isolation was a gift. Boredom too. I was dreaming of more. Always bigger stages and beautiful people. I'm still surprised each time I travel. I suppose I'm just a girl who never forgot she was little."

I smiled and saw that Ruth was also smiling. She was not like the others after all, coming here to laugh and mock how we lived. It was the feeling of being with an old friend whom I'd forgotten how much I liked being around.

"Let's walk down to the river."

She gripped my forearm and we turned toward the uneven brick roads of the Market District, gray office buildings fading from view behind us. The sound of her voice was low and soothing; the instrument she used to enthrall audiences was a weapon kept hidden from view, a secret power concealed inside her. She told me about her father, how he'd left her mother for a second family, and it surprised me how easy it seemed for her to talk about intimate things.

I pointed the way to the trailhead below.

"What's it like having a child?" she asked. "The love. You must feel so much love."

I lied and told her it was true, that having a child made you realize how much your own parents must have loved you.

"I wanted kids at one point. I worried I might never perform again. I was afraid. I thought my husband was homosexual when we first met—can you believe that?"

I nodded, unsure what to say.

"But he has sex with me. We'll go for a walk in Central Park and keep our eyes out for this big Labrador, a true squirrel hunter always bursting through a bush or cluster of purple wildflowers. I can see him now, bounding in pure energy through the park. We'll come back up to the apartment and shoot a scotch, and then my husband will take me from behind with my cheek pressed against the window. Window glass has such a cool feeling no matter the temperature outside. Have you ever noticed?"

"No," I said, buttoning my coat.

There was a chain-link fence enclosure just off the trail, a collection of wires and power transformers kept inside.

"How did you propose?"

"On a golf course," I said. "It was a few days before I left for the military. I haven't been back to the course since."

I looked at the cylinders and springs made of metal rooted in a bed of white gravel. So much electrical equipment only thirty or so feet from the water's edge.

"We just woke up together one morning in the city. Said 'Why not us?' Easy sort of thing. We walked down to the courthouse that day and did the arrangements. Received our paperwork the very next morning. Here we are."

She looked at me over the edge of her sunglasses. "Do you have sex with your wife?"

I lied and felt my cheeks flush, wanting to say more. Pressure was building inside me. We walked in silence for what felt like hours.

The river stretched out beside us like a long, brown tongue, sliding back and forth against the darkened soil of the banks.

The electric machinery hummed and buzzed but there was no laughter, no boats on the river that day. No barges down from Canada to haul scrap metal or coal to southern ports on the Mississippi. Only wind and the sound of our footsteps. Ruth picked up a rock out of the tall grass off the trail and slung it into the muddy water, then pulled tight on her sweater and tucked her chin into a long, purple scarf, its tails draped over her back. We came upon a bronze sculpture at the center of a small garden wilted and bare from winter.

I kicked the lip of the metal plaque with my toe. Just a small American flag sticking out from the ground and a pair of bronze combat boots. I never knew it was there. War memorials had sprouted up at every park in the city, and they christened sports fields, libraries, and town halls. How similar it looked to the one we had built. The meaning of it would be lost on Ruth.

"Memorial," I said.

She knelt down and touched the metal etching. Clouds blocked the late day sun and the back of her hand had turned red with chill.

"Grave should be good enough for the job. Such a lonely thing out here by itself, like a decoration left up after the end of a season."

"We built one for someone I knew. Far from here. In a park not far from his grave. He loved wearing boots. He loved the whole uniform. His priest told him anyone who died while wearing it would be on a rocket ship to heaven, if you believe such a thing. So, we buried him in it."

"He died violently?"

I nodded.

"You were friends?"

"I was responsible for him," I said.

"You watched him?" she asked, as if the question had occurred to her like any other.

Again, I nodded.

"Can you tell me?"

It was a question I had been asked before. First by Grace and then by myself, over and over again, hoping for an answer that would solve the problem. I had waited years for a time when I would be interested enough to answer honestly. The wind had turned Ruth's cheeks red and she squinted, looking at me with the same patient expectation I saw the first time we met.

"It happened on patrol," I said.

And the words came easily.

"It was all flat desert around our base. There was a hill above us. No rivers or trees and no grass, just the one rock hilltop, and I had wanted to get on top for months. It was only a few hundred feet tall and nothing special to look at. The hill made me wonder what the ground would look like from up high. I wanted to see things from above. Everybody did by the end, and I'd never seen anybody go up there. Maybe somebody grumbled that we hadn't cleared the ground, but we'd walked through so much shit by then we didn't care. We had our shaving cream and our metal rods. The man at the head of the patrol had called a hundred halts by then, everybody had frozen a hundred times, holding still inside their footprints while the lead man swiped his rod over every grain of sand, and it always worked.

"Everybody was in a good mood when I told them we were going to stand on top of the hill. 'We'll know what it feels like to stand up there and look down on this shithole,' I told them and everybody grinned. I'd been in country for six months and hadn't seen anything I could take home with me, the stuff you tell your friends and parents to let them know how lucky they are you're still here. There had been combat and everybody but me had seen it. I'd gone to a memorial service for one kid who'd been shot in the neck, and I'd placed a hand on the lid of his helmet stuck to the end of a rifle at his memorial, and I might have cried a little, but it wasn't real. I hadn't been with him when it happened. By the time we marched up that hill, I'd been imagining for months how much the dudes liked having an experience that wasn't mine—gunfights, explosions—how it gave them something to hang over my head when they came back to base. 'The sir's never actually seen combat. He can't understand what we go through out there.' I'd been hearing it inside my head and the voice kept getting louder.

"I'm laughing now because I can still see him. He's got his helmet on, the chinstrap dangling and tobacco spit coming off his lip. I tell you the right side of his face was blown up like a puffer fish. He kept himself grungy, so unclean that you'd think not even the bad guys would touch him. Maybe that's why I liked him being nearby, because I thought it would keep me safe or something.

"I was walking fourth in line that day and one place ahead of West, who was smack in the middle. 'You're in my world today, Sir—you know the drill.' He was the guy everybody wanted in charge of the patrol, so I did as he said.

"We set off single file, like a group of schoolchildren walking across the playground, one right after another. It had rained the night before so the ground was thick with mud. It felt like I was walking through peanut butter, every step sucking at the bottoms of my boots. The point man had the metal detector stuck out in front of him, waving it back and forth like a flashlight in the dark. We only walked where the metal detector allowed us, each man planting his foot into the footprint of the man in front of him and that was how it worked: one footprint at a time, hoping the ground wouldn't give out from underneath. I can't remember what I was thinking about before it happened. The weight of my pack, maybe, how it felt like carrying a limp body on my shoulders, that's how heavy the gear felt. I wasn't thinking about fighting. I was uncomfortable but not afraid. 'Keep up, Sir. Speed is the name of this game,' was the last thing West said.

"We crested the hill and were approaching the plateau. Halfway to the center, there was a flash of white light, then heat, a wave of fire that burned the hair off the back of my neck. I felt something kick the side of my head and then, all of a sudden, I'm sitting on the ground. I feel the force of the blast on every part of my body, like a punch to the head and ribs at the same time. One second passes. My first thought is, 'I'm dead.' Another second passes. I hear rocks and debris, clumps of mud splattering onto the ground around me. The air is reddish brown, a fog, like I'm inside a filthy cloud, picking wet mud out of the inside of my nose and spitting it from my mouth. More seconds pass. My conscious self slams back inside my head and I realize for the first time that I'm alive. I have memory. I remember I was walking, that I'm with my team and we're near the end but we've been hit by something. More time passes. My ears are ringing and I notice that my head hurts, like I haven't had a cup of coffee in months, and the ache is enough to make me stretch my forehead and close my eyes. A doctor told me later that the blast from twenty pounds of explosives shattered my eardrum, but for now, I'm just drifting in and out of focus. I hear voices, the sounds coming from a tunnel, inside a shaft. They're getting louder as the sound expands, but still I'm staring into the fog and seeing nothing until I turn to see what's going on behind me.

"'I'm good!' I scream at the outline of a figure, sweeping my hands over my legs and in front of my face, then my chest. 'I'm okay,' I whisper to myself. I made it. I look behind me and finally see the image of someone emerging through the fog. 'Hey, buddy. I made it,' I call out. He's quiet, just sitting there. His back is stiff and perfectly upright, like he's just chilling, and I think to myself, 'Hell of a time to sit around, isn't it?' He's holding something in his hands—a helmet turned upside down like a bowl with a bootlace hanging out of it, and it's odd. I push myself to my feet so that I can stand above him and then I understand. West isn't sitting. His upper body is planted in the mud, like he's sprouting up out of the dirt, right up from his ass, and there's something black and red tucked inside the boot he's cradling in his helmet. I keep staring at the boot in his hands.

"My mind flips back to something I heard. "Sir, my orthotics don't fit these issue boots, so I'm gonna need to buy a special pair. Check this sweet-ass pair of boots." The only dude in the platoon with boots that looked like Air Jordans. It's his left foot he's holding in that helmet, the tan leather is a dark red color, but otherwise in perfect condition. The toe box and throat of the boot are plump. The laces are tied.

"He couldn't have been more than five feet away. I dream about it sometimes at night, reaching for his tourniquet off the front right shoulder of his plate carrier, fingers dancing across the stub of his right thigh before I rip my own tourniquet off my plate carrier, fastening it across what little is left of his left leg, doing what I can to stop the bleeding. I do it right every time in my dream, but it didn't happen like that. Seconds passed and I didn't move. More seconds passed and I couldn't move. Eventually, the lead man in the column is there in front of me, giving the aid I'd plotted out in my head but hadn't been able to deliver.

"Have you ever had that dream where you're playing a basketball game and you steal the ball? There's nothing but open court between me and the basket. Not a single defender stands in my way. Sometimes my legs are rubber, other nights they're wood. He bled out on the helicopter, arteries sliced just as clean as cut grass is what the medic told us, said it was a 'victim-operated IED.' Victim-operated, like West had decided to kill himself when he stepped on the pressure plate, when he stepped into my footprints. We both stepped on the plate. Only West was able to operate the bomb that killed him."

Ruth was standing behind me now, her arms around me and hands on my chest. I fell back into her, hearing nothing but my heart banging inside my ears.

"You survived," she said. "You lived."

But there was more to surviving than not being killed.

We went back to base, took off our helmets and flak jackets, and collapsed on the ground. I felt nothing. It was nighttime and steam was rising off our chests and backs. Somebody got out cigarettes and passed them around. It was cold but nobody complained. I fell asleep, unable to walk into the barracks or crawl into my sleeping bag. We woke up early and went back to work.

"We're supposed to owe a debt to the dead but it's West who has a debt," I said, my breath short. "Mouth stretched out like that. His teeth pressed together flat as granite. I keep his picture on the wall in my office. The picture is big and bright. I look at his picture every day to remind myself…to remind myself how the real West looked."

The downtown was vacant and night had fallen, streetlights casting a glow that shimmered off the metallic street. Workers had long since left for home, locking the doors on storefronts and offices. We were alone but everything had become strange. I glanced from street signs to buildings, looking for direction, anything to regain my bearings in a city that seemed unfamiliar at night.

Ruth was beside me.

Her eyes turned dark blue and holding my attention. I felt her calming me. Power and Light loomed beyond her in the distance. She put a hand gently to the side of my face.

"Take me inside."

CHAPTER SIXTEEN

*W*e passed underneath the red exit sign buzzing above the doorway.

I led her down a darkened hall.

I stopped outside my office doorway, fluorescent bulbs flickering, and my eyes adjusted to the sudden burst of light. I turned to show Ruth the way and she walked right past me, stopping by the banker's box of medical papers on the floor. She hovered over the papers for a moment before moving to the bookshelf. She examined the row of statute books handed down from a dead partner, touching the cracked leather binding on one volume after another and running her knuckles along the edges of text as if her hands were made for reading. She picked up one book, then another. I pointed to the framed picture on the wall behind my desk.

"Here."

She stepped closer, staring at the picture with the interest of an earnest student, her face inches from the glass. She tilted her head to one side, examining his face and uniform against the black background. I leaned against the edge of my desk and waited for her to satisfy whatever fascination she had for the young man in dress uniform, colorful flags draped behind him. There were millions of pictures just like it. Nobody paid attention to them until a television station needed to put the face to a name.

Ruth folded her arms. She stepped back and stood next to me.

The heat rose up from my chest, then into my neck.

"A boy's face," she said. "Smooth."

I looked at our reflection in the glass, afraid to move any nearer. I wanted to tell her it was time to leave, make up a story that the night cleaning staff was coming, or tell her the truth, that my wife and son were waiting for me at home, but I couldn't speak. From the black screen of the computer, I watched myself standing there. I held onto the edge of the desk while Ruth's thumb beat a rhythm against the wood.

Tap.

Tap.

Her fingers covered the top of my hand, sliding into the grooves of my knuckles. Her hand moved to the underside of my wrist, the touch light, her breath so cold my neck muscles tensed. I was caught, afraid the moment would end if I moved or spoke, watching the scene play out on the black computer monitor as Ruth's fingers crawled across my shirt to release one button, then another.

I winced.

I wanted to reach with both arms and smother myself against her body.

The metal clasp clipped open and fell away.

The rush of air and plunge into a pool of ice water, begging for the surface so I could breathe again, my hand jerking in vain to jostle the keyboard.

"Shhh," she whispered.

My body wheezed.

I tried to close both eyes and avoid the defeated form reflected in the monitor.

The feeling was gentle, like the careful turning of a key. Then harder. The heel of her hand slammed into my chest and pushed me backward. A shock of pain choked up from the root of my cock until the pain released and I fell forward. When I opened my eyes, Ruth was standing in front of me, holding my cock in her palm like a borrowed tool she'd finished using.

"Do you have the time?" Ruth asked abruptly.

She pulled a comb from her pocket.

I watched in hazy, slow motion while she straightened her jacket and brushed the strands of hair from her face. She stepped back from the desk and walked calmly to the doorway. I fumbled with the buttons of my shirt, stuffing it into my pants as I hurried to collect myself. I followed her out the door, looking anxiously around the room and hallway for any sign that we had been seen.

Minutes later we were back on the street, alone.

"Good night then," she said, flapping both arms to her sides.

Her face was plain, drained of all the interest and passion she had shown earlier in the evening, colored yellow by the glow of the Power and Light sign overhead.

"I'll see you this weekend at the show." The words tumbled out of my mouth awkward and foreign.

I was tired now; my head ached and I lacked the energy to say what had taken place between us, to even touch the woman who, moments before, I had wanted to make love to. She left me standing there, watching speechless as she crossed the empty street and disappeared from view.

CHAPTER SEVENTEEN

A voice croaked into the speakerphone at work.
The room was dark.
I'd been staring at the blank computer monitor, head aching.

"Mr. Ward is waiting for you in the fifth-floor confer-ence room. You're late," Viv said.

I picked up the binder and scanned its pages as I walked upstairs to the mediation.

Our plaintiff was fifty-seven years old and in good health. His address and name were missing, redacted by Viv, I assumed, but his medical history was complete. Three years ago, he was diagnosed with stage four pros-tate cancer. He had chosen the most aggressive course of treatment, battering his prostate with round after round of radiation treatments that left the organ "beaten to a pulp," according to one assessment. "The shape of an overripe prune," according to another. He suffered cramp-ing and sexual dysfunction. "Extreme sexual dysfunction," according to his physician. The incontinence was so bad it had turned the man's penis into a leaky faucet.

"It's the leakage I can't tolerate," he said during an earlier meeting. "Spots showing on my trousers when I'm sitting at my desk isn't so bad, but when I'm presenting at a ceremony? Standing front and center in a room filled with hundreds of well-dressed people? Like, come on, Doc, there's been times I was afraid to step away from the podium because I feared five hundred people—community leaders, mind you—would see that I, the [REDACTED], share something in common with their four-year-old grandkids."

His doctor recommended the Pride, and he had the tiny rubber and metal harness installed into his scrotum. He did not see his physician once in the next several months and it appeared the surgery had worked.

Enter Ms. Niki [REDACTED], midthirties. The two had met years prior when she accepted a position as an executive assistant at company [REDACTED]. Their relationship was professional from the time he received the cancer diagnosis through treatment. Things changed once he made his recovery.

"He told me he wanted to sleep with me in the office, then wake up on the floor the next morning and drink coffee while we looked out his big window and watched the rest of the city cram through the streets, late for work," she said in an earlier deposition.

The affair cost the plaintiff his marriage.

"It was the happiest day of my life," he said of the couple's wedding day. Their future was promising. His physician, his surgeon, everybody he trusted had told him the Apollo Pride would cure the incontinence and not leave him sexually unavailable to his new bride.

"Client had no cause to place the device under heavy workload prior to marriage to Mrs. [REDACTED]. Client was shocked when device began to cause immense discomfort. Client and Mrs. [**REDACTED**] had expectation to produce children during their union."

The memorandum went on like this for pages.

"Knifing pain in the scrotum" appeared on one of the final pages. "Plaintiff described pain, 'like my balls are slicing open from the inside.'"

The man's Pride, which was a polyurethane strap wrapped around the urethra and anchored into the pelvic bone by two tiny fishhooks, had dislodged from the stress of activity. The hooks had come loose, pricking the soft interiors and causing blackout agony. For his pain and suffering, the man demanded a settlement of at least $5 million, but not for himself. He wanted to "do something meaningful for my kids."

I flipped to the bottom of the binder and found what I needed: the confidential memo suggesting the treatment was too risky for men who had undergone radiation therapy. This was our silver bullet, the defendant's acknowledgment the plaintiff never should have been advised to have the surgery in the first place. I set the document on top of the stack of papers under my arm and pushed open the conference room door.

"Hey you! Willy Loman!" Ward yelled from his high-back leather chair at the head of the long table, his eyeglass lenses magnifying the size of his eyes. "Where ya been, kid? Made a sale yet? You know who I'm talking about, right, Gray?"

Ward swiveled in his chair to look at the man sitting on the opposite side of the table dressed in a sport coat without a tie, his white collar unbuttoned.

Graybar pursed his lips.

"I sent the young lieutenant here all the way to Grand Junction, when was it? Two years ago? How many ticks was it kid, two and a half years?"

"Last fall," I said, sliding the report toward him.

"I sent the kid out one and a half tanks of gas from here and said, 'Don't come back without a sale!' Ya know, farmer smells somethin' and heads out to investigate, starts sniffin' around until it's too late because there's an underground pipe leaking anhydrous ammonia. Stuff turned the old man's lungs into pink goo, but I told the lieutenant here to sign up his widow."

"Sure, Mick," Graybar said. "Read about that one in the paper. Quite a—"

"Allen, excuse me. I'm not finished telling the story, okay, brother? It's a short one, only a minute, okay? Can I finish this one, please?"

Ward wiggled in his chair, which seemed twice the width of his narrow shoulders.

"Where was I, the tractor, then the gas leak...."

"Vaporized his lungs," Viv chimed in from one of the chairs along the wall, laptop across her legs, typing.

"Farmer Brown smells this gas and starts walking into the cloud, but he calls his assistant out there, uh, Diego, to help in the investigation, and poof! Soon they're both vapor. I tell you what, I mean, we gotta figure out how to treat these people who come into this country, Gray. These immigrants working the toughest jobs, getting no..."

The long glass table had nothing on it except for my binder and a few papers placed in front of Ward. There were fingerprints along the edges, smudge marks left over from yesterday's luncheon or a morning conference. They should have been wiped clean. I noticed my own fingers were smearing prints into the glass.

"...well, we've had this conversation before, brother," Mick continued, wagging his finger at me. "Point is, kid couldn't make a sale, Gray. Jury came back with ten million for wrongful death against the pipeline company—a big ol' pot of money for some other lawyer because this kid couldn't close the deal."

Graybar dabbed his fingers in the glass of water and ran them through the few strands of hair atop his reddish head. He looked at me furtively before drying off with a towel.

I felt the ball of my calf muscle tightening.

I was tired and wondering where I could find a glass for myself.

He shifted nervously in his seat, hand trembling where he held the towel in his lap. This was not the man of ceremony and confidence I had seen nights before, stopping a crowded room to take Ruth into his arms. It was as if a second, smaller man had been released from inside him, this one the true version, the one exposed and uncomfortable in front of just a few people in a conference room, where a heavy privacy curtain had been drawn to limit the number of witnesses to his vulnerability. Graybar had made his reputation on a concept of himself that had not been true. He would refuse to humble himself as long as he could.

The mediator had slipped in while we were talking, lowering himself into a chair between Ward and Graybar, another old man wearing a gray suit that tightened around his heavy midsection and thighs.

I wiped sweat from my brow.

"It's the final stop, gentlemen," the mediator said in a tone both bland and serious. "If we can't put away our swords and agree on something reasonable, then we're going to turn it over to twelve strangers, three of whom are probably crazy."

"Let me get a word in here, Michael," Ward said to the mediator. "Take a look at Allen. Right now. Let's start this thing on the right foot and look at the man. Devastated, debilitated. For God sakes, Michael. Gray has got a clip on his dick."

"Do those guys know I've got a clip on my dick?" Graybar said quietly, referring to the attorneys for the company that manufactured the Pride, sitting in a room across the hall. "They know about the clip, don't they?"

"Gentlemen, I guarantee you they know," the mediator replied. "But you have to give me something meaningful, a number that says you guys mean business, and then I can take it over to the other side."

Ward leaned back in the chair with his hands clasped behind his head, a boy at the head of the boardroom. "Five million."

"Five mil—? Mick, please be serious. These guys are going to start at fifty thousand dollars, you understand that?"

Ward hopped out of his chair. "Jesus, Michael. These guys couldn't hit me with a three wood from fifty grand. I been honeydicked by the slicksters twice already and now I want them to hurt a little for what they did to us. We're not doing this for the money. One dollar, one billion dollars don't make shit difference to us, Michael."

"Do they think they're dealing with some hayseed? If these guys think we're Hicksville out here they're wrong, okay?" Graybar fumed.

"Gray, buddy, hush. Michael, I want what they took from my client, and I want him to get back his pride. It's about a man's pride. I know you been there."

The mediator nodded. "Been a couple years since my diagnosis."

"Me too," Ward said, holding his hand in front of his face. "I'm literally starin' this sucker down! Right here! This man is the least of our brothers. Those big-city boys across the hall, well, they left a wounded man on the battlefield, physically wounded and psychologically. He has the PTSD, Michael. A man's sword, after all. We're talking about manhood here, I mean—Gray, you okay, brother?"

Ward squeezed Graybar on the shoulder and shook his head with a look of pity. He pointed to me and I picked up the document, placing it in front of the mediator. Graybar glanced at me as I leaned back over the table to take my seat, scowling as if to warn me against stepping too close, as if I might finally see the truth of fear and embarrassment written on his face.

"I want you to go back and tell these slicks they never should have operated on Gray, not in his condition, and that their own study says so, the study written by their own doctors and whatnot. This file has enough coal on it to burn all winter long, Michael, and I've seen a few."

The mediator squinted at the memo and pushed the papers back into his folder. He stood up and shuffled into the hallway, presumably to deliver the same speech to the opposing attorney. The routine would drag on for hours without progress.

"Are they kiddin'? It's me here. It's Micky, and I ain't sittin' on my ass all afternoon for no fifty grand. I'll go drill a hole for fifty grand!

Graybar rubbed his eyes.

"Say, Gray, buddy, hang tight. You okay, buddy?"

Graybar started to open his mouth.

"You gotta stay with me, buddy! No sleepin' on Micky, okay? And this yahoo. Don't like dealing with mediators, Gray, and this yahoo is playing both sides, he's playing us off each other and I know it."

Ward popped up from his chair and strutted over to the door. He pulled back on the privacy curtain and looked into the main hallway. "How much you pay for that pool?" he asked.

Graybar didn't seem to notice the question. He was sitting hunched forward in his chair, picking at the edges of his fingernails.

"Gray."

Ward snapped his fingers toward the other man. "Bro, how much that pool set you back? One fifty? More? Beautiful new pool in your backyard."

"Somewhere around there," Graybar replied.

"But you're in it every day?"

"Mmmhmm," Graybar nodded.

"Getting' your laps in every morning? Olympic size and all. Heater works so well you gotta take a cold shower afterward just to cool down your nerves, right, bro? Guess you're probably heatin' that thing eight months outta the year?"

Graybar chuckled. "Niki likes to watch the steam rising off the water during winter," he said. "I tell her to enjoy it. She's watching dollar bills literally evaporate into thin air.'"

The intercom system interrupted the conversation. Someone was on the line waiting to speak to Ward. Reception said it was urgent.

"Brother, lemme check on that for one minute and I'll be back."

Ward pulled the curtain aside and disappeared into the hallway. Viv followed him out the door. Who knew if Ward had a client on the phone line, or if he had instructed the receptionist to page him just so he could leave the mediation, take a phone call, and dive into the middle of somebody else's crisis.

Suddenly, it was just the two of us left in the room.

"Embarrassing," Graybar said, breaking the silence. "No. This is unbelievable. We're sitting in this office arguing while I've got a fishhook loose somewhere inside my cock and these fuckheads won't just admit what they did and pay me to go away."

I sat still, not knowing how to respond and hoping someone, Ward or the mediator, would come back into the room. He was looking at his hands.

"You were in the service?" he asked.

My head ached. I was unable to get my mouth working well enough to speak. I nodded.

"Love vets. Love 'em because you all know how to go to war, you know how to fight for something, am I right?"

"Yeah."

"What'd you call the bad guys overseas anyway? Haven't heard enough about what our guys were callin' those shitheads on the other side."

"Pardon?"

"The bad guys. You know, called them gooks in Vietnam. What did you call 'em over there? Ragheads? Sand niggers? When you were really pissed off, when you were throwin' down with these backward fucks in some house-to-house shit, bullets flyin', buddies dyin' sorta thing. What did you call them?"

"You were in Vietnam?" I asked.

"I served. Too late for the war, but I know what we called the North Vietnamese, kid. Do you know what I'm driving at here?"

He looked at me in a way that raised questions about my intelligence and my patriotism.

"We said haji, sometimes."

Graybar reached for another bottle and poured water into a tall, clear glass. His hands were thick and square, bulging with veins that ran up his wrists and into his forearms. A sharp pain cut through my forehead again, and my whole mouth felt dry. I wondered how he had not one but two bottles of water.

"Well, fuck these hajis!" Graybar yelled, slamming the empty bottle onto the table. "Fuck 'em! These fuckers made my life an embarrassment. The buildings, the investments, projects. I own half of what's happening in this city, all got my name on it, and I'm an embarrassment. Try telling a woman, beautiful young woman, blonde, that she has to leave the party because your diaper is so full it's like you're walking with a bicycle seat stuck between your legs. Having to tuck a restaurant napkin into your belt because you've got a goddamn soil mark on the crotch of your pants. Woman like that deserves to walk out the front door of the finest restaurants in town, every man in the building with his tongue hangin' out his mouth. Instead we're slinking out the back like we're afraid to be noticed!"

There was an air of fear that surrounded him. The way he smacked his lips in between words, how he refused to look at me. I saw the tiny beads of sweat forming in the pores of his reddish cheeks, which he swiped at with his fingers. How easily he talked like this in the corporate boardroom. Everything he spoke was nasty, the way he wanted to punish people, to steal anything that he could use for a time and then reject. He was a man who took whatever he was allowed to get away with, a man whose conscience had been shaped by getting and spending and all I could do was wait for him to finish. But he kept talking. He reminded me how generous he had been to the city, how marrying a younger woman was part of that generosity.

"I could have had anyone," he said, sitting up a little straighter in the chair. "I took Niki because of her beauty. I had more left to give and I wanted to give it to her. My time, my money, how it's bubbling over inside me and I wanted her to have some of it, not sit around and talk about my kids, burn up my time watching somebody else do the living."

I was too weak to offer up resistance, so I sat in my chair expressionless, realizing Graybar did not respect himself enough to just be quiet, to shut up, to behave like an ordinary man.

"But you have kids," I finally said.

"Yeah. Niki hates kids. What's your point?"

"I guess everything worked, when it needed to."

"Wooo!" he yelped. "Sex!? Is that what you're wondering about? You wondering whether I'm still having sex, kid? Look, I don't know what you were reading in that file, but the sex is the only reason I'm worried, if you know what I mean."

"I thought that was why we were here. The pain and—"

He rolled his chair away from the table and edged closer to me. He leaned forward, as if to tell me a secret. "I'm worried to get this thing fixed, ya know. The orgasm is unbelievable. A knockout, like my balls are inside a vise grip and splitting open type of unbelievable. Unreal. The intensity of it sends me high as a fuckin' airplane. I can get it two, three times in a row. I don't know what the deal is and I never, ever heard anybody talk about it, but this metal," he grabbed his crotch, "might be bad for pissing, but it is great, I mean *great*, for fucking. I'll put up with a lot of pissy diapers for that kind of a fuckin' high."

I reached up with both hands and rubbed my forehead, the pain sudden and blinding. Without warning, the room in front of me blurred and a sharp sound rang out inside my ears. I staggered up from the chair and braced myself against the conference room table.

"Excuse me," I said, running out of breath.

Graybar stood up and turned away, removing his phone from a coat pocket and pacing to the other side of the room.

I pushed through the doors and sprinted down the back hallway to a bathroom. Feeling sick, I covered my mouth with one hand. I gripped both sides of a toilet and knelt onto the cold bathroom tile, letting my chin come to rest on the porcelain, my stomach muscles seizing from dehydration.

How did this happen, I asked myself, pushing up from the toilet and staggering to the sink.

I looked around the empty bathroom. Everything had become unfamiliar, like a place I had never seen before.

I retreated into my office. The red light of my phone was flashing like a beacon. I knew it was Viv or Ward, asking where I was and telling me to get back to the mediation. I yanked the cord from the outlet and shoved the phone into a bottom drawer. I stood up then sat down. I stood up again and looked over my shoulder, seeing my reflection in the glass encasing West's picture, my face small and wide-eyed like a lost child stunned by his sudden aloneness. I ripped the picture from the wall and tucked it underneath my arm.

Past the steakhouse and the banks, past the pickup trucks parked outside the municipal building, I walked quickly down the street. My clothes felt heavy and too big for my body. I walked by the store where Ruth bought me a book I never read and through the Market District, not stopping to look inside the windows of coffee shops where she might be sitting. I kept walking until I reached the banks of the river, swollen by rainwater and colored so dark it looked as though the Earth had melted into brown liquid. Alone, I watched gray clouds spread across the sky, their shadows moving along the trail we walked the day before. A squirrel rustled the branches of a bush nearby, indifferent to my presence.

"I never expected her to come into my life," I muttered to myself.

I laid the picture on the ground beside the trail and tugged up on the empty beltloop of my pants. The smell of dusty books and sweat mingled together in my nose. My eyes fell over the gaze of a dead young man, his bright brass buttons gleaming beside a stack of ribbons. The picture had lost its meaning. He would never have to change, never need to start over again. Death had spared him the grief of watching life become a disappointment, and I wondered for only a moment whether to save it, donate the whole thing to a junk store, or sell the frame at a pawn shop. Neither seemed right. The picture had only ever been mine.

I spread my feet and straddled the outside of the frame. Bucking up my knee, I threw my fists out as the heel of my shoe came down like a pickax, fragments of glass and wood flying in every direction, the sound so high and sharp that I shielded my face behind my forearm. I did it again and again. Up and down until the paper was punched through and disfigured in a way that left me confused. I had wanted for so long to improve, to grow up, to commit myself to something larger as a release from the memories that disturbed me, but all I felt was dissatisfaction. I wrapped my jacket across my chest, kicking the mangled frame off the trail and looking back to watch the crumpled paper of his photograph roll harmlessly across the brown grass.

I put my face in my hands.

My chin and cheeks were rough with stubble and my neck felt stiff.

I rubbed my eyes, bloodshot and tired.

What's happened to me? I wondered, as if the person I'd become were a disguise, the real me having disappeared inside someone else. Time was speeding up now. So many of the lies I'd told to Grace had a way of making life spin faster and faster until I'd lost track of where I was going. I hadn't realized how quickly the world could rearrange itself.

How long had it been?

Just a day ago I thought I knew who I was.

Now, the sun was falling behind the bluffs and the sky was streaked with blue and orange.

The hardest part had just begun.

CHAPTER EIGHTEEN

That evening, I stood in the kitchen while Grace poured water into a glazed pot on the windowsill.

"I missed you last night," she said.

Her eyes were shadowed by fatigue. She had been too proud to call, to ask me the question directly. It had been her habit to wait for me during late nights away, refusing to say out loud whatever she felt.

"Do you feel better now?"

I couldn't know what she meant.

I was exhausted from the last twenty-four hours and wondered if time would ever regain normal speed. I wanted to sleep. I wanted to retreat someplace free from responsibility, to find a cure for my own foolishness before having to confront Grace like this.

"How was your ministry last night?"

I rubbed my head, forgetting yesterday had been grief ministry, an evening I should have been sipping cups of tea with the parish widows instead of chasing Ruth through the city.

"Fine," I told her, too tired and too afraid to say more.

"What are the names of the others in the group?"

Hadn't we been through this before?

"What are their names?" she asked.

Grace's face hardened. She leaned forward on the sofa to set her elbows into her knees, eyes fixing on me from across the room.

"Tell me their names."

Moments passed in silence.

I shifted uncomfortably on the couch opposite her, crossing my legs then uncrossing them, moving from one pose to another in a vain attempt to release the tension building inside me. Her peace bothered me. She knew the answer but wanted me to speak, to satisfy her curiosity with the certainty of an admission. But what was truth anymore? It had been years since I lost the willpower to stop lying and reveal to Grace the difference between truth and the stories I used to hide myself from her.

"I can't remember last night," I told her, as if that was all the answer she deserved.

"Mary called me. You wouldn't call me, but she did. I guess you put my phone number as your emergency contact. She called to say you hadn't shown up since last week, that she was worried. Someone was worried about you, imagine that. She said something was bothering you." Grace sighed. "Do you understand how stupid I must seem to her? Asking why you'd run out of a counseling meeting would have been, what, asking for 'every last detail'? I would have been going out of bounds again, prying into your personal life."

Through the window over her shoulder, light cast on the small plot of soil Grace had turned over for Charlie's garden. The season's last frost was still a month away, so only red and yellow pinwheels sprung from the ground, their fan blades spinning in the breeze.

"You were with her," Grace said.

It was funny. Neither of us knew much about planting, but Grace was determined to learn, and planting pinwheels was her opening ceremony. Soon she and Charlie would move on to beans and carrots, probably tomatoes. Several months ago, I asked if they had considered flowers. "Maybe sunflowers or petunias that will bloom in the summertime and then die when the weather turns cold," I said. They both shrieked with laughter. It was as if I had suggested they plant lumps of coal in the dirt and pray the Earth made them into diamonds. They were never more alike than when they laughed together, sitting side-by-side at the kitchen table.

She rubbed her eyes with the backs of her hands, the reflection of tears lining her cheeks. I wanted to console her but said nothing when Grace threw herself into the pillows beside her on the couch, wrapping both arms around them and squeezing hard, burying her head so I could not see her face as she sobbed. The sight of her like this was strange, so unreal that I wanted to laugh out loud. She was like a teenage girl whose boyfriend had called to say they were breaking up, an overdramatic child seeking comfort in the teddy bears and pillows piled on her bed. I wanted to grab her by the shoulder and laugh together at her reaction, so out of character it had to be performance. Grace processed emotion. She considered it, carefully. She worked feelings into something sensible and then spoke of how to move on, how to get on with things, and I had never seen her any other way until now.

"There's nothing to worry about," I said finally. "Please. Stop crying."

Her eyes were welts, hands tucked inside her sleeves. "I want to know what you were doing," she started. "I read your emails. Every message that's gone between you the last week, including the latest one you haven't answered. She wants to know if you're doing okay after last night, by the way. Nice of her to check."

Nothing mattered. Whether I changed the password or bought a new phone or stopped using a phone, I knew she would find them. I could have printed and saved the emails in an unmarked file alongside the dozens of manila folders that lined my desk drawer, a place no one would think to look for something interesting. I could have deleted the emails, but it didn't matter now that Grace knew.

"We walked..."

"Where?"

"The street. Downtown. I don't want to talk—"

"About what?" she shot back. "About sleeping with her? Or maybe you held her hand, maybe kissed her on the cheek?"

I begged her to stop.

"Did you ride bicycles with her? Did you go to your office or did you go straight to her hotel room? Where else was there to go? You'd already gotten coffee, already walked all over the city like two kids in love for Christ's sake, trading passing thoughts you couldn't hold inside.

It's all there. What was left but go back to her hotel room and get it over with?"

"We went to the office," I said, whispering. "We looked at the pictures on my wall. She wanted to see what they looked like."

"So that's where you fucked her? Her ass tipped up high in the air, right in the office you hate so much, right on top of your desk, right there in that tiny office, shoving all those goddamn papers right off the desk, the ones you're always complaining about."

"Grace—"

"I know—you didn't have a choice! 'Oh, she cornered me! There was nothing I could do to resist! She backed me against the wall, told me to put my hands on her shoulders, pulled down my pants and sucked me off right there, right across the hall from old Slaven. 'Boy, if he ever knew what I was up to last night!' The things she did to you with that mouth of hers. It would make more sense, anyway, that she'd be the one taking charge of you."

"No."

"I believe you," she shot back. "No, really, I do. You just wanted to see her again. You just wanted to look into those blue eyes one more time. Maybe you wanted to... kiss her?" Grace flashed a brief smile, then ground her teeth. "You wanted to kiss that mouth."

I tried to calm her and describe what happened, but there was no way for me to explain something I did not understand, that I had actually done nothing in the office yet knew I was guilty of all the betrayals Grace had conjured in her imagination. I had done nothing but accept her touch, and still my distress could not be relieved, not by a thousand excuses, not by protesting Grace's assault.

"You're not acting like yourself," I said.

"Myself!?" she screamed, standing up and walking past me into the kitchen, where she stood with her back turned. "What will your mother and father say?"

I had no idea. I hadn't seen them in weeks. They were busy with their own lives.

She told me what I expected, to leave, to go "anywhere but here," that she "didn't want me here." She said it all so quickly that I knew her mind had been made up before I came home. She walked down the hall and went up the stairs to our bedroom. I listened for the bathroom light to switch on, the faucet to run, the bedroom light to turn off. I heard her footsteps walk across the floor, and I listened as she pulled the sheets down on our bed and climbed inside.

Alone in the darkened room, I felt myself disappearing.

For months I had been seeking an escape, slipping out the front door to walk through a vacant neighborhood, peering through windows and doors hoping to lose myself in the lives of others. These nightly escapes became longer and more elaborate as my self-absorption grew, until even my presence had become a burden. Grace's attention had shifted away from me and refocused on our child. He was innocent of my failings, full of promise for the future. Every time Grace asked if I was okay, or if work was going well, or what my plans were, I knew it was for their sake and not mine.

I found my car keys on the kitchen table and left through the front door.

The days that followed began the same way, the sound of Slaven's leather satchel dropping onto his desk at 7:30, rousing me out of the sleeping bag laid underneath my desk. No one knew I was there because no one had stopped by to say hello or ask why I was spending nights behind the locked door of my office. Truth was, I was glad to finally be alone, confined to my own private space. Besides, I had the noise of the firm to keep me company, the workday sounds of phones ringing, footsteps padding the carpeted hallways, keyboards jamming, the electric whir of a printer as it rolled out paper to fill the attorneys' files. The sounds of other people's business continuing without the slightest concern for my humiliation. For the first time in months, the urge to stay put was stronger than the urge to run away.

By the middle of the week my peace was interrupted.

Summoned to Ward's office, I found him looking out the wall-sized window on the fifth floor, the light dwarfing his small figure. There were stacks of documents everywhere, a litter of yellow legal pads on one desk and a tray of empty envelopes on another. The room smelled of rotting paper and the kind of leathery aftershave from Dan's childhood, a scent so strong it made me lightheaded. I thought for the first time of my own father and what he must have looked like in his office, a man reaching the heights of professional success and fully in command of his life. But I was a lost boy now. I sat awkwardly in the chair, rubbing my unshaved chin and trying to straighten my collar, which had yellowed with sweat around the crease.

"One minute you're there and the next...poof," Ward said.

He tucked his hands into his back pockets and paced the room. He was different than before, less certain of himself. Somehow quieter, smaller than before.

"You know what I do, don't you?"

I waited for him to look at me but he didn't. Ward's eyes had fixed on something on the street hundreds of feet below.

"I ring the bell!" he shouted. "That's who Mick is. A bell ringer, a high-dollar, big-money type o' guy. I got million-dollar cases stuck so far into my inbox Viv won't touch 'em for another two weeks. It doesn't bother me because I'm already so deep in the money. As I speak to you, there's enough unsigned invoices in that outbox on my desk to pay your salary through your kid's sweet sixteen. It's just who I am, but it took a lot of time, kid. You're wonderin' what was Graybar's deal, how does that fit in? That was a favor to a friend, kid. My friend, and that's where you happen to come in, because I'm never gonna get to the next verdict while I'm employin' guys like you to sneak out the back stairwell and..."

He paused to close the door.

"Look at him. Take a second to collect yourself, straighten up, and look," he said.

Ward pointed to a portrait of John F. Kennedy hanging on the wall, head bowed in thought. He kept the picture concealed behind the frosted-glass door. I'd never seen it until now.

"You two got a couple things in common. What you don't got in common is that you look like a bag of shit and I'm not surprised. What you do got in common is that you went to war, Counselor. You and that man both went to war, so that tells me both of you were brave, both of you earned your spurs the hard way. Where the rest of us play-act combat in the courtroom, you two did the real thing. You're also a family man, a churchgoing man."

Ward took off his glasses and wiped the lenses with a handkerchief.

"War veterans and family men, all-Americans. You're cheats too. Maybe it's somethin' you picked up in your travels, but fact is you're a liar, okay? You're bed swervers, but pay attention because I'm proud of you. That's right, proud. There's a lot of pussy to be had out there and you fellas are doin' what men do to keep the fightin' spirit alive. You know all about that, how it keeps a man hungry, eager for the next hill to climb, the next big case, you follow me?"

I did but it didn't help. Ward had caught me. The only question was how much he knew, how many betrayals and lies he had seen through even as I denied them to myself.

"Brings me back to Graybar. It's why I put you on the case! I knew something about you, Walker. You got the look of a hunter and we recognize one another."

Ward was still pacing across the room, waving his hands and talking about sex like it was an elephant hunt, the smiling faces of his wife and kids sitting on his desk.

The pictures were everywhere in this room. On the bookshelf, taped to the inside of the glass window. He pointed again to the picture of his favorite president.

"But nobody's supposed to know until you're dead."

He walked toward my chair. The small man now towered over me. He stuck a finger in my chest.

"You been caught and there's hell to pay. The secret's out. Don't ask me how I know. The only thing to do now is go to ground because they caught you with your hands on another man's property, took somethin' that didn't belong to you. This is just part of the deal. We're the establishment here at Tailor. Tailor men are the open palm of the business class and we protect whatever is dear to our clients, and that means whatever they want it to mean. In this case, you grabbed a collector's item, staked your claim to a rare gem that's been held on reserve for a very long time. You took what wasn't yours. You're on your own."

He rubbed his palms together like washing his hands. "She's Graybar's girl, you follow?"

The phone rang.

I grimaced and nodded, stumbling to my feet.

"Hey, it's me—it's Micky. You got it in spades, pal..."

He glanced over the phone, holding up a hand and brushing his fingers to sweep me out the door and back into the world.

I sat there for a few seconds, stunned but uncertain what would come next. He turned his back to me, fitting the phone into the crook of his neck, planting his hands on his hips, and staring out the window. I thought I might quit, tell Mick his firm was shit and the clients were shit and the whole experience had been an embarrassment, a waste of my ambition. But the ideas failed to become words. It was their manner, Graybar and Ward, that stopped me. How these men had staked a claim to anything new that happened in the city. How much did they know?

Gripping the armrests of the chair with sweating palms, I wanted to strike back at Ward, leave him standing there in his big corner office with his mouth hanging open, the big shot's ego cut down to size by the only honest witness to the petty business that made up his life's work. But the seconds passed as he jabbered into his phone. I released the chair from my grip, feeling dizzy and off-balance. I turned toward the door and walked away.

When I pulled into our driveway that evening, the light over the front porch was on and the garage was empty. I walked through the dining room and kitchen, wiping the counter and laying out three plates and silverware as if any moment they might walk in. Grace had not called or left a note. There was no sign when she and Charlie planned to come home. I found a jar of peanut butter left out on the counter, so I pulled a knife from a kitchen drawer and spread it evenly on two pieces of bread, then rolled the sandwich up and shoved it into my mouth. I kept one eye on the front door and listened for the grinding sound of the garage door lifting open.

I sprawled out on the couch wearing the same suit I put on two days ago. I tossed my phone on the floor and pulled the tie from around my neck, stuffing it into a coat pocket. My suit had begun to feel as soft and worn as a pair of pajamas.

My eyes fixed on light coming from the house behind our backyard, where an older man and woman stood with their backs turned to each other in their kitchen. The man pulled a plate out of the sink, his head down and face expressionless under the yellow light. He wiped the face of the plate with a green sponge, his hand moving in a circular motion, then set the plate down on a mat laid out beside the sink, where the woman picked it up and dried it with a towel she kept tucked into her waistband. The man never took his eyes off the sink, reaching into the suds for a cup, a spoon, another plate, scrubbing it then setting aside. The couple did this over and over again. I closed my eyes and pictured the silence, the household sounds of water dripping, the muffled clink of porcelain touching on granite, the clatter of plates stacking in a wooden cupboard. The couple worked together in harmony. I wondered if they enjoyed it, if I was witnessing a routine they kept instead of watching television or talking about their day, people who could have done anything but chose to stand there silently in the kitchen, scrubbing and drying and placing the few dishes in their proper place, tending their collection. They'd probably been like this for years, decades even, next door to me since childhood, and they were still here tonight.

I closed my eyes and faded into sleep.

CHAPTER NINETEEN

The next morning there were pancakes frying in the kitchen.

I kept my eyes closed, listening to the sound of oil snapping as Grace poured a thick coat of pancake batter into the frying pan.

Could this be real?

Charlie smearing syrup on his cheeks and nose as he ate the tiny wedges Grace had cut for him. I giggled at him and Grace was laughing too. His hair was mussed and sticking up in the front.

What day was it—Saturday?

Yes, today must be Saturday, a Saturday like any other. Charlie was here and so was Grace, calm at the stove and as effortless as she had been last weekend, and the weekend before that. Every Saturday since Charlie was old enough to eat them, she had made pancakes.

"Here you go," she would say, flipping one onto my plate.

Her eyes weren't bloodshot anymore. Her tan skin looked smooth again. Her eyes were rested. Here she was, the beautiful woman I knew years ago.

I thought of what Dan had told me.

"Everybody gets caught, dude. Nobody confesses. Shit only happens in the movies."

I pictured Grace moving with her usual grace, acting like all was normal, seemingly unaware of what she said to me nights ago. Perhaps this was the normal course of things, the reconciliation I had hoped for but least expected after what she'd said. If she was here now then that was good enough, though I still wanted to know where she had been.

I told her the pancakes were delicious.

"Your mother's recipe. Did you know that?"

"No," I said, licking the syrup from my plate. It was so good of her to borrow Mom's recipe, and I was proud of Grace for doing it. She knew what I liked after all. My phone vibrated inside my jacket and I caught myself before reaching because it was important to be present. How had the waitress described it? To be mindful. I had avoided looking at my phone for fear a message from Ward or Graybar would be waiting for me, what I expected to be the final notice that I was finished with Tailor. It had been days since last I heard from Ruth.

"First time trying them. Figured I'd change up my usual recipe, try something new."

Grace cut the last pancake into two unequal sizes, passing the small one to Charlie and the large one to me.

One for Charlie, the other for his daddy.

"Still planning to take Charlie to the zoo today?" she asked. "He's been talking all week about seeing the lions."

I smiled and agreed.

What a good idea she had, and I wished it had been mine. I couldn't remember if I made the promise to Charlie.

It had been months since I'd done anything alone with my son, and suddenly I wondered whether Grace was plotting something new against me, encouraging that I leave the house so she could disappear somewhere for most of the day, a new abandonment that I could not bear. For too long I had failed to examine her motivations, to notice how carefully she planned out everything she said, and that was my fault, but to try and probe her now would be useless, except to reveal my own insecurity. I put the last tasty piece of pancake into my mouth and savored its flavor.

Mmhmm.

It was childhood.

Yes, it was the taste that brought me home again, the same as all those Saturday-morning pancakes Mom had made.

"Would you like to come?" I asked, smiling now, glowing.

Grace was scraping the pan with the spatula. She shook her head. "It's better that you two spend some time alone. Besides, this way I'll have time to prepare a big dinner for when you come home."

She dumped the pan and spatula into the empty sink and I shuddered at the sound. She walked around the table and rubbed a damp rag through Charlie's hair before kissing him lightly on the cheek.

"Love my boys," she said, pulling her sweater tight across her chest and walking past me to the pantry.

She was gone again and I couldn't find her.

I put my fork down on the plate and grabbed our coats without a sound.

The zoo was crowded with families.

Mothers and fathers walked miles of paved trails that ran the perimeter of the park, pushing strollers and chasing children from one exhibit to another. They came from all over, men and women wearing dark-colored suits and plain, floor-length dresses—Amish families from a town nearby. There were young boys dressed in matching sports uniforms, groups of children celebrating birthdays, and plenty of parents wearing hiking boots and big backpacks loaded with sandwiches and bottles of water.

I carried Charlie on my shoulders, maneuvering behind a line of people piling up to peer through iron bars at a steep green hillside, where rhododendrons grew around a half-built stone wall structure, a red panda asleep on the branch of a fir tree. It was almost three in the afternoon by that point and earlier than I wanted. A golf cart whizzed past us, then I separated from the crowd to walk down the long trail lined with prayer flags floating on a wire.

"Lions! I see them!"

Charlie wriggled down from my shoulders and sprinted to a short wrought-iron fence. Three lions stood atop a stone platform at the center of a field, surveying the visitors who stopped below. He nudged his way to the center of a crowd and I stood steps back, surprised by the scene: a male flanked by two females. The male was licking his nose with his eyes half closed, as if he had woken up from a nap moments before, oblivious to the visitors and unaware his caged life was on view for anyone standing behind the fence. He had been brought here to perform, to climb the stack of painted rocks and make us tremble when he roared.

Today, though, he showed no interest in performing and instead lay dreamily on his side, tongue lolling out of his mouth in the dirt. He was either too embarrassed or too lazy to perform what we expected from him.

A man about my age adjusted thick black sunglasses that wrapped around his eyes. I checked the time on my phone and noticed a new message.

"Date with Dad?" he asked.

I looked at him.

"Date with Dad. Just the two of you, right?"

I nodded, hoping he would see I wasn't interested in a conversation. My presence here was an obligation, one I was anxious to end. I took a couple steps closer to Charlie, wishing I could have joined the gaggle of children standing with him at the fence. The zoo had been a place of celebration during childhood, where my parents took me for birthday parties with friends, a group of boys running from the entrance gates to one exhibit then another, so drunk on excitement we barely stopped long enough to observe the animals in their intricate habitats.

I looked down and swiped the phone.

"Us too," the man said. He pointed to a little girl standing next to Charlie. "Saturdays. We always do something on our day together. Zoo, hockey game, the park. You know how it is. Cuts out all the boring stuff, right? I hated that part—all the boring time—the time you didn't know what you were supposed to do with her, those breakfast and dinner times, but that's all gone now. Now we've got just the highlights."

The man bobbed his head, agreeing with himself.

I looked back at the phone and her message: *Will I see you tomorrow at the show?*

My heart beat faster.

"Daddy!" Charlie yelled, pointing to the animals clustered in a neighboring exhibit. "Why do the deer stand there? Why don't they run from the lions?"

The antelope he noticed had their backs to the lions less than a hundred yards away, a five-foot fence the only separation between exhibits. The man with the sunglasses came even closer and squatted down next to Charlie. His keys were clipped to a carabiner on his pocket and they jangled against the pavement.

"When you're happy like they are, you just don't care anymore."

I was becoming impatient. We had been at the zoo too long, tagging along with families we didn't know, groups of people following behind one another like railcars. I hadn't received even a message from Grace, nothing to let us know what she had been doing all day or if she was waiting for us to come home, where she'd gone. I was ready and it was time to leave, so I grabbed Charlie by the waist and hoisted him onto my shoulders, feeling him squirm under my grip.

"But Daddy!" he cried, thrashing his arms and legs in protest, his tiny body trying to swing itself loose from my shoulders. I struggled to keep hold of his legs. I wrapped my hands around his thighs and squeezed tight.

"You're hurting me!" he yelled loudly enough that people turned to look.

"Take it easy," the man said, extending his arm and guiding his daughter to stand behind him. "Not in public, not in front of my kid, okay?"

"Fuck off," I said, storming past him on the sidewalk toward the exit, wrestling Charlie down from my shoulders midstride. I hugged him tightly to my chest and covered his mouth with my hand to prevent his screaming from inviting the attention of more people. He was crying when we reached the car, and I shoved him into the back seat. I gripped the nylon straps and yanked hard, tightening the seatbelt across his chest and lap, digging into the soft flesh of his legs so he couldn't move.

"You're hurting me!" he screamed between sobs, his cheeks red, tears mixing with sweat on his face.

"I hate you!" he screamed. "I *hate* you!"

His voice pierced the air and reverberated in my ears, the sound blinding. I closed my eyes and thought about slapping him across the face quickly, just once to shut him up and stop the horrible sound. Charlie cared only about himself. I felt my fist open and my hand raise, hanging there for moments before I cupped my ears to dampen the noise that flashed inside my head. He didn't care if he hurt me. He didn't care what he made me do. When I finally opened my eyes, an old woman was standing in the parking space next to us. She stared at me with an expression that combined curiosity with horror. I dropped my hands to my waist. I stepped back from the car seat, humiliated and suddenly aware not just of what I had done, but that it had been in public. The woman turned away from us and scowled at me over her shoulder, disgusted by what we both knew was true.

I loosened the strap around Charlie's waist and closed his door.

I found Grace in the kitchen finishing dinner.

She dished food onto our plates with the same smile pressed across her lips from earlier in the day. After clearing the table, she volunteered to put Charlie to bed. I waited for the sound of their footsteps on the top of the stair, then opened the door to the garage and walked out to put my hand on the hood of her car and listened for the clicking sound of its engine still settling down. The car was quiet, the hood cold. I went back into the kitchen and opened the doors of the pantry and the refrigerator, inspecting boxes of crackers and bags of cheese, checking their dates to deduce whether any of it was new. Everything appeared to be in order.

Could that be all it took? A little lost sleep and one argument before life snaps back to normal?

Grace and Charlie have their life, and I have whatever is left of mine.

A dog barked in the neighbor's yard and my phone glowed in front of me. Perhaps this was how she would punish me, with meals and bedtime routines, restoring all the conversations with nothing to say that made the foundation for our family life. She must think I'm a fool.

It was her life, not mine, holding onto old habits as if they were prayer beads meant to bring order when all I wanted was to feel happy. I looked at my phone and read Ruth's message again. My heartbeat quickened as I looked at photographs of her opening night, amazed how her expression and costume transformed from one frame to the next. She was living a different, alien life from the one I had chosen and still she was here, right in front of me, waiting. I thought back to the first time I heard her voice, how I could have gone through life never hearing that music, not knowing how good it would feel to lose control. Every day had been stale and unimaginative until Ruth appeared, and now I could not go back. My desire for love was stronger than love itself.

"Would you like some light?"

Grace stood at the edge of the hallway before entering the kitchen.

I wanted to ask her what she had done all day, where she had been last night, and whether she would leave again tonight or tomorrow, but I couldn't say the words.

"He was exhausted," she said.

She bent over to pick up Charlie's coat from the floor and draped it around his chair, then made her way into the kitchen.

"Do you dream?" she asked. "When you sleep, I mean?"

"No," I said, caught off guard by her question.

"Maybe it's the stress or something, but I keep having the same one…"

She pulled a glass from the shelf and filled it with water. "Tell me."

"Do you interpret dreams now?" Grace snapped.

"You brought it up."

"Well," she sighed. "It's silly even to talk about, for me at least, but I guess you're used to listening. You charge by the minute while people run up their bill talking to somebody they think has abilities he doesn't actually have."

She brushed hair from her eyes and took a long drink.

"So, my dream. It's getting close to the end of semester. I haven't been to a single class and I'm afraid the instructor will fail me, that the other students will think I'm dumb or lazy, which makes it harder just to show up to class and get on with it. Finally, I go. It's almost finals by then, and I'm sitting at my desk in the back of a lecture hall, and I'm dressed in a ball gown. Everyone turns to look at me. They're nice, actually—they all stand up and congratulate me, the students and instructor, they clap and clap, on and on, as if they've forgotten we're in school. It's not at all what I expected. I'm surprised by it each time. I watch them stop what they're doing, stand up, and applaud me. Every last one."

"And then what happens?" I asked.

"I wake up. Get on with my morning. That's the end, until a couple nights later when I have the same dream."

She rubbed the band of muscle running at the base of her neck and across her shoulders, eyes closed and head leaning to one side as if trying to summon a distant memory.

"What's happened to us?" she asked.

"I've had a bad year," I said.

She looked in my eyes.

"I haven't been myself. I didn't do what you said and I want you to know I never even touched her."

"Yeah. Well, whatever it was I want to—"

"Put it behind us."

"—do what's best for Charlie," she said, sounding out of breath.

She stopped to look at me and my throat caught, wondering not whether I needed to tell her the truth, but what I wanted to tell her and how much. I was already invisible. Alive but not living, at least not for a purpose strong enough to make me confess what I felt. The only thing left for me to want was to be with Ruth, to see her again.

"I'm afraid they're going to fire me before I get the chance to quit."

"You don't know that," Grace said, sounding reassuring for the first time in days.

"Mick practically told me so. I left the mediation and never went back. Everything they've given me to do I've put off or ignored. I sit in the office and nobody talks to me."

Grace turned off the lights. She walked toward me, touching my face with her fingers, running them along the stubble of my cheek. I wished for a moment to pull her close, wondering what would happen if I reached for her shoulders and wrapped myself around her like we had done a million times before.

Her arms dropped to her sides. "Just go back. They know what you've been through."

"That's why we need to be there tomorrow," I said.

"What?"

"I've already told people we would be there," I said.

"Oh?"

"Ward and some of the others will be there," I lied. "My job is on the line."

Grace drew back, her eyes to the floor. "You think this is the right thing?"

I was surprised by how easily persuaded she seemed, how effortlessly I made the case, speaking about work and my desire to set things right. I said everything I could imagine to convince Grace my motivations were pure, that I needed her by my side, that we were a happy couple, that I loved her.

And she agreed, nodding encouragingly as I parroted Graybar's words about the importance of showing up, how necessary it was to get a W for the community. Everything I told her was meant to distract from the truth. My explanations were a lie, an elaborate contrivance to soothe her fears while I pursued the fantasy I hoped would save me.

The ride was quiet.

Grace squinted into the afternoon sunlight, one hand clamped on top of the steering wheel. The venue was north of the Market District in an industrial area of downtown, an abandoned furniture factory just a few hundred yards from the river. We pulled into the lot and parked near the rusted gray water tower that loomed over a broad, brick three-story. The building's windows were cloudy, some broken. Grace slammed the car door shut behind her and surveyed the place as if she had seen it before.

"Did you lock the door?" I asked.

She pulled the key from her back pocket and held it up for me to see, pressing the button.

Inside, a line was forming to bleacher seats that opened in front of the stage, where a concrete floor was surrounded on four sides by walls made of thick clay blocks twice the size of bricks. The roof was flat. Someone had hung a single crystal chandelier from the middle beam at the center of the room, the only source of light and just enough to reveal the silhouettes of three grand pianos positioned between us and the stage. The stage was unusual, a square raised platform with a milky color that extended deep into the background where a white curtain descended from the ceiling. From our bleacher seats, I watched gray hairs blowing on pink scalps and scanned the tops of heads for someone familiar. The audience was small and unrecognizable to me, fanning their faces with programs folded in half.

"What time is it?" Grace whispered, straightening up against the metal seat back. The room was hot, much hotter than anyone expected.

The light from the chandelier dimmed and the room darkened, the grand pianos before us casting three long shadows.

Muffled coughs echoed across the stage.

Someone's fingers snapped.

Floodlights from underneath the bleachers burst light onto the stage like headlights shining onto a playing field.

Three pianists stood in front of their instruments. They faced the conductor, who pulled a pencil-thin baton from a pocket of his jacket. The pianists lowered themselves into their seats, hands raised above the keys. My eyes focused on the woman at the center piano, her black hair swept back over her long neck, forearms floating parallel to the floor, muscle rippling from hands to wrists.

I wiped the sweat from my eyebrows.

The players' hands came down onto their keyboards and the music began, each piano strumming a repetition of notes.

Up and down.

High and low.

Up and down. Over and over the sound rose and fell, going deeper with each loop, each cycle, each revolution in chords. I watched the slender woman playing between the two men, her torso rigid and still while her arms worked back and forth as the conductor's baton looped right and left, driving the instruments' voices until they merged into one. I nodded in rhythm. The hypnotic movements were beginning to pulse inside me.

The light changed and the platform stage took on a silvery luster under the glare of the floodlights. Shadows appeared behind the white curtain. Man and woman emerged first, barefoot and wearing thin garments in gray and brown, sweat like specks of crystal gleaming on the man's thick shoulders, the same man I had seen a week earlier at the playground. The woman followed behind. I saw the full curve of her brown legs, the shake of her thigh as limbs bent and folded, bare feet thudding to center stage, where the dancers embraced, wrapping legs and arms around one another as the music dissolved into a whisper. They were pinned against each other, barely a breath of air separating the tip of her nose and his lips.

Then I saw her.

Ruth swaggered out from behind the curtain dressed in a crimson trench coat over a man's suit. Her hair had been slicked back behind her ears and she strutted, glaring at the others as the music swelled and her lips curled to a grin. She hurled something I could not see at the man, who fell to the ground, seemingly wounded, as the narrator spoke.

"Strikes him full on the breast. A heavy blow. A marble-fisted blow. A marble-hearted blow."

The couple stripped down to undergarments and lay together on a bed. Ruth was silent, scowling as she disappeared behind the curtain without uttering a word. I scanned the edges of the stage for her as the instruments whirled through arpeggios, building up and breaking down, again and again.

"They were like two halves of the same body."

They caressed each other on the bed, at first touching then grasping, grabbing, clawing at each other in ways that made love and violence indistinguishable. Drops of sweat ran down my back and Grace was quiet next to me, resting her chin on a thumb and forefinger, studying the stage when Ruth returned, transformed and resplendent. She was gliding across the stage, her crimson hair loose and free. She opened her mouth and, as the music swelled, her voice swept through the theater, richer and stronger than the others.

She looked at the man.

He stopped and looked back at her.

Then she looked at me.

"Fate had chosen its weapon well. Aimed it. And struck his heart."

I met her gaze, heat rising through me, the object of an appreciation so loving and intense it became a welcome interrogation.

What do you see? I thought. *What can you find?*

"A brilliant starlit trap is laid."

The man clutched his chest with both hands, staring at the ceiling in pain. He reached into the drawer of a bedside chest and found a jar. He plucked a pill from inside the jar and swallowed it. He took another, then another, until a handful of pills had been taken into his ailing body, and a tremble that started in his fingers worked its way into his wrists and forearms until his whole body was racked by convulsions.

The center piano rumbled in a percussive crescendo.

I searched for Ruth; shadows flashed against the curtain like searchlights.

The second piano tapped out an anxious staccato.

The third trilled on high.

The woman shouted words unintelligible to the audience and struck her stomach with clenched fists. Their fight was a game. Life's tragedies never play the way we imagine, she seemed to say, and the pianos hammered against the woman's screams when Ruth returned.

"Doctor!"

I leaned forward as her mouth opened, voice erupting into its ultimate sound.

Our eyes met. Energy flashed through me. *It was for me*, I thought. *The story, the music, everything was for me.* We were two people in a room of strangers, and she sang for me. Ruth sang the words I had waited a lifetime to hear, her eyes so big I saw myself reflected, the music a promise of our future together.

This was my chance.

Together we would leave this behind, my marriage and the problems I had created.

I had to go with her.

I felt myself lift out of my chair, air rushing past as I lifted higher and higher, above the music, above the stage and pianos, floating above the crowd and chaos, the disorder of life below.

"Love's grandeur lies beyond our understanding."

I watched the woman raise a pistol above her head and my heart stopped.

Higher and higher it went until the lights extinguished.

The music stopped.

The trigger pulled.

The hammer slammed forward and broke the silence.

Bang.

The chandelier brightened.

The audience stood.

I blinked, my eyes adjusting to the burst of light as my dream suddenly ended. I searched the stage, desperate and disoriented, finding Ruth bowing to the crowd in wave after wave with the rest of the cast. I looked for the exit to the side of the bleachers and considered running toward it, away from this place and back to the life that waited outside. But I couldn't leave, not while Ruth waited for me, giving me one last chance to leave everything behind. I summoned the courage to start walking toward her, cutting across the flow of people moving toward the exit, sliding my body between two people stuck in place.

"Excuse me," I said, trying to sound polite when all I could think was how close I was to Ruth, how only a few more seconds and we would be together on stage.

But something was wrong. Head down, I stopped. Whether for fear or guilt, I couldn't force myself any closer.

I took one more step but turned back.

"Grace," I said to an empty row of seats.

I glanced at the faces of people around me, the faceless crowd.

"Grace!" I said more forcefully. There was no answer.

I looked at the seats where we had sat minutes before, then at the exit. It had been only minutes since we were sitting together and she couldn't have gotten far, I reasoned, turning once more to the stage, then back to the seats, whirling back and forth as I looked and looked until the room spun, the realization dawning on me that Grace was gone, disappeared. I wanted to see Ruth, to tell her I was sorry, but she had gone, walking away with the other performers, her arm around the shoulder of the man, both of them smiling as they disappeared behind the white curtain.

I stood alone in the theater, anxious and confused.

Both hands shoved into my pockets, I turned toward the theater doors and shielded my eyes from the glare of the sun outside. A plastic grocery bag blew across the vacant lot. I checked the seats. I felt across the dashboard and steering wheel. I checked everywhere for a note, some hint where Grace had gone. There was nothing to be found. No text messages or missed calls from Grace. None from Ruth either. I rolled down the window and let the cold air brush over my neck and face, tears forming in my eyes as I drove away.

At home, I pulled into an empty driveway.

The front door was locked and I knew what I would not find.

I could press my ear to the door and listen if I really wanted to confirm it.

But what good would it do?

I stepped out of the car, walked onto the grass, and let my keys fall to the ground. They were useless now. The sidewalks surrounding me were neatly swept and trash cans had been arranged in a row at the edge of my parents' driveway. I looked it up and down, the street that had been my link to childhood. Coming home was supposed to protect me, draw out of me the innocence and peace I thought had been lost. I spent years wandering these streets in search of something that never appeared, horrifying myself by how little I understood, how little I recognized in the people and places that sent me into the world.

The clouds had cleared and a light breeze shook the trees, buds forming at the ends of their naked branches.

I should never have seen her. I should have paid attention to them.

The present was speeding up and all my mistakes were appearing before me for the first time. It was useless to concern myself with old choices, not knowing exactly where I had gone wrong. Again and again, I realized too late how each decision brought only misfortune and trouble, how helpless I had been to save myself.

I walked across the lawn to the side of my parents' house and lifted the rubber mat that hid the spare key underneath. The door opened and light spilled into the darkened garage. Dad was out somewhere. Mom would not be back for another day. I walked over to the tool rack so neatly kept and kneeled. Gripping the rough edge of the dial with my fingertips, I turned gently until the lock popped open, gun resting inside the case. The magazine was still loaded from when Dan and I went to the range a little more than a week ago. I pulled it out by the barrel and cradled it in my lap, running my fingers over all the notches and holes I knew by heart. I breathed in and out, my eyes closed, not wanting to move or think, not wanting to do anything but fade away.

Seconds passed.

Then minutes.

Slowly, the darkness inside the garage turned yellow and blue, the scent of gun oil and gasoline changing to smoke and leather car seats baking in the summer sun. My head rushed as time wound itself back and seasons changed to what had been gone for decades.

It's an evening in summer.

My window is cracked.

I see my younger self reflected in the rearview mirror.

I'm riding in the back of our old sedan and Dad's up front, one hand on the steering wheel, radio tuned to a station I barely hear.

He's young again.

Warm air blows against my hair and makes me squint like I'm staring into a fan. Outside, I see the highway lined with streetlights that slip by one after the other, glowing bright orange like the tip of Dad's cigarette. Evening is coming but summer light is slow to fade. Houses on one side of the highway, brown fields on the other, and the road rolls out underneath us just as far and straight as I can see.

"It goes all the way to California," Dad says over his shoulder.

He flips the turn signal with a wave of his hand and the car glides off the highway.

My eyes open wide for the first time.

There's the stoplight at the intersection, the grocery store and gas station. Turn here and our street is only a mile away. Dad could drive this way blindfolded. One left-hand turn and a straight shot to our driveway, Mom waiting behind the front door. I can feel and smell it now, the scent of fresh-cut grass hanging over the baseball fields and green lawns of my hometown. Only a few minutes now. The sun is falling behind the houses on the edge of the horizon, and I hang my arm out the window to feel the warm rush of one hand floating on the wind.

The wheels roll smoothly. Closer, closer.

My dream is interrupted by the grinding sound of metal gears turning.

I blink and the scene disappears.

I watch the metal gears of the garage slowly turn.

The door begins to lift.

Daylight floods the garage and my lungs shudder, muscles shaking. I look up to see a vehicle gently rock to a stop. The engine cuts and a door pops open. It's different from the one I saw in my dream. I find myself staring at the heavy metal grille, the face of a pickup truck, as if it were the face of a stranger on the street. The driver steps out and lingers for a moment, putting his hand on the hood and just standing there as I wonder where he's come from, how he knew. I'm not ashamed anymore, just cold and exhausted and hoping to fall asleep where I sit, listening for his steady footsteps. A cloud melts in the distance over his head. The man's heels strike the cement and echo inside the garage. I can feel my heart rate slow to keep time with him.

Finally, he reaches me.

"It's okay, son," my father says.

He touches a hand to my shoulder and the sensation rushes through my chest and neck like a pulse of energy.

I draw a deep breath.

"You're home."

ACKNOWLEDGMENTS

Thank you to Patricia, Erin, Cheryl, Kara, Margaret, and Cecilia.

Thanks Alex, for believing the story.

ABOUT THE AUTHOR

*J*ohn J. Waters graduated from the U.S. Naval Academy. He served in the Marine Corps on deployments to Afghanistan and Iraq. He lives with his family in Nebraska, where he was born.